A Maiden's Prayer

A Family Story Set in 1970s Sri Lanka

Srianthi Perera

Published by Evocative Journeys, USA.

Editor: Marsha Gilliam
Cover Design: Jenny Quinn, Historical Editorial
Map: Uma de Silva
Author photo: Elaine Kessler, Elaine Kessler Photography
Logo/Website Clip Art: Sumeera Perera/Gayani Leonard

Published by Evocative Journeys, Arizona.

ISBN-13: 978-1-7354120-0-9
E-book ISBN: 978-1-7354120-1-6
Manufactured in the United States of America

Dedication

This book is dedicated to my darling Mummy who wove an endless tale of her own to quench my never-ending thirst for stories during childhood.

"Once upon a time in a faraway land, there was a sugar factory," she would begin. "Nearby, was an ant hill."

I knew what would follow, yet I was all agog.

"One day, an ant came into the sugar factory and took away a grain of sugar. Then, another ant followed and took away another grain of sugar. Then came another ant that took away another..."

And thus, she would go on with her continuous story until I begged her to stop.

The world is inescapably linked to the motions of the worlds above. All power in this world is ruled by these motions.

Greek philosopher Aristotle (384 B.C. – 322 B.C.)

Sri Lanka,
Formerly Ceylon

India

Indian Ocean

- Trincomalee

Anuradhapura

Kandy

Pettah   Borella
Colombo   Battaramulla
        Panadura

Telikada
    Galle

Prologue

O ur extended family is celebrating Berty Uncle's son Chanake's seventh birthday at their beautifully renovated estate in Panadura. I watch Chanake play *The Teddy Bear's Picnic* on the piano, moving his little body to the exuberant beat. He's flanked by a beaming Olga Aunty and a proud Norah Aunty, while Berty Uncle seated nearby has his hands readied for clapping. I try to filter out images of teddy bears frolicking in the woods and focus on this gifted boy who took to the instrument like a duck to water.

My mind wanders to the months leading up to his birth. Berty Uncle, rich in one sense, poor in another; even as he sought to improve the fortunes of others, his own was to undergo an upheaval.

But before I can relate the circumstances of Chanake's birth or the unraveling of Berty Uncle's good and bad karma, let me first unburden myself of my own discomfiture at the time.

About the time that Ceylon became Sri Lanka to cast off its last ties to colonialism and turn into a free, sovereign, and independent republic, I graduated from girlhood to womanhood. Unlike the peaceful name change of my country in 1972 when politicians sought to discard the moniker given to us by the colonizing Portuguese, my transition, as it seemed to me then, was revolutionary. It was, in fact, a regression; Sri Lanka became independent, while I, on the other hand, lost the little personal freedom that I had.

The State, by Constitutional Law, received the designation, "The Democratic Socialist Republic of Sri Lanka," while

1

keeping intact the umbilical cord with the British Commonwealth.

I remained Tamara de Silva.

CHAPTER 1

THE ANGELINA, SIZE 28

January 1973

When it happened to me it wasn't at all amusing like those times when I had huddled with Minaka and Aruni, animatedly discussing the mysterious week-long absences of our grade six classmates, one at a time. When they returned there was a curious glow on their faces, and, more often than not, pairs of shiny gold bangles gracing their arms and matching earrings dangling from their earlobes, even though wearing jewelry was against the school rules. But the best part was the bra. The Angelina, size 28.

We couldn't always see it through the white poplin uniform. So Aruni, the "forward peter," had devised a way of discovering if the girl in question was wearing one; she would utter a cheery "hi" and thump the embarrassed victim on her back.

I thought it would never happen to me. But the sticky stuff seeping out of my usually trouble-free body and the thick wad of cloth that Amma, my mother, had strategically placed to absorb the flow—all these, shamefully, were real.

I had not moved from my bed since the morning wash. Keep the cleansing to a minimum, Amma had warned. "The Dhobi woman will do the needful on your Big Day."

Ever since the calamitous moment three days ago when I discovered an angry red stain in my underwear and uttered an ear-splitting scream in the bathroom, the whole household

3

had been in an uproar. Asoka Aiya, my brother, had immediately been dispatched to phone Olga Aunty who lived some distance away. The remaining pair of maternal aunts had been alerted too, using other means of established communication. The males were strictly excluded except for Thatha, my father, and Asoka Aiya. But given half a chance, I had no doubt Amma would have tried to male-proof the house, if not the entire neighborhood, in her frenzy to "do everything properly."

With Olga Aunty's heaving bulk installed in the confines of my room and issuing to me strict instructions not to step outside, my parents were free to go about preparing for the occasion. Shopping must be done, an astrologer consulted and a special dress in a lucky color tailored, Amma said. During all of this, I was not left alone in the room even for a minute without a female companion.

"But Aunty, why can't Dhamith come into my room like on other days?" I mustered my best impudent tone. After all, my youngest cousin wasn't from another world, although he sometimes behaved like he was. "Why should I eat this boiled vegetable stuff for every meal? And why is there an iron thing under my pillow?" It was all wail and downhill from there.

I lay on the bed, not because I was tired, but because there was little else to do. Olga Aunty regarded me over her glasses with a weary sigh. I knew what she was thinking. I was her fourth niece to attain age and clearly the most troublesome. Malkanthi, Renuka and Jasmine had taken it in their stride, embracing age-old rituals with good grace and even took advantage of the situation to collect some money. There would be gifts of money after the rituals. But I, Tamara de Silva, had to be difficult and different.

She wriggled her mass to a more comfortable position on the cane chair at the foot of my bed, repositioned the spectacles slipping down her nose and began: "Tamara, males are not allowed into the room because this is a symbolic and essential training that you're being given—to be aloof from them from now on. Fried food and meats are not good for you at this time ... *err* ... because they are more difficult to digest."

"But I thought Aruni said it's because they attract spirits."

"Tamara, if you know the answers, why do you ask so many questions?"

"I'm bored. Why can't I leave my room?"

"You must understand that you are no longer a little girl." Olga Aunty closed the errant middle button on her flowery housecoat and tried again. "Twelve years is not too young to attain age. You must realize that this is a very important transition in your life, and it's nature's way of telling you that you must leave your carefree, little girlhood and enter the threshold of young womanhood. Don't you think this in itself merits some recognition?"

"But Aunty, several of my school friends grew up and their parents didn't behave as if the world had changed. Their mothers bathed them the very next day and soon they were back in school. They didn't even have a Big Birthday party!"

Olga Aunty shook her head and rolled her eyes. This time she didn't even bother to reply.

It was hopeless. Day Three was incredibly long. I longed to ride the winding lanes on bicycles with Anura. Instead, I was held prisoner and forced to listen to nonsense. The night before, all my cousins came, and I had listened longingly to their play and banter from my jail. Eight-year-old Dhamith, caught peering through the keyhole, was told that I had contracted an infectious disease, hence the quarantine. Martin Uncle dared to open the door, put his head into the room and wink at me, only to be immediately shooed away by an annoyed Mary Aunty, his wife. Asoka Aiya, who was fifteen, kept his respectful distance, but still, I overheard him chuckling away to someone about my unceasing complaints. He probably wanted me to hear, since he made it loud enough.

Anoma's visit redeemed my spirit. The young woman who lived in the house opposite, who was seldom allowed to go out anywhere by herself, had dropped in unexpectedly. Amma, who had kept vigil the whole day and whose patience was wearing thin, gladly left her with me and went about her neglected housework. When I asked Anoma how she managed to come and see me, she replied that she had insisted until allowed to visit. Although Anoma was years older, I could always connect with her as a friend. She was the gentlest person I had yet met. I wished for a sister like her. Her stay was nearly two hours long, but it seemed just minutes. When I grumbled about having to sit inside a room for days, she replied that her whole life was spent mostly within the four walls of a house.

Anoma's kind consolation had made things more bearable to me, even for a short while.

The other thing was Berty Uncle's surprise gift. Just after Anoma left, I heard a deep voice at the front door. Berty Uncle, the only member of our extended family who has money to spare for life's little luxuries, had delivered a wrapped box to Amma with a verbal message to "smile."

The box seemed heavier than a pair of shoes. I tore open the brown paper packaging, broke through the sturdy cardboard and retrieved a sleek, white baby grand piano. It had golden flecks on its feet and the keyboard was exposed. But if it was a toy musical instrument, the notes were stuck together and wouldn't play. What was the use? Then Amma noticed a tiny ring atop the piano that she lifted and wound up. Two little pink ballerinas sprang up from the top and twirled to *A Maiden's Prayer* without running into each other.

How did Berty Uncle know that I was familiar with this piece of music? Was it a coincidence? It was so much better than the floral dress lengths or pairs of shoes—the things I need rather than the things I want—that he usually gifted.

I played it over and over again until Asoka Aiya demonstrated his irritation by banging on my bedroom door. Old Frisky, our dog, whined in agreement. I played it again, hoping the porcelain maidens weren't getting too tired of pirouetting for my entertainment.

But that was yesterday.

I sat up on the bed and tried to concentrate on the Enid Blyton book of adventure balancing on my knees but having already read it five times before, the secrets and intrigue of *The Secret Seven Fireworks* had the impact of a damp squib. From the kitchen, I heard the rhythmic motion of pestle on mortar; Soma, our borrowed servant, and a luxury we could not afford, was pounding spices into a paste. Looking up, I saw that Olga Aunty had nodded off. I left the bed and gingerly peeked through the part in the curtains covering the doorway. It wasn't the best timing, because Amma chose that moment to come in the front door. She snapped the umbrella she always carried as defense against the merciless sun. Thatha was following behind.

"I told you, Duwa, you have to be inside the room. *Where is* Olga Aunty?"

"I'm here, sister." Olga Aunty, looking sheepish, quickly ushered me back inside.

"The astrologer said that she could be bathed on Friday. It's also a holiday, being Poya Full Moon Day, which means that everyone will be able to come. So you have only two more days to go." She looked placatingly at my indignant expression.

Amma fetched the Dhobi couple once she managed to locate their address. The Dhobi, a tall, wiry man with a sturdy neck whom I privately called Mr. Wash-a-ton, had appraised my recent spurt of growth, nodded his head and decreed: "Baba, you should write down my address."

It was found scribbled in Sinhala in my handwriting in the back pages of the hardbound book she used to record the lot of clothes the washerman bundled and hauled away on his back every three weeks. I used to wonder how he kept track of our clothes; it was seldom that he brought a piece that wasn't ours. Then I noticed the mark that distinguished our clothes from all the others: a cross with dots in each quarter. The mark was placed on the garment's inner neckline or on the corner of a sheet.

Every sixth page of that book was silver-coated, and I remembered once how I had been peeling away the coating with my nail while Amma was gathering the dirty clothes. They had a major part to play in this drama, bringing me some strange girl's clothes to wear while I was in detention. So this was why my frocks were often late when I gave them to be laundered. They were sent around the city to be worn by others in similar distress. Apart from arriving frayed after

8

being smashed on a rock in some riverbed, boiled in a cauldron, faded beyond recognition under their steaming-hot coal irons and starched to paper, my frocks were also worn by others. There should be a law against the whole Dhobi clan.

Years later, I found out the thinking behind the Dhobi family's role in my becoming a woman. It had evolved and had been promoted by the Sinhala caste system, which necessitated that the lower castes seek the succor of the higher ones for sustenance. Traditionally, the Rada or Dhobi caste washed clothes of the higher *Govigama* (farmer) caste in exchange for food and other requirements. Therefore, during occasions such as these when cleaning clothing was necessary, it was only natural that their services were called upon. Their presence was also comforting to the higher echelons, because they were a convenient scapegoat during this time when a girl was vulnerable to the evil eye and other spirit-like influences. Apparently, the Dhobis had seen beyond that; they had exploited the situation and it had stuck as a privilege – of the underprivileged.

***

On Friday when Amma awakened me, I could discern a ribbon of faint crimson light braving the darkness outside. "Get up Duwa, everything is ready. You have about fifteen minutes until your bath time."

"*Ummm?*"

Realization struck. It was The Day. A tremor of fear coursed through my body. Shivering, I got up and walked over to the mirror only to find a blank wall instead and remembered that Amma had removed it from my bedroom. All sensuous thoughts were taboo, and mirrors propagated narcissistic thoughts which, in turn, led to thoughts of the opposite gender—that is why males were banished from the room.

At the auspicious time, Amma shook my long hair loose, wrapped a white cloth over my lean body and shepherded me into the bathroom. Dressed in a flowery cloth and blouse in the typical village fashion, Mrs. Wash-a-ton presided in all her glory. I looked around. The bathroom was now an unfamiliar place, an altar to some goddess who no doubt patronized hapless girls like me. What on earth was the bough of a jak tree doing here?

The woman unceremoniously removed my cloth and bid me sit, shivering on a stool placed in front of a cauldron filled with water. She also held an earthenware pot, which without further ado, she tipped onto my head.

Out tumbled a concoction of leaves and powders that had been floating in cool water.

"*Aaaaaah!*" The cold liquid cascaded down my hair. Pink particles of sandalwood powder, roots of turmeric, margosa and lime leaves escaped the strands and came to rest on the slight contours of my body. Before I could recover from this onslaught, she dipped a pitcher into the cauldron and proceeded to pour more and more cold water over me. I must say it was a welcome rain.

After the flower bath, the woman wrapped a fresh white cloth around me and handed me a knife that I recognized as the one Amma used to break open coconuts. She pointed to the jak branch. What was it I remembered from our whispered conversations in school? If I could cause the milky sap to break out from the branch with one blow, it would indicate a plentiful supply of breast milk in the future.

A few more bizarre rituals later, Amma kissed me and led me to my almirah which contained a brand-new dress in the lucky colors of gold and white. But before I could dress, she smiled and handed me a flat, pink box. I knew what it was—an Angelina bra, size 28.

***

Three aunts, four uncles, five cousins of various ages and a dog greeted my bashful reappearance in society with something of a standing ovation. Deep male voices juxtaposed with treble female ones that in turn were outdone by high-pitched shrill tones. Not to be left out, old Frisky barked his two-cents-worth.

"Tamara, you seem to have grown a couple of inches taller these past few days!"

"Congratulations!"

"There you are, at last. I was beginning to wonder when you would emerge from your hibernation."

"Are you okay Akki? Did you recover from measles?"

Obliging custom, I greeted my elders by presenting them with a sheaf of betel leaves and worshipping at their feet. Beula Aunty took out a pair of flower-shaped gold earrings from a little red box and fastened them on my ears. They went well with the pair of bangles that Amma had slipped on my wrist. Nelson Uncle handed me a brown envelope. There were many other interesting-looking packages on a side table. Everyone smiled and stared at me in turns.

Olga Aunty, famous for dispensing unsought counsel at the drop of a hat, thought this an opportune moment for one of her sermons. She adjusted her spectacles, blew her nose into a white handkerchief that imparted a lilac fragrance and began: "Now that you are a young lady, remember that you

11

can't gallivant about the neighborhood as you used to, especially with boys. So, tell Anura, when he next comes a-calling, that ..."

Fortunately, Thatha, who was beginning to get impatient and had other things on his mind, interrupted. "Oh yes, yes, Olga, I'm sure Tamara knows all that." He hustled everyone toward the dining table laden with the traditional milk rice and sweetmeats like *kavum*, *kokis* and *athiraha*. As we began serving ourselves, I spotted the Dhobi couple lingering in the kitchen. Thatha could neither dispose of them without giving them some food nor invite them to eat before the family had eaten.

I knew what was on Thatha's mind. He rarely had a crowd of males, extra money to spend, *plus* a holiday, at his disposal. It was the ideal opportunity to have a drink.

Shortly afterward, the Dhobi couple left with a flourish of triumph. Bundled on her back, she bore all the spoils of the affair; the soiled garments I had been wearing the past five days, bed linen, white cloth, slippers and even the band that had held back my wavy hair. He bore on his back the other 'burdens,' the gifts of rice, dhal, dried fish, coconuts, and a generous allocation of all the sweetmeats. Less palpable was the folded hundred-rupee note my mother had slipped into the woman's eager palm and was quickly tucked away in the crevices of her bosom, unseen by the husband. The happier she was made, the stronger her blessings, but she was not to know that Amma had surreptitiously made me remove my gold earrings and chain just before my tradition-enforced detention. Rightfully, those would have been hers to claim too.

A Maiden's Prayer

They were hardly out of the gate when Thatha ran into the bedroom and returned brandishing two bottles of Mendis Special coconut arrack.

"Let the show begin—I bought this for the special occasion!"

A wave of appreciative murmurs rose from the males, but the sisters gave each other wooden looks before preparing to move away from the sitting room. "It's Poya day too, how can Buddhists behave like this?" I heard Mary Aunty whisper to Beula Aunty. "Ting-ting ... ting-ting ... ting-a-tingting ... ting-a-tingting ...." As if in empathy, the gong pealed in the neighborhood temple to summon children to the mid-morning daham class. Poya day, or the Day of the Full Moon, is significant to Buddhists, who are encouraged to suspend normal routines and use the time for religious undertakings such as fasting, meditating, visits to the temple, worshipping and listening to dhamma discourses. I can safely assume that a party with alcoholic underpinnings is not an option the Government had in mind when it sanctioned the holiday.

Olga Aunty couldn't resist the chance to butt in; "What is this, Oswald, must you drink today as well, now that you also have a grown-up daughter?" She admonished my father, the fall of her sari quivering with her outburst. Amma paused with a hopeful look.

"That's exactly what I'm doing; celebrating my grown-up daughter!" he replied, to the amusement of the uncles.

"Did you hear about Walter Fernando? He passed away recently, all because of drinking. He had liver problems."

"What men! Those who drink will die and those who don't drink will also die, depending on their genes. So, it's better to enjoy life and conk off gracefully when the time comes."

"Is this the example you're setting for your son? Do you like him doing the same thing? Do you want his ruin?"

"Of course, he should take a drink. If he doesn't, let him wear a housecoat and be in the kitchen!"

Olga Aunty's face changed. She knew it was hopeless to battle with my father on this topic. "All right, all right, Oswald, I don't want to talk about this. Have it your way!" she called out as she left the room.

When my father presided over family gatherings, drinking sessions and the inevitable boisterous singing followed. When he was absent, the females ruled and the atmosphere rarely got rambunctious with their discussions of "life in the good-old-days," English teaching methods or the merits of graduate English teachers against those of trained teachers (those who pronounced "not" and "pot" as "note" and "port"). The four sisters, apart from sharing the same mother, had a common career as English teachers.

But my father knew how to whip up a party much like a gale could stir up a monsoon.

"Ice, Duwa, get us some ice," he requested, and in his haste, trampled old Frisky's tail. The dog yelped in pain and retreated outside. "And while you're there, get five glasses as well."

My "period of banishment" (forgive the pun), was already history to him. It was back to business.

"Blossom, could you make us something for a bite?" he called out to my mother. My mother had not been married for nineteen years to my father for nothing—she was already thawing some sausages. "Make it very hot and don't forget to put some Marketing Department chili sauce."

Olga Aunty maintained that Mendis Special, a pure arrack distilled from the fermented sap of the coconut flower, warmed the gut, and wagged the tongue. I wondered how she knew when neither she nor any of her sisters partook of any. I had no way of testing the first assertion apart from taking Asoka Aiya's word for it (he had tried it on the sly), but in listening to the conversation that ensued, the latter part proved true.

"These bloody Communist fellows in the government, they have a good time going on foreign trips every month," Thatha began. "We don't even have anything decent to eat, so what harm is there in having a drink now and then?"

"True, true," the voices chorused. "We are supporting local industry."

"At any rate, it's cheerio to all the imported stuff—forget the Globe butter, the Kraft cheese, and Maldive fish," Nelson Uncle acknowledged, with the sorrow befitting one who loved his food.

"Sirimavo Bandaranaike came into power in 1970 promising rice from the moon. But the first thing she did was halve the free weekly measure that the previous government used to give to the poor. Now the emphasis is on austerity as if a war is on. How things have changed in two years!" Thatha sounded exasperated.

"They ration everything and want us to live on *manioc* and *koss ata*. Catch me growing yams!" said Martin Uncle whose property had a spacious back yard that could accommodate a considerable plantation.

"I can do without a lot of these things, but not the Bombay onions," lamented Nelson Uncle. "I want Bombay onions in my *seeni sambol.*"

Seeni sambol is a sweet and hot relish that does wonders for any Ceylonese meal. Bombay onions, a large, pinkish-purple variety imported from India for its pungency and flavor, are finely diced and tempered with a sprig of curry leaves, garlic, a piece of cinnamon, chili powder and Maldive fish, a tuna fish preserve that is imported from the Maldivian Islands. Sugar is added at the end to take the sting out of the chili. The cooking aroma is heavenly, and it advertises itself to the entire neighborhood.

Nelson Uncle was still going on about the scarcity of the onions.

"Yesterday Olga went marketing in Borella and couldn't buy any Bombay onions from the bloody black-market fellows who are hoarding it, as usual, waiting some more time so that they can raise the price further."

"Let's hope the onions will become rotten while they wait!"

"Think of the poor—or rather the rich—people who are going to lose all that land? What can you do with fifty acres when you are used to having thousands? Think of the produce from all those estates? The dowries they were planning to give? We only miss our Bombay onions, but they have to give up their ancestral land."

Martin Uncle was referring to the controversial Land Reform Bill that was introduced recently, which placed a ceiling on land ownership at twenty-five acres of paddy land and fifty acres of other land. Children over the age of eighteen could own the same acreage, but few had written the land in their children's names.

"Ceylon used to be such a wonderful place to live." Martin Uncle sighed.

"Haaa, we're not even living in Ceylon now. The independent member of the British Commonwealth has become Sreee Lanka!" Nelson Uncle dragged the "e" to show his displeasure of the government changing our country's name in 1972. This had happened a few months back, so no one had quite got accustomed to it yet.

"Harpasix fellows!" Thatha offered his favorite expression, which had no origins in the Sinhala or English languages. I have never heard anyone else use it, and I suspect he had made it up. Asoka Aiya loved that expression because he thought it contained just the correct amount of ridicule to belittle someone.

"Fortunately, these things don't concern me too much now."

Everybody looked at Berty Uncle as if seeing him there for the first time. He had kept quiet during the preceding conversation, lapsed in deep thought as he sometimes was. Berty Uncle is Nelson Uncle's younger brother who for the past three years had lived and worked in Saudi Arabia. He was on vacation for three weeks and was by and large unruffled by our country's many ills that the others complained about.

At thirty-two, Berty Uncle was tall and nicely built, not too thin, yet not so large as to appear awkward. He had the money, so he was always dressed in imported shirts, trousers and shoes that had a different cut and quality to those worn by everyone else. But the forehead above his well-cut eyebrows was gradually increasing in size; grey hairs were popping up, and we cousins were monitoring the bald patch on the back of his head as well. What began as smaller than a twenty-five-cent coin had now become more like fifty-cents. It appeared to be in competition with his receding hairline.

Berty Uncle was supposed to be on the hunt for a wife. So he provided our family with a constant occupation, which had intensified after a near brush with matrimony a few years ago. It's difficult to imagine Berty Uncle settling down and I thought that the woman, whoever she was, had been spared a husband with a roving eye. The story circulated was that he had changed his mind at the last minute, but one day I heard my mother tell someone that the woman had found out about his numerous affairs, including the ones on-going, and her parents had hastily called off the planned engagement party.

Everybody, including the grownups in the family, knew that Berty Uncle had had many girls; they were frustrated that he hadn't married any of them. Now they turned a blind eye to his affairs and continued to promote him to the world as "a wonderful prospect" and "a good catch." We cousins referred to him as "Dirty Berty," a terrible sounding adjective and one that was unkind and not altogether fair, because Berty Uncle was the closest we had to a family Santa Claus.

I thought Berty Uncle would marry soon. As my cousin Renuka whispered, that fifty-cent coin was showing every possibility of turning into a rupee.

Thatha began humming the refrain of a *baila*, denoting the natural progression of gaiety. Martin Uncle asked me to fetch a plastic bucket from the kitchen, which he turned upside down and started thumping in time to the song about Babi Aachchi's bicycle. Nelson Uncle shouted to Soma to bring a couple of spoons, which he turned into an impromptu musical instrument by clicking them together in a ripple effect. As Thatha's inebriated voice rose in the neighborhood, drowning out the intermittent peals of the temple, Old Frisky began howling in the kitchen.

If there was one thing we couldn't avoid, it was music, even that induced by alcohol. We cousins were drawn into the circle like bees to flowers, even though our mothers had drifted into a bedroom, where they attempted to shut out the din.

We also got the opportunity to closely examine Berty Uncle's expanding "coinage" from many rear vantage points.

CHAPTER 2

THE MUDALIYAR IN THE RAJAKARUNA FAMILY

When Olga Aunty married Nelson Uncle in 1964, our family got its own Mudaliyar. Nelson and Berty Rajakaruna could trace their ancestry to the mid-nineteenth century, when James Peiris Siriwardene Rajakaruna, their great-grandfather, was a Mudaliyar under British rule.

When school history lessons touched on the Mudaliyars, I stopped daydreaming for a while and paid attention to the teacher. The Mudaliyars, comparable to English country squires, were chief headmen of ancient Ceylon under a patriarchal form of government. The Portuguese in 1505, the Dutch in 1658, and the British in 1796 were the three colonial powers who sailed into, subdued, and ruled the inhabitants of our tiny Indian Ocean island. They realized the advantage of using the native Mudaliyars to rule the Ceylonese and vested in them military powers on top of the feudal rights they possessed over the peasantry. They were also confined to the elite Govigama caste, traditionally cultivators and herdsmen, and considered a cut above most except for royalty.

Particularly under British rule, the Mudaliyars became an indispensable link between the rulers and the ruled. They collected revenues, settled the taxes and contributions, assembled locals for government service, provided coolies for labor, quelled uprisings, and represented the locals' interests to the masters.

In return, Mudaliyars were gifted with land, granted a license entitling them to acquire more duty-free land and gained favoritism in trade over their competitors.

Nelson and Berty Uncles' great-grandfather had certainly excelled while discharging his administrative duties and rendering services to his masters. Mudaliyar Rajakaruna was a pampered headman who had accumulated great wealth and property that had sustained his family as well as successive generations. Chief among them was an estate in Panadura, sixteen miles south of Colombo, along the coast. It encompassed several hundred acres of coconut and paddy fields and a mansion that the patriarch had built to accommodate a growing family.

When they were children, Nelson and Berty had been entranced by the family stories related to them by their father. In keeping with the Mudaliyar image, their great-grandfather had a stiff mustache like a pair of bicycle handlebars and a strict countenance to match. His uniform consisted of a black epaulet-decked coat with six cords and silver buttons and a sword belt that went across from his right shoulder to the left of his waist. The sword had a hilt and scabbard of silver and was encrusted with jewels.

Apart from land, Mudaliyar perks included personal tomtom beaters, hautboy players and soldiers, called lascarins, who accompanied them on public tours designed to heighten their dignity among the villagers, who didn't always appreciate their haughty demeanor and iron rule.

It was told that whenever Mudaliyar Rajakaruna appeared in public in his jurisdiction, he was escorted by four lascarins.

Thus, he inspired awe and fear and the villagers sprang aside like water parting at a swimmer's advance.

The authoritarian allowed his power to spill over to his personal life. Nelson Uncle and Berty Uncle loved to retell the story of the pre-breakfast drill he had inflicted upon his five male offspring. Every morning, Mudaliyar Rajakaruna, erect and commanding in his riding gear topped with a fashionable Trilby hat, would mount his horse and set off at a brisk trot on a two-mile journey through his property, his sons in tow–a perfect picture of alfresco bonding between father and sons, except that the sons had to run behind on foot to keep up with the paternal rider. Were they to stumble, scrape, or cut themselves in the thick shrubbery of the estate, fatherly concern or first aid would not ensue; they were expected to pick themselves up and continue. Not surprisingly, the boys often arrived home bruised, and after a quick clean up, were expected to seat themselves at the table where their mother and two sisters, clad in lace, would await mutely behind bowls of hot porridge. When the last exhausted member of the family had arrived and seated himself, the father would pick up his spoon.

Despite the severe upbringing, the five sons were provided adequate properties to launch them into landed ownership, while the daughters were given in marriage with treasures (in native parlance) equal to the weight of an elephant. These included cars, jewelry, gold and silver coins, brass ornaments, and household furniture and utensils.

Over the next two generations, with the outer parameters of the estate sectioned off to settle successive offspring, the inheritance dwindled and the wealth decreased. This was in keeping with the situation for much of the Mudaliyar progeny.

By the middle of the twentieth century, more stories than wealth circulated about these colorful personalities.

In the Rajakaruna family, following Sinhala tradition, it was customary for the main house to be passed to the youngest son in the family. The tradition was for the girls to be married first and the sons to follow, according to age, and set up households on their own. The youngest son would inherit the parental home and be entrusted with looking after his parents in old age. Thus, Berty Uncle had inherited the old home from his father, who was the youngest grandson of Mudaliyar Rajakaruna. Berty Uncle was then expected to produce a male heir who would continue the upkeep of the place and thereby, the family tradition.

The house still bore the trappings of the revered patriarch. In a glass-fronted almirah in the rear sitting room, the Mudaliyar's uniform, complete with silver buttons, cords, sash, and cap, awaited with a hundred stories of former authority and pomp. Beside it lay his constant companion and witness to his deeds – his sword. On the wall above hung a pair of magnificent crossed swords, believed to be a gift from his British masters for efficiently subduing an outbreak of civil disobedience in 1870 occasioned by the misbehavior of outside officials.

In 1923, Berty Uncle's father, William Rajakaruna, had inherited the main house with its stories and the sixty remaining acres of land. He had received other properties too, which had disappeared with his lavish living, but in respect of his familial tradition, he had spared his ancestral home.

Nearly three decades later, with the demise of his wife in a car accident that had left him crippled, Rajakaruna Sr. had promptly divided the property between his three children.

Leaving the middle portion with the main house for his youngest son, Berty, he had apportioned twenty acres from either side to his elder son, Nelson, and daughter, Elisa.

Both Nelson Uncle and Berty Uncle were proud of their ancestral house, admittedly crumbling and a shabby version of its previous grandeur. The white paint and concrete of the balconies and balustrades were chipped and broken in large patches; the children had been cautioned not to run up the wooden staircase anymore because it was rickety and some steps were moving; the back verandah had a sloping roof that I admired, but the gutters were blocked and broken, so rainwater came crashing down without order and over the years had caused erosion holes in the ground; the double doors leading from the front verandah had several patterned glass window inserts, but they were cracked in places, and someone had glued paper to hold the glass together.

The house, had it anticipated the comforting pitter-patter of fifth-generation sons to lead it into the future, had so far been disappointed.

When the tragedy of the accident occurred, Berty Uncle was a playful nine-year-old with much older siblings. Nelson Uncle, at twenty, was already working, while Elisa Aunty had finished her schooling and was being displayed in the marriage market. Elisa Aunty, however, had a mind of her own and announced her intention to marry one Tony Abrew, a cooperative inspector for the Panadura region.

Rajakaruna Sr. was outraged. Tony, in addition to being undersupplied in the education department, was also lacking in caste and means. Tony hailed from a family of cinnamon cultivators in the Galle District and belonged to the Salagama caste, according to the old Sinhalese social system.

Unlike tea bushes and coffee trees cultivated in our country by the colonizers, the cinnamon tree is native to Sri Lanka. The colonial Portuguese, who prized Ceylon cinnamon as the best in the world, exported it to Europe. They used the labor of Tony's ancestors, cinnamon planters, who often adopted Portuguese last names such as Mendis, Silva and de Zoysa.

Europeans used cinnamon to preserve and flavor food, and possessing it amounted to a status symbol as it was so expensive. I guess it didn't automatically follow that the Ceylonese cultivators were of an equally high social status, because Rajakaruna Sr. bemoaned the entry of a "low-caste pariah" into his family.

I learned in school that the Dutch, who were even crazier about cinnamon (how a pungent- smelling bark of a tree could generate such greed, I can't imagine), allowed those associated with cinnamon planting to achieve economic power and gave them the ability to buy land, and thus gain greater status. But I guess these historical facts were lost on Rajakaruna Sr.

Though his daughter was podgy and bereft of beauty, he thought her dowry would cover those deficiencies that cosmetics couldn't. But with no willpower left to fight the resolve of his daughter and with little opposition from Nelson Uncle, he reluctantly agreed to the union.

After the marriage, Rajakaruna Sr. urged his daughter not to leave home as was customary. Despite the many servants he employed, there was nothing like a daughter for an ailing father. Besides, young Berty would benefit from having the sister keep an eye on him. Nelson Uncle had passed his London Matriculation and joined the Coconut Development Board as an inspector, which meant living outstation. Writing from the coconut groves of Kurunegala, sixty miles northeast of Colombo, he, too, advised Elisa Aunty not to move away from home.

Tony, who did not own a house, was more than happy to live in his wife's home that had the added attraction of proximity to his workplace. Consensus was that they would build a house on the adjoining land Elisa Aunty had received and move there later. Rajakaruna Sr. fondly envisaged his three children amicably settled in a triangular utopia.

For some time, there was even tenor. Elisa Aunty continued her role as the lady of the house, with a firm grip on matters ranging from her father's fixed deposits and the salaries of the servants to the extraction of coconut oil. She was her father's crutch until he died four years later.

A few years after his father died, when Nelson Uncle got a transfer to Colombo, it was too uncomfortable for him to live in the same house as Tony. Also, his daily commute to work was too long. Nelson Uncle sold a part of his land and built his own home in a posh area called Borella, in Colombo. It had taken him several years to work out the transfer to Colombo and marry Olga Aunty who was working there as a teacher. Berty Uncle was now fourteen, and after their father's death, Nelson Uncle took him under his wing, deeming he needed more fathering than mothering. Rajakaruna Sr. had enrolled Berty Uncle in a premier boy's school in Colombo — Royal College — but he had been placed in the school hostel since the bus commute from Panadura was daunting to the boy. Berty Uncle was happy to live with Nelson Uncle and Olga Aunty, whose house was only a couple of miles away from school, but he came to Panadura during the school holidays.

But years later, their sister was still the mistress of the estate and had not bothered to build her own home. She had produced two daughters and was firmly ensconced in the house, which for all intents and purposes belonged to her. Her Cooperative Inspector husband turned out to be a good-for-nothing schemer who had married her for her means.

***

It was late afternoon. Old Frisky was in the kitchen with Soma, lapping at his water bowl. It was still my party, but it had long ceased to center on me, apart from Amma seeking me out from time to time to touch my forehead as if I had a fever or hug me close into the folds of her sari for no reason at all. By then I had changed out of my golden dress with its stuffy, elbow-length sleeves into a sleeveless poplin frock with a long and full flared skirt.

The four sisters remained in the bedroom, where they lolled on the bed directly underneath the ceiling fan like walruses at the beach and continued to reminisce softly among themselves.

"Remember the vadai with a dried prawn on it that cost one cent a piece?" Mary Aunty was saying. "We used to buy them at the school gate during the lunch interval."

"The leftovers of the previous day went at two for one cent," piped in Olga Aunty.

Dhamith, my youngest cousin in the extended family who gets away with everything, made a diversion by tickling the four pairs of lined up soles with a mango leaf to surprised yelps and loving protestations. He then nuzzled against their cool, butter nylon saris.

The boisterous group in the sitting room was still at the bottle (there were two empties on the floor) and the savory bites that Amma had to intermittently supply. Eyes reddish, hair awry and shirts unbuttoned, they expunged each other's political viewpoints with fresh ones of their own.

Berty Uncle was saying that the reason for Sri Lanka's food crisis couldn't be blamed solely on the current government. We Ceylonese had become accustomed to free rations, he said, and the population had risen drastically since independence from the British.

"I read that the cost of food imports is out of control, while exports earn only a limited income," he said.

"The British only wanted to continue the tea and rubber exports; they neglected to support agriculture," Martin Uncle added.

I surveyed the scene.

The group had munched their way through two strings of sausages (that was all we had at home and shops were closed on Poya day, so Soma could not be dispatched for more), ten fried eggs sunny side up and a packet of salted cashew nuts. Only Thatha smoked, but the air was thick with cigarette smog.

Berty Uncle, however, had stopped drinking and was looking pensively at his empty glass and glancing at his wristwatch one too many times. Jasmine noticed it too and whispered that he may have an upcoming appointment with a lady friend. Asoka Aiya commented that it seemed an opportune time to deflate a tire in Berty Uncle's mustard yellow Ford Capri. I quelled the potential mischief by threatening to tell on him.

Despite the derision, I admired Berty Uncle. He led his life without bowing to anything or anyone. He was his own master. Of course, the money helped. If tradition didn't suit him, he chucked it by the wayside, which was more than I could do for myself.

Berty Uncle was never nasty to anyone, not even to Elisa Aunty, who was practically stealing his property. Although it was a battered old house, it didn't follow that he should surrender that easily to Elisa Aunty's scheme. To borrow a phrase from Olga Aunty, "it was a matter of principle."

***

Berty Uncle attended university from 1962 to 1966. During these years he stayed with his sister during his term breaks at the insistence of Nelson Uncle who knew that Elisa Aunty had designs on the house. Once, I overheard Berty Uncle say that the house that had seemed enormous when he was a child now appeared crowded and bursting at the seams.

There was nary a stick of cinnamon, but there was a burgeoning brood of kinsmen.

One by one, on some pretext or the other, Tony's village relatives from Galle had descended on the house, reminding Berty Uncle of the Arabian Nights story of the encroaching camel that displaced the Bedouin from his tent in the cold of the night. If you let the nose of the camel in the tent, pretty soon you are living with two humps, I heard him say.

Berty Uncle said he felt like the displaced Arab whenever he went to Panadura.

The front room was occupied by one of Tony's nephews who had found an easy work commute and even easier board and lodging. Two more rooms were in use by Tony's cousins' pig-tailed daughters who were in school. If that was not bad enough, in lieu of his "temporary visitor" status, Berty Uncle had to share his room with a younger brother who neither worked nor schooled and seemed to while away his waking hours inside the room, quivering his leg and contemplating the ceiling. When the rippling motion had annoyed him beyond endurance, he had complained to Elisa Aunty who had merely retorted, "So what's wrong with sharing a room? You have been so spoiled! At Peradeniya, the undergrads share their rooms?"

Amidst this parasitic clan, Berty Uncle's visits dwindled, and those that took place were the result of Nelson Uncle's coaxing. Olga Aunty was not happy to visit as Elisa Aunty was resentful, though not openly hostile.

I heard that one day when Nelson Uncle and Olga Aunty went into the storage shed where coconuts from the estate were usually kept, there were none to be found. As usual, Elisa Aunty had begun complaining about the diminishing yield due to the beetle infestation and the expensive manure she had to buy.

It was an unwritten rule in the family that they all shared the property's produce. When their father was living, every acre of the land provided a bi-monthly yield of about seven hundred to one thousand coconuts that were sold to a wholesale buyer at the prevailing market rate. Nelson Uncle remembered his father sending a male servant every morning to pick up the few fruits that the pluckers had missed or that had fallen from the trees during the night. These were stored in the shed. Even after a generous allowance for personal consumption, they would have enough to offer their relatives or sell to whoever wanted to buy.

Although the beetle infestation of 1971 had done great damage to crops, especially in the Coconut Triangle cities of Kalutara, Kurunegala and Chilaw, with the import of the counter-parasite from Fiji and the subsequent elimination of the pest, yields across the country had increased in the previous months and were nearing normalcy. Hitherto, without any effort on anyone's part, coconuts would get collected in the storeroom and languish for months without attention. Now someone had sold them or had taken great pains to hide them. The same was true of the cashews, jackfruit, mangoes, breadfruit, olives, and other produce that had grown for decades in the fertile soil.

Nelson Uncle was even more distressed to learn that Tony had sold a two-acre plot of Elisa Aunty's share of the property from its outer fringes. Enormous gouges of red soil were missing as well, leaving empty scars where firm ground had once been. Tony and his clan were living off the land in more ways than one.

Nelson Uncle was saddened by the gradual decay of the house. It looked neglected and badly needed a coat of paint and repairs. Moreover, silverfish were attacking the treasured Mudaliyar uniform. The key to the almirah had been misplaced, so it could not be rescued or repaired short of breaking down the ancient cupboard, which in itself was a family heirloom. The jewel-encrusted sword had long been robbed of its luster. The crossed swords above were rusting. No one seemed to care.

During a couple of visits, Nelson Uncle had brought up the subject with Elisa Aunty as to why they did not build their house as planned. He reminded her that the house belonged to Berty Uncle. The standard answer was not having enough money; she was not working, and they had to live on Tony's small salary. Besides, what was the hurry, as Berty was either living in Colombo or out of the country?

In this atmosphere of strained relationships, Nelson Uncle and Olga Aunty recognized that the last remaining path for Berty Uncle to lay claim to his inheritance was marriage and the production of an heir or two. If he had a family, he had a legitimate reason to claim the house. If the heir turned out to be male all the better, as he would carry on the Rajakaruna lineage.

But with Berty Uncle, this was easier said than done.

CHAPTER 3

DIRTY BERTY

B erty Uncle — who had no idea that he was "Dirty Berty" to the younger crowd — began adulthood on a promising note. He was the only graduate in the family. He studied in the vast halls of Peradeniya University in Kandy and graduated with honors in Civil Engineering. Nelson Uncle said it was a rare feat considering that this was one of only two indigenous universities producing engineering graduates in 1960s Ceylon, the other being the University of Colombo. Nelson Uncle also reportedly said it was difficult to decide whether he or his brother was more surprised. I suspect Nelson Uncle had resigned himself to a lifetime of untangling his brother's romantic entanglements and Berty Uncle's intellect and inborn mathematical talents came as a surprise.

By all accounts, if Berty Uncle's career progressed well, his numerous love affairs progressed even better. Nestled in the salubrious climate of the cool Hill Country among verdant vistas and plenty of rose bushes, Peradeniya Campus had provided a fertile breeding ground. To the disappointment of the family, none of these affairs resulted in the socially desirable state of marriage.

His single status wasn't due to a lack of marriage proposals either, as none were sought more avidly than engineers, doctors, and accountants, the elite matrimonial triumvirate of the day. Of course, everyone conceded that Berty Uncle had all the qualifications to be selective.

But thus far, Berty Uncle had managed to dismiss them all with a quick wit and ready rebuttal. One prospect was "so thin that her bones could be heard rattling in the wind;" another had a bossy, rotund mother and he predicted the daughter stepping into a similar role five years hence; one was bespectacled and her glasses were compared to the base of a bottle, and yet another had *a sister* with a protruding lip. (As far as the girlfriends were concerned, such idiosyncrasies were irrelevant; he found them easily and discarded them just as readily.) In truth, Berty Uncle was fighting commitment; to him, the lynchpin of matrimony was the blight of marriage.

Of course, everyone conceded that Berty Uncle had all qualifications to be selective. Olga Aunty, the self-appointed family consulter of horoscopes and firm believer in planetary placement concerning destiny, had declared, on borrowed authority from her astrologer, that there was no favorable alignment of planets for marriage in his horoscope until he passed the age of forty.

Behind their backs, when only Thatha was around, Berty Uncle scoffed that he was single due to his own choice and that "the placement of planets—aligned, misaligned, or otherwise—had no bloomin' part to play."

His stance was, "Why buy a cow when milk is available in plentiful supply?"

"Well, may I point out the danger in consuming possibly contaminated milk supplied by various cows on the loose?" I heard Thatha retort one day, a sensible comment for him.

"It's worse if I get sour milk from the same cow, day after day, isn't it? And then, it might proceed to hoof and mouth disease." Berty Uncle could not be outwitted and propounded longer on the cow theory, but I couldn't follow much more because Asoka Aiya caught me hiding behind the door curtain and threatened to yell unless I parted with my weekly pocket money.

After he sauntered out with my coins jingling in his trouser pocket and with some nefarious plan or the other on his mind as to how best to spend them, I returned to my perch behind the curtain. The sacrificial two rupees, which equaled a week's worth of popsicles and salmon buns from the school tuck shop, was worth what was to come.

Nelson Uncle had broached a promising new potential with attractive family connections, and Berty Uncle didn't have the heart to argue with his brother.

"I can't carry on this bluff forever," he confided to Thatha. "I will have to settle down. My congenial band of friends has all but disappeared. Those days, they were more than happy to pursue girls with me or spend hours drinking at the Venus Club."

"One by one," he announced in a dull voice, "they succumbed to the pestilence that is marriage."

Whenever he visited their homes, there was always a seemingly suspicious wife hovering in the background and a mewling baby or irritating child clamoring for attention so that the uninterrupted conviviality of the previous days could not be recaptured. On the rare occasions they conceded to meet him outside, their brows were furrowed and conversations peppered with "finding a good Colombo school," "saving for university education," "building a house," and other such necessities that revolved around money and responsibilities in which he could not join.

In his heart of hearts, Berty Uncle told Thatha, he realized that marriage would give him a firm place in society and a family of his own that would settle his listlessness.

"I feel as if I have an umbilical cord with a question mark attached to the other end," he declared.

I was so captivated with that poetic image that I almost fell from my perch on that wobbly stool placed behind the door curtain. I also realized that it would be dangerous to remain on the stool; if Amma came into my room, as much as she would discover my eavesdropping, she could also bump into me and injure herself. So, I pushed the three-legged danger aside and lay supine on the bed with my hands bent under the head to frame what I imagined to be a casual, restful look. If interrupted, I could close my eyes and pretend to be asleep.

Berty Uncle admitted to Thatha that if not for Olga Aunty, he would be lost. Olga Aunty, who had always wanted a brother, had firmly steered and installed him in our family circle.

But still, there were the odd moments when, looking around at his adopted family circle, he felt he did not quite belong. He was sandwiched between the older members who were well into their forties or early fifties, and the younger generation who engaged him in their banter but called him "uncle."

Thatha assured him that he was always welcome at our house and would be treated like a brother. I noticed that Berty Uncle had begun to be at ease and find his tongue in the garrulous presence of our family thanks to Thatha who was on the same carefree wavelength, albeit often alcohol-induced and sans a financial foundation.

***

Thatha was often privy to Berty Uncle's escapades with women. So was I. He often referred to a woman called Liberty Lisa who masqueraded as a masseuse and ran a shady parlor called Liberty Massages down Galle Road.

Ramani, Kamani, Priya, Jayangani, and Thusitha were a quintuplet with more sensible sounding monikers; I gathered they were decent women whose only crimes were looking for husbands.

Old flames he reignited – or rather, they refused to extinguish, no doubt on account of his ever-expanding wallet.

I got to know them all and jotted down notes on their adventures, because, one day, I planned to be a writer. I instinctively felt Berty Uncle's stories would be grist to any writer's mill. But now, looking back a few years later, I wonder whether these notes are true reflections of the deeper sentiments that he must have harbored.

And then, new flames lit up his life, and in a different way, lit up mine too.

During one of his vacations, he related the following story to Thatha. I'm glad I made copious notes on this one.

"Can you remember that girl I was going out with – the teacher named Shanthi?" Berty Uncle began after a meal at our place. Amma and Asoka Aiya had dispersed to do chores, and everyone assumed that I, being out of sight, was out of sound too. They also had no idea about the conveniently placed frayed spot in the door curtain which I had rounded into a tiny peephole.

Thatha nodded and settled back in his chair in anticipation.

"Shanthi's parents had started to bring proposals for her, so she had told them about me. Now, you know me, I never utter the word 'marriage,' but these girls have a one-track mind and they think ..."

"Okay, okay, get on with the story; I know all about that." Thatha smiled and reached into his breast pocket for his pack of Player's Navy Cut.

"When Shanthi told her mother about me, she had said that they wanted to meet me. For my bad luck Os, the girl's elder brother, who's a seaman, was home on leave, and the mother said that she would send her son to meet me first."

Thatha paused from his task of smoothing his cigarette. "And you got cold-feet?"

"Cold-feet and arms ... why should I get married to her? I'm not crazy," declared Berty Uncle. "I was dizzy and more seasick on terra firma than the seaman fellow would be at sea when I heard that he was coming to meet me."

I nearly burst out laughing, as Thatha did, but controlled myself in time.

Berty Uncle's brains didn't stop at engineering construction projects. He contacted a friend and devised a plot.

The next day, as appointed, the seaman had turned up at Berty Uncle's friend's office in the Colombo Fort, where Berty Uncle was already present.

Perfunctory introductions performed, the seaman had inquired for a quiet place to talk.

"We can go to the Fortune," Berty Uncle said.

"At this time?" the seaman said. The popular bar located among offices in the Colombo Fort supported a steady clientele of working alcoholics, such as my father.

"It's 10 a.m. now, what's that? We go even earlier on other days."

Reluctantly, the seaman had accompanied them to the premises. Berty Uncle demonstrated his familiarity with the place, thumping the barman on his back and addressing him rather loudly with his first name.

"What can I get for you?" the barman asked.

"A beer," the seaman replied.

"A beer? Only children drink beer. Let's have a shot," Berty Uncle said, ordering a whole bottle of Old Arrack, ignoring the protestations of the nonplussed man.

Three generous glasses were poured. Berty Uncle and his friend drank theirs in a few hearty gulps and refills were poured while the seaman nursed his first.

"How's sea life? It must be fun visiting so many ports around the world. How long were you working? I wish I had that opportunity. Gala time, girls in every port, that kind of thing." Berty Uncle even winked at the seaman for special effect.

The first bottle was fast depleting, and the weather-beaten seaman's face was getting darker by the minute. He acted as if to leave, but Berty Uncle motioned him to stay and tried to order another half-bottle.

That was the last straw. He got up, thanked the two of them, and made his way out of the bar.

And that was the last Berty Uncle had seen of the seaman or his sister. Shanthi had phoned him and scolded him as only a woman could scold.

Thatha choked on his cigarette while attempting to smoke and laugh simultaneously. Berty Uncle beamed.

If Berty Uncle's life was a book, Thatha — and I — were appreciative readers.

CHAPTER 4

STORIES FROM SAUDI ARABIA

Berty Uncle's unique status of living abroad helped endear him to everybody. It wasn't just the gifts. It was also the stories. To us, he was Sinbad the Sailor. Most of all, we were enthralled by his reports of abundant food and magnificent meals.

In 1973, Ceylon was three years into Sirimavo Bandaranaike's socialist government. Farmers were urged to cultivate more rice and the masses – that includes us – were encouraged to grow alternate crops like sweet potato and manioc on every available inch of land. The starchy and fibrous tubers were to be our new staple. Now we had a Ceylonese diet.

Bandaranaike had stopped imports, thereby stripping store shelves bare of foreign labeled goodies. There wasn't much else on those shelves because black marketeers hid the remaining and charged a small ransom for them from moneyed folk. In this rice-dependent nation, ration cards limited the quantity of rice the public could buy at an affordable price. Faced with food shortages, substitutes, price hikes, and queues, we were a hungry people.

So, when Berty Uncle declared that he often ate a whole fried chicken by himself for dinner, we screamed.

"The whole chicken to yourself? That's unheard of – we are lucky to get a piece here!" Someone summed up our thoughts loudly.

Chicken curry – tender meat suffused in spicy, coconut milk-laden gravy – is the high point of a Ceylonese spread. The delicacy was more of a luxury now with poultry so expensive. Berty Uncle said he paid ten Saudi Riyals for an oil-dripping, fragrant and golden fried chicken that broke apart at slight pressure. Amma couldn't even remember when she had last purchased a whole broiler.

The roti in the bakery is as big as an LP record, Berty Uncle announced, making a circle with his hands. Dhamith promptly asked him to bring us an "LP roti" the next time Berty Uncle came on vacation. The roti we make at home is smaller than a tea saucer, someone remarked wistfully. The grass is always greener on the other side. Even though our roti is small, it doesn't lack taste and fills you up with its generous share of shredded coconut mixed with wheat flour.

Berty Uncle tasted Indian food in restaurants. Although India is our nearest neighbor and its cuisine influences ours, we were unfamiliar with Indian food. The herby marinated lamb, the puffed puris and the cottage cheese in creamy spinach sauce that he described made us hungry. Kulfi, the Indian version of ice cream, sounded wickedly good.

We didn't envy Berty Uncle's good fortune, but we wondered – and sighed – at the bounty he described.

Palm trees bursting with soft, honey-filled dates, some golden, others burnished copper, yellow, red—dozens of varieties that no longer made their way to Ceylon. Of course, Thatha and Nelson Uncle had memories from the past.

The fish markets slippery with gleaming fish caught fresh by fisherfolk that hauled their nets into the marine life-rich Red Sea. With its coastal location, Jeddah is a fishing haven, Berty

Uncle explained. The fishermen sold the fish cheap and by the whole; tuna, mackerel, sole, shark, mullet, and bream.

Ham, cheese, baked beans, green peas, and corn packed in tins and brought over from England, America, and Australia.

Camel meat.

There was a pause. Berty Uncle said it tasted "peculiar."

Thick and gooey chocolates from England, Switzerland, and Austria: Toblerone, Kit Kat, and Mars. He brought us ample quantities to testify.

Green, red, and yellow apples bought by the kilo and a daily staple, a crunchy and juicy thirst-quencher in the desert. That was lost on me. Apples were always red in picture books, and I had never eaten an apple of any color.

He was our Scheherazade, spinning tales of Arabia to a flock of curious relatives who never tired of his stories and regarded him with a Godlike reverence because he had crossed the oceans.

He wandered about the souqs, the medieval markets of the Middle East, where for hundreds of years, camel trains used to bring the riches of the world to the Middle East and the Ottoman Empire.

His entertainment consisted not of television programs or films (that were in Arabic anyway) but meandering through the serpentine alleys of old Jeddah town. Camel stools jostled for space with bolts of fabric. Ripening fruit and vegetables begged to be taken home. Incense wafted through the air and cast a dizzying spell. Pyramids of fragrant spices and dried fruit were displayed in gunny sacks. The white-bearded shoe merchants sat against a backdrop of neat rows of leather chappels pinned to the ceiling.

A Maiden's Prayer

"For you, special price," a trader would beckon, unraveling a magnificent carpet with crimson tassels. "You want nice coffee pot? Just look my shop," another would say, holding aloft a brass beauty. Bargaining was expected and nothing was accomplished without a smile.

Berty Uncle dazzled us with descriptions of the gold souq; a veritable Aladdin's Cave that he first entered, mouth agape at the row upon row of gleaming 22-carat bangles, bracelets and chunky necklaces that the jeweler would sometimes wear around his neck like a lion's mane.

In this Islamic country, the mosques were enchanting. He spoke of their grandeur and architectural splendor. In ancient times, muezzins used to call the faithful for prayers from the minarets. But now, he said, the task has been taken over by loudspeakers concealed in the intricate designs of the turrets.

Muslims, however, did not need a mosque to pray five times a day: at dawn, midday, afternoon, sunset, and evening. Often, in a corner of a room, they would unroll a colorful prayer rug, face Mecca and touch their forehead to ground. Mecca, lying inland east of Jeddah, is the place where the Prophet Mohammed was born.

When Ramadhan came and the hours between sunrise and sunset were set aside for fasting, non-Muslims couldn't eat in public. Even smoking in public was taboo. Day became night and night became day, Berty Uncle said.

In the office, the Kerala coffee boy didn't make the morning sustenance and serve everybody in the clattering assortment of tea mugs that he usually did. But the coffee boy loved Berty Uncle (for his generosity, no doubt) enough to make a secret cup for him and beckon him to an isolated room.

43

Life came to a near standstill during Ramadhan. The few nationals in the office made rare appearances. The expatriates bore the brunt of the work, as they often did. The lazy afternoon siesta in the Kingdom became even more slothful. A little after noon, everybody was driven back to their quarters and expected to lunch and nap until the scorching afternoon sun abated. Shops and restaurants remained closed. Nothing stirred. The endless desert landscape held her breath awaiting evening, save for an occasional stream of dust energized by a puny breeze.

At three forty-five p.m. the driver would toot the horn and Berty Uncle and his colleagues would be whisked back to the office, where they worked until seven.

During Ramadan, Muslims took *iftar*, light snacks and cool drinks, shortly after sunset, and a heavier meal later. Shops and restaurants opened and the shopping malls filled up till late into the night. Mosques were a hive of activity. Day became night and night became day.

***

Our family's Arabian Nights could have continued for a thousand and one nights if Berty Uncle hadn't had a job to return to.

Often, visits from these relatives extended beyond Olga Aunty's family. Those whom we only met at weddings and funerals undertook long journeys of a Saturday to chance on Berty Uncle being home. Most in reduced circumstances, they expected to receive money or gifts in kind. Berty Uncle never disappointed. Hundred-rupee currency notes were folded and placed on their palms or shirts, and trouser lengths were proffered and received deferentially with both hands and bent head. They lingered afterward, sipping copious cups of tea, and were easily persuaded to partake of Olga Aunty's lunch or dinner spread.

Former servants of the Rajakaruna family would also slink into the property from nowhere. They would loiter about the front doorsteps, hesitating to go in and hoping to catch the eye of someone inside. The door was kept open until the evening's arrival of mosquitoes. It was a mystery how the servants found out where Berty Uncle lived or when he was visiting. Like ants that tapped each others' antennae to pass vital information, people exchanged news from one another. More money was doled out and more shirts retrieved from that bottomless pit of a trunk which had its airline labels still stuck on.

***

The main reason Berty Uncle went to Saudi Arabia was to build a modern house on his inherited estate in Panadura. He had dreams of renovating the crumbling family home with its outhouse toilets and village-style kitchen and adding alongside a contemporary house with modern bathrooms and pantry.

This is why he needed financial resources, and the job overseas provided just that.

It came to him unexpectedly.

With the oil boom, Saudi Arabia was one of the earliest to open to expatriate labor in the 1970s in a big way. With wealth from "black gold," the country was planning huge infrastructure and industrial development projects but had a totally inadequate workforce to carry them out. Berty Uncle was among the first waves of skilled and unskilled immigrant labor from other, less fortunate Arab and Asian countries that were to flood the rich Gulf countries during the next several years.

A friend from university had noticed a tiny advertisement in the *Sunday Observer* asking for civil engineers to work in Saudi Arabia. Together they had dropped off their applications at a local recruitment agency. To his surprise, Berty Uncle had been called for an interview immediately, while his friend wasn't contacted. He was personally met by an enormous, pot-bellied Saudi Arabian agent who was wearing a headdress that looked like a red-and-white checked tablecloth, and with whom he was closeted nearly two hours in an interview that was more like a meeting between long-lost friends. Berty Uncle said he felt an instant affinity with this red-faced, bulbous-nosed man who kept thumping him on the back, laughing a lot and speaking even more in his Arabic-accented English.

The job offer followed immediately. His friend was never interviewed.

Olga Aunty called it destiny.

***

Afterward, he had been half-minded about accepting the job as Nelson Uncle and Olga Aunty had been totally against this sudden turn of events and strongly advised him to remain in Ceylon and settle into matrimony before thinking of going abroad.

"How will we ever find a girl for you if you leave now?" Olga Aunty had wailed. But his colleagues, on the other hand, hearing of the generous package that included accommodation, food, and transport, had nudged him to take the job. In the end, Berty Uncle decided to accept the offer. He had never been abroad. What would stop him from leaving if he did not like it? He assured his brother that he would return after the year's contract was completed. In fact, he could leave after eleven months, as the last month was vacation time.

No one in our family had been to the Katunayake Airport, much less climbed aboard an airplane and whisked off to another land. Also, at the time, I thought that all those who hopped on a plane went to England. That was the only country on the map that mattered. Radio Ceylon belted out a pop song by an Anglo-Sri Lankan called Bill Forbes, who was also known as Kal Khan. It went thus:

Oh to be in England, now that spring is here!
Oh to be in England, drinking English beer!

Forbes never gave away the gloomy skies, the incessant rain, or the teeny-tiny homes of his beloved "Yingland." Instead he concerned himself with Yorkshire pudding, roast beef, tans, and television. Everybody sighed for England, with its roses and daffodils, the Queen, the London Bridge, and Buckingham Palace.

How romantic was petroleum oil, endless stretches of sandy desert, a burning sun, shrubby frankincense trees, and camels? What of magic carpets and bands of thieves? They were not real, but fairytales that lulled you to sleep.

Time passed before Berty Uncle noticed the comforts and appeal of his new surroundings. Those first few weeks in Riyadh were the hardest. He saw the glass half empty.

He wrote frequent letters to Thatha on scented notepaper that featured background pictures of Bedouins and camel caravans. I saved them all for the rich descriptions they contained. Berty Uncle made a fine writer.

Here's one such letter, written in those early days:

The city is an unfriendly congregation of imposing steel and glass structures. The landscape is dusty and barren and I cringe and yearn for the green tropics of home. The modern highways are grandly suspended mid-air but devoid of life, except for the gleaming cars that whiz past, the occupants concealed by black-tinted windows. Where are the people?

In the souq, women draped in black from head-to-toe slide past, ghost-like. On the weekly Friday holiday, the hundreds of Indian, Pakistani and Bangladeshi laborers while away their time in the commercial district staring desolately; they send their earnings home and have nothing left for their own gratification. The Muezzin's call to prayer mournfully reminding Muslims to pray five times a day clutch at my heart. The days are scorching, and the nights chilly beyond anything I have ever experienced.

The woes piled up, outweighing the contentment. Berty Uncle missed the cushy life in his brother's home, with Soma the servant climbing a mountain of drudgery each day, silent and uncomplaining. Now he had to wash and iron his clothes, tidy his room and clean the bathroom. Under Olga Aunty's watchful eye, every meal was balanced to contain all the food groups. Although he did not have to cook, and the food in the Mess was tasty in the beginning, he soon tired of curries swirling in oil. *The meat – goat, lamb or chicken – would differ, but the dishes, spiced liberally with garam-masala, managed to taste the same*, he wrote. Once he had an uncharacteristic urge to hurl a tandoori roti at the Pakistani cook who slapped down a particularly greasy preparation with a wide grin. The *parathas* were flaky and delicious but ended up around his waist. He thought the Mess was aptly named.

Unlike some of his cronies in Ceylon who lived in perpetual intoxication, Berty Uncle was not addicted to liquor but enjoyed a companionable drink. But alcohol – and gatherings – was prohibited in this authoritative Muslim society, making parties and similar revelry as infrequent as desert rain.

He sent me a picture postcard of a camel race with the following words scribbled on the back: *Tamara, overleaf is a picture of a race you might never see: The Camel Race. Even I haven't seen it. My entire life here is a race anyway, so I won't miss much in not seeing it. Berty Uncle.*

I think Berty Uncle fared better in the office, although he had trouble readily connecting with people of other nationalities. It was a case of being transported from home to work and work to home, much like the camels that gazed dolefully through the backs of the pickup trucks he saw on the highway. By the end of the third week, he had made up his mind to leave, but he could not muster enough courage to tell the man who had recruited him. He felt guilty for taking the opportunity away from somebody else who would have weathered the life there out of financial necessity. He was also faced with the shame of returning; his friends would deem him a sissy who could not face life alone.

Back in his room every evening, as the glaring sun finally set and the last call to prayer pierced the eerie silence, Berty Uncle would decide to write his resignation the next day. But at the office, he could not force himself to act, for he thoroughly enjoyed the work.

Ultimately, it was his work that saw him through. By all accounts, Berty Uncle put his heart and soul into his duties. As time passed, he made friends with his peers and demonstrated an excellent work ethic. He was equally liked by his superiors and peers.

He shaped himself to the environment and began to enjoy himself to a certain extent. He passed the difficult driving tests and bought a car. He met other Ceylonese who were trapped in similar circumstances, away from their loved ones. It became routine to meet in one of their rooms after work and chat or play cards. Occasionally, they were able to find a bottle of whiskey at an exorbitant price through a contact or smuggle the brewed liquor that some resourceful individuals sold in Coca Cola bottles, which considerably lightened their clandestine parties.

Within six months, Berty Uncle was promoted to junior management as the predecessor was leaving. He was offered a fresh contract with better perks, including a fifty percent jump in salary, three-weeks paid leave and a ticket to visit his home country every six months. As the superintending engineer at Al-Abra Engineering, supervising a ten-member team of engineers of Indian, Bangladeshi, Pakistani and Filipino origin, his considerable tax-free salary was almost wholly saved.

So Berty Uncle settled into his new circumstances, tentatively planning to leave at the end of six months. But at the end of that term, the next, and the next, he had been unable to relinquish the comfort, security, and salary that came with his position.

Back home, his family and friends were battling harsh times. The government of Sirimavo Bandaranaike had fought a radical youth uprising in 1971 and jobs thereafter were scarce, food was in short supply and the cost of living had skyrocketed.

Thatha called him "the ant lucky enough to have fallen into the treacle pot."

CHAPTER 5

THE MANUAL

March 1973

In school, the days of discovering Angelina support were supplanted by something more engrossing. Sex, the forbidden – and, quite curiously disgusting – action of human intimacy became the focal point of our hush-hush conversations. In the absence of any written material, a documentary film, an elder sister-turned-teacher or any other source, we were floundering along with the bits of classroom flotsam and jetsam. Even perusing the biology books in the library didn't help much as there was little else than well-marked diagrams of the male and female bodies. Whoever ordered those books knew what they were doing.

The defining moment in our education came when Aruni, the forward peter, pinched a book entitled *The Manual of Love* from her elder sister's bedroom.

She produced it during the lunch interval, the subject matter concealed in a thick, brown paper.

"Open it, let's look now," Minaka said eagerly.

Aruni looked around her. Although the lunchroom was now deserted except for a few straggling rice-pushers, the matron was still hovering about. She had sensed the ripple of excitement coursing through us and was already casting suspicious looks at our table.

"No, I don't think it's a good idea now. Let's go outside."

We took our lunch boxes for inspection; the school didn't trust us to eat all our food and had appointed a matron to oversee that the entire egg, beetroot salad or green leaves, as the case may be, went down our gullets and not into the dustbin. Under the ever-running tap, we rinsed our boxes at the washbasin and washed our hands. Then, we made towards our favorite corner of the grounds, a huge, *kottamba* tree that had listened to the secrets of generations of Bishop's College girls.

But the brown paper-covered manual was attracting too much attention.

"Are you coming to play rounders? What have you got there?" Deshini, the bossy clique-leader we generally tried to avoid except when it came to playing our favorite game, was looking at Aruni's somewhat guilt-ridden face.

"It's only my social studies scrapbook; I was just going back to the class to put it back. I'll be back," said Aruni, rushing off with the all-important publication.

While she was away, the two of us noted the kottamba nuts that had fallen under the shady tree, thanks to the good work of birds and squirrels. We usually took great pleasure in bashing the nuts with a stone to break the shell, taking care not to smash fingers or stain uniforms with its sap. The spindle-shaped milky kernel tasted good and smelled like Amma's almond essence.

But Aruni returned fast, and we had other, more pressing, matters to discuss.

We were trying to decide who would take it home first, when the screech of several vehicles coming to a sudden stop and the merry beat of a musical band distracted us. Looking towards the sound, we saw ten or twelve white-clad schoolboys opening the school gates and flooding in. They were grinning from ear to ear and waving like mad enormous black and blue checked flags. Some had draped the flags, sarong-like, around their waists.

It was the week of the Royal-Thomian cricket match – the only time that boys summoned up the guts to gatecrash into girls' schools in search of support, monetary and otherwise.

The intruders fanned out, working the little clusters of girls who were unsure whether to embrace or reject the cause that was shamelessly peddled before them. One approached us with his cap outstretched:

"Sister ... please help us ... contribute ... after all we are from your brother school, no?" he grinned impishly, waving a sweat-soaked cap under Aruni's nose. His eyes were reddish and he reeked of liquor. It was easy to guess why he wanted money and what state his piggy bank was in.

Aruni hesitated. After all, most of us had brothers at home who were up to just the same mischief during their schools' big matches when even teachers would temporarily turn a blind eye on their misdemeanors.

She was fumbling in her pocket for some change when from a distance, the leader of the pack yelled "Three Cheers to St. Thomas's, hip hip ..." and a loud chorus of "hoorays" rang from his dispersed comrades.

Just then, alerted by the noise and a prefect, the vice principal and several teachers made their collectively stern appearance. So did the gatekeeper, who had been at lunch and had omitted locking the gates, and whose job it was to prevent these types of intrusions in the first place. Between the few of them, they managed to usher the boys out of the gate, and they obligingly retreated, waving their flags like Neil

Armstrong did on the moon and not more than a few rupees richer. The jeeps took off with another din and a final deafening clash of cymbals, after treating us to a five-minute rendition of *I've Got a Lovely Bunch of Ericanuts* as the gatekeeper helplessly looked on. He couldn't do anything once they were out of the school gates.

The three of us stood near the gate and stared at the spectacle until it dawned on us that the scrutiny of the teachers had now been transferred to us girls.

###

For all our daring and impatience, coupled with Aruni's haste to restore the *Manual of Love* to her sister's bedroom, we were sensible enough not to turn its explicit pages in school. So Minaka and I took turns to take it home, where conditions were no less precarious. With significant parts underlined in red and Asoka Aiya hovering about, it wasn't easy to read it at home during the allotted time limit. I seldom locked myself up in my bedroom and to do so now would only arouse suspicion. So, I relied on my power of hearing and delved into it in short, eager bursts.

This must be the reason why I misread "pubic hair" as "*public* hair" and caused an outburst of giggles when practicing the newfound word on my two best friends.

The crumbling and dog-eared volume had been published in 1938 and had obviously served more than one generation. But it didn't matter. The subject — and our curiosity — were timeless.

CHAPTER 6

HATCHING PLOTS

Although Olga Aunty was not the eldest in the family of sisters – my mother Blossom was – sister number two assumed the matriarchal role early on after their mother succumbed to pneumonia at the age of fifty-one. After Olga Aunty took charge, she never looked back. She didn't have children, and that position provided her with more time on her hands when compared to the others, which she used to run their lives.

Whenever there was anything of importance to be decided, the family turned to her. Her counsel was as good as anybody else's, but her decisions were unwavering and the lack of ho-humming that characterized the others' thought patterns had made her the obvious choice to lead.

In the case of her brother-in-law Berty, however, there was no easy solution. The matter had dilly-dallied far more than she had anticipated. It seemed hopeless at times, but Olga Aunty plodded – and plotted – on.

She chose to ignore the astrologer's assertion that Berty Uncle could not have a successful marriage until he was above the age of forty. While remembering the astrologer's warnings about taking particular care in finding the partner, she encouraged the adult members of the family to hold aloft a perennial searchlight for Berty Uncle's future mate. Like Jane Austen, they firmly believed that an unmarried rich man was a waste to society, like beef tenderloin on a Hindu ascetic. It was not as if the four sisters' marriages had turned out to be particularly rosy examples. Oswald, my father, lived from one drink to another, Olga Aunty had husband Nelson Uncle firmly under her thumb, and it was rumored that Mary Aunty's husband, Dinesh, was seeing another woman. Beulah Aunty, the youngest, had yet to start complaining publicly about her husband, Martin Uncle, but rust was appearing in the conjugal armor.

They had their own hands full, but they were all united in an almost vicarious desire to install Berty Uncle in the married state. Olga Aunty's problem had become everybody's problem especially because of the long-standing issue with Nelson Uncle and Berty Uncle's near-estranged sister, who had staked unfair ownership of their ancestral home in Panadura.

Thus, they left no stone unturned; matchmakers were sought, feelers were sent around staff rooms in school, neighbors were appraised, and distant relatives were informed of the existence of this eligible bachelor. Proposals kept cropping up, though not all worthy of consideration and the chaff had to be removed from the grain. They ranged from divorcees with or without children (mostly chaff) to homely but wealthy girls trying to fling off the old maid status (sometimes grain) and poorer hopefuls trying to climb the social ladder (definitely chaff).

Even after a process of stringent winnowing, there was enough to keep Berty Uncle occupied during his vacations in Colombo. The six-month labors of his dismayed brother and sister-in-law, ably aided by the extended family, ensured that a plethora of marriage proposals – some on paper and others

A Maiden's Prayer

less tangible – awaited him. He was whisked from one bride-viewing appointment to another.

***

The promising new potential with attractive family connections that Nelson Uncle had sounded Berty Uncle about was a relative of Olga Aunty's staff mate, Sushila. One day, during a shared free period in between teaching, Sushila had spoken about this girl.

"She's a quiet and well-behaved girl, very well educated and in a good job. It's a pity that they couldn't get her married yet. The parents are quite worried now that she's past thirty," Sushila had said.

Olga Aunty had pricked up her ears. Berty was coming on a holiday soon, she told my mother later, and it had seemed natural to suggest him as an applicant. Olga Aunty had been even more interested when Sushila mentioned that the girl's mother was the sister of the current Inspector General of Police.

I can picture Olga Aunty's moment of realization that here was an opportunity to seize. She would have resettled her glasses and blown her nose on that white handkerchief of hers before going to great lengths to boost the prospective bridegroom to absurd heights. She wouldn't have stopped until she led Sushila to believe that Berty Uncle was poised on the tree of elitism on an equal branch, if not on a higher limb. She would have thrown in the Mudaliyar connection, hinted at the Panadura property, albeit without revealing its crumbling façade, and even revealed his Middle East-derived salary. They would have parted with a conspiratorial agreement to take matters to the next level.

57

In retrospect, I wish I had shared with Olga Aunty my post behind the door curtain when Berty Uncle visited our place. She would never have dreamt of mining among her staff mates for a wife for him had she known even one or two of the escapades that Berty Uncle related in confidence to my father. I could have spared her humiliation, but I didn't, for one obvious reason. My eavesdropping would have been stopped, and I was enjoying it far too much.

My thirteen-year-old conscience reasoned that it was for the greater good of mankind. A writer had to observe and listen to everything without discrimination. Especially to Berty Uncle's "Dirty Berty" side.

CHAPTER 7

A MAIDEN'S PRAYER

Every day at the twilight hour, with the regularity of vespers, Anoma, the young woman in the house opposite ours, would tenderly play *A Maiden's Prayer* at the piano. Through the white lace curtains, her long tresses and shapely form could be seen bent over the instrument, while the notes of the melody would waft out of the window and wrap the neighborhood with its sweet melancholy.

Precisely at that same point in time, Quaver, Anoma's maiden aunt of questionable sanity, could be seen led out of the house by the dogs. Her real name was Norah Dias, but hardly anyone referred to her by this appellation; the middle-aged music teacher was either "Quaver" or "Old Maid" behind her back and "Miss Norah" to her face.

It was a debatable matter whether Quaver was taking the dogs for a walk or the dogs were airing Quaver after her long day teaching at the piano. Viewed from a distance and seeing how eager the canines were to sniff at the lampposts, the latter description more accurately fit the bill. After a certain time, both parties had hit upon a mutual degree of equilibrium. Quaver had perfected a dogtrot to keep up behind the leash. At its most harmonious, poised at a 45-degree angle to the land, her only view of the scenery was of the dogs' exposed derrières and curled tails. The curly tails formed perfect "O"s, denoting that they were pariahs and not of noble pedigree, but they were considerate of her circumstances and well-mannered enough to never cause her to fall.

Quaver was always dressed in the same long white twill dress, which had acquired a brown border of mud after many moons of these travels. She had long hair too, which, let down at the twilight hour, was not conducive to aesthetic pleasure. But no one had made any pointed remarks, as almost everyone in the neighborhood had had a son or daughter learn music from her. The neighbors simply surmised that "Quaver had lost her comb again," because the music teacher was in the peculiar habit of borrowing a comb from her neighbors, after which she would neatly plait her thinning hair by her side of the fence and return the comb.

Along with *A Maiden's Prayer* and the emergence of Quaver and the canines, another group of rather unwelcome members materialized. The murmur of mosquitoes also started precisely at this hour, as they rose out of the water-clogged drains, thrown away coconut shells and shrubbery; a ravenous army in search of dinner. Therefore, instead of being charmed and soothed by the drifting overture, when they saw and heard the spectacle just described, the neighbors were in a momentary frenzy, irritably swatting themselves while hastily closing the windows.

Anoma, at twenty-six, could be excused for praying in refrain for a suitor, but why did the music drive her aunt out of the house? Was Quaver escaping from the past? Did she have her own maiden's prayer thwarted once upon a time? These were the questions on the lips of many a neighbor. "Do you think there is a Dickensian type of link?" Mrs. Vithanage once dared to ask Amma in a hushed whisper. "Was she a Miss Havisham? She certainly has an Estella!"

A Maiden's Prayer

***

Quaver lived with her hoarse voice, her niece, her servant and her driver in a tiny two-bedroom house. Despite its size, its sitting room was attractive with its well-polished red floor, cane furniture softened by cushions in a cheerful bamboo pattern, and potted croton plants. But unlike Miss Havisham in *Great Expectations*, who let cobwebs grow and dust gather in the house after she was jilted, Quaver was diligent in getting her house cleaned. To ensure its spic and span upkeep, her middle-aged, gregarious servant and the tacit driver labored regularly.

The daily dusting and the sweeping were done early before the first students arrived. The polishing was affixed for the last Sunday of the month. The tacit driver, who lived in the garage, had other surfaces to polish apart from the Morris Minor. I sometimes spied him, hunched and crouching on the front stoop, dabbing red polish on the doorsteps from a tin and rubbing at them with an old rag, the process engaging his whole, shirtless body – muscles, sinews, bone, skin and all.

From daybreak to late afternoon, Quaver's students would sail in and out of her front door, taking care not to slip on the shiny floor. My concern was centered more on her coterie of brass ornaments that could be easily dislodged by swaying skirt or careless hand than on injuring myself in a fall. It had happened once, to my embarrassment. With a sudden movement, I had ousted the brass bowl sitting on its throne of three outstretched elephant trunks. The bowl clattered to the floor and Quaver's eyes grew wide and hands flew up to cup her chin. From that day, I steered clear of those pachyderms in their regal pose.

Quaver herself wore pointy high-heeled shoes that made a tock-tock noise, but then, I've seen her maneuver herself on more rugged territory. A word about those pointy shoes: I have always held that those who preferred the ready-for-an-emergency, weapon-like shoes to the kinder-looking blunt ones were possessed of a fiendish temperament.

Every September, the music teacher would order a more intensive polish and re-polish of her floor, a cleaning of all the cobwebs within and without, and even a washing of the outer walls of the house. She then threw open her house to visitors with a big *tamasha* that celebrated her birthday. With few friends to choose from (the only friends were past pupils who were now adults), the bulk of the invitees were her older pupils, but never their parents. She steered clear of inviting the gossip-mongers, the curious and the less-fortunate from down the lanes. The only other relative who would be present was an old uncle, who was her dancing partner on this occasion. He was known for his penchant for making a whistling sound while twirling his niece on the slippery floor. Mercifully, no one got injured during this exhausting-to-watch exercise, which I was privileged to witness four years in a row.

In the beginning, I was one of her reluctant pupils pushed to learn music. I wonder if she suspected that my mother was the instrument for all this. I didn't exhibit any prodigious childhood talent; we didn't even own a piano. Amma paid for those lessons with the sweat of her brow because she herself "never got a chance to learn." Looking back, I think it was a Victorian vestige of her upbringing that she wished to impinge on her only daughter. I suspect there was also a dim connection between pianoforte and an arranged marriage to come. It would justify her use of the word "accomplished" in the proposal letters she would write.

Despite her pointy shoes, Quaver was not a wicked teacher. Others reportedly kept a twelve-inch ruler handy to tap knuckles at the slightest stumble. But here was a girl who would have preferred to master the finer points of cleaning fish, or even weave reed baskets with a group of village women in a vocational institute, rather than study piano music. Asoka Aiya often poked fun at me, saying that my fingers resembled a bunch of small *ambul* bananas. For once, I agreed with my sibling. I did the least study and minimum practice to survive the exams.

During those early days of my music instruction, I had another bugbear. I was becoming acutely shortsighted and had to stick my nose into the sheet music to read them. I had increasingly inched my piano stool to the keyboard in a valiant attempt to read the crotchets and quavers. Resolute that the posture was not in keeping with the playing and equally determined, Quaver would pull the stool back, much to my dismay. At times, I had resorted to playing by memory, with dubious results.

The tussle with the stool had continued until Amma had saved the money for a visit to an unlikeable ophthalmologist, who lectured me on poor eating habits and promptly recommended glasses. On the day she saw the vision aid, Quaver's sigh of relief rustled the manuscript. She leaned back and settled passively on her chair. The tug-o'-war with the piano stool had ended.

For me, the redeeming factor after the battle with the minor scales, the arpeggios and distinguishing a perfect cadence from an interrupted or plagal one, was being able to chat with Anoma.

She had the knack of saying just the right thing, in any circumstance. She applied the salve to life's little wounds. It was even more remarkable because Anoma never went anywhere, did not interact with people and did not immerse herself in books as I did. Her greatest talent, besides the gift of music, was an inborn capacity to understand.

Also, there was something singular about Anoma that one could not pinpoint. Apart from her shy smile and that faraway look in her eye, which I privately attributed to playing *A Maiden's Prayer* in that melancholy manner far too many times, she had the ethereal quality of a person who exists temporarily, almost on loan.

During the first year, I had passed the Eat-Good-Bread-Dear-Father stage (the bread shortage notwithstanding) with ease and thereafter was rapidly completing the various levels of examinations rather like an ascending scale.

But it was many moons later that I mastered *A Maiden's Prayer*, the climactic moment in Quaver's musical instruction which deemed that every young lady of good family and unstained moral character was expected to play. Although she countered that the music was simplistic and banal in comparison to the great composers of Tekla Badarzewska's time, such as George Bizet who produced "Carmen" and Johannes Brahms who produced four great symphonies and countless masterpieces of chamber music, Quaver's love for the Polish composer was unwavering.

"Pieces like these do capture the fashion of their times and are deserving of the attention they once had," she whispered to me, hoarsely, on a day that her voice was acting up.

A Maiden's Prayer

Tekla Badarzewska seems to have lived life, from 1834 to 1861, to give herself just enough time to compose "Modlitwa Dziewicy" for the boon or bane of young women around the world. "A Maiden's Prayer" was published in 1856 in Warsaw. The medium difficulty short piano piece for intermediate pianists became one of the biggest selling pieces of piano music of all time. In Sri Lanka, its charm is undisputed, but European critics have described it as "sentimental salon tosh."

The Andante piece becomes Piu Allegretto somewhere towards the end, and Quaver hastened me on even though my ambul banana fingers couldn't cope with flying over the keyboard.

But as soon as I mastered the piece and could pull it off as well as the next girl, Quaver asked me to set it aside. "There are other pieces worthy of your time, Tamara," she said, and I detected a quiver in her voice.

Quaver could teach a thing or two to the metronome that rested on her piano. Precisely at two-twenty p.m. each day, she would nod off, drowsing, nay snoring, even while the hapless student thundered scales down the ivory keys. Her boat-necked, tight-around-thighs shifts made of drill cocooned her body, ensnaring her to the chair.

Fortunately or unfortunately, during any given lesson, the servant Dhanawathi could be depended upon to find an excuse to barge into the sitting room and wake up her mistress. Her name, meaning "rich woman," was a misnomer bestowed upon her by hopeful parents; she was rich neither in mind nor material.

Dhanawathi found the vicinity of the piano a suitable place for domestic consultation. Most queries were related to the day's cooking. She would report, in her deep voice, that there were three potatoes and not four. Quaver would awaken from her slumber and instruct her to cut each into four pieces. (That way she could keep a tab on the number and pilfering was out of the question. The servant was excellent in all mathematical manipulations up to ten.)

One day, the excuse to butt in was a pair of squished tomatoes she had discovered at the back of the refrigerator. "Nona, Nona, look at this," she cried in Sinhalese, holding aloft the bruised fruit. "This must be two months old. I found it in the pridge!"

"Aney, Dhanawathi, take that away. Let me do my work."

"But Missy, you wanted to buy tomatoes today, no?"

"Dhanawathi, go, go! Leave me in peace."

Crestfallen, the woman ambled off: the detective denied reward.

Another day, a commotion was heard in the kitchen, seemingly caused by the dogs' active participation. As the rumpus steadily picked up in volume, Quaver ignored it for the most part, except to open her eyes wider and place her palms over her ears. But trying to filter out the domestic din this way resulted in obliterating the piano music as well. After more noises of scratching and jumping, an explanation – and proof – was proffered: the dogs, which inhabited the tiny backyard, had caught a much-sought rat. Dhanawathi appeared in the drawing room carrying the mangled prize by its tail. With her mouth full of the red aftermath of a betel chew, it looked as though the woman, and not the dogs, was the huntress.

"*Eeeeek, cheeeee,* Dhanawatheeee, take that away – you're scaring the children here also. Quicklee!"

"No, no," grinned the red-mouthed Dhanawathi. "Children not scared, it's only a mouse, and a dead one at that.

CHAPTER 8

TWO SETS OF TENANTS

In the months that followed my much-celebrated entrance into womanhood, Amma kept a close watch on me. There were all kinds of new rules and regulations in force: climbing trees was banned and riding the bicycle was taboo. I could no longer be "alone" with my boy cousins, could not go out of the gate, especially after twilight, and was delivered and picked up like a parcel whenever I had to go somewhere.

She especially did not tolerate Anura's friendship with me anymore and, worst of all, Anura had begun to avoid me as if I had caught the plague. I knew that something was amiss and was determined to find it out.

The opportunity presented itself, somewhat unexpectedly.

***

In tropical Ceylon, *thalagoyas*, or monitor lizards, and their larger land cousins, *kabaragoyas,* are a common sight, often slithering across people's back gardens or basking in the sunlight on parapet walls. They spend their daylight hours roaming about shrubbery or marshy land eating snakes, mice, grasshoppers, roaches, and other little creatures and return to their hideouts before twilight. While the Sinhalese believe that *thalagoya* tongue is a memory enhancer that also improves articulation and covet it to be fed to young children with impaired speech development, they steer clear of *kabaragoyas* because it can deliver a gash with its tail, cutting the flesh to the bone. A deadly poison is obtained by lighting a fire under a *kabaragoya* hung head down.

In the clammy space between the ceiling and roof in our house, a family of *thalagoyas* had noisily made their home. Every morning, between the hours of six and eight, they made a hullabaloo similar to the one made by the household in preparation for the working day. On most mornings, they could be heard going from one end of the ceiling to the other, and a few minutes later, a lizard (or two) could be seen sliding down the whitewashed rough wall outside the back door, its legs making a scratching noise like chalk on blackboard, forked tongue flicking in and out and head moving to and fro.

Whenever she had a moment to spare during the morning bustle, my exasperated mother rushed out of the back door with a basin of water and threw it at the descending reptiles. Indignantly they would draw themselves up, inflate their throats and hiss at their landlady and withdraw hurriedly, their thick skins sustaining only temporary discomfort. Amma was careful to maintain a fleeing distance as they could easily jump on to her.

When the monitors deemed it safe again, the second attempt would set the family at an accelerated descent down the wall, and a rush to the concrete fence.

The climb over was usually not without incident too, as their clawed feet often entangled in the profuse passion fruit creeper that ran along the fence — its flowers and tendrils were bruised, and immature fruit dislodged before time; another source of irritation to my mother who made passiona from the fruit for all our visitors and *mallum* from its leaves. Amma's passion fruit vine was the envy of the whole neighborhood, and she would often present part of the yield to neighbors in reciprocation for a couple of juicy mangoes, a heap of *veralu* (wild olive) or a breadfruit plucked from equally fecund flora. I must add that Amma's vine would bear fruit throughout the year, unlike the seasonal fruit trees of our neighbors.

With a final clumsy slide down to the rotting carpet of pulpy fruit on the other side of the fence, the lizards would creep into the undergrowth of the vacant plot behind our house.

Around mid-afternoon, the day's meals taken, and other sundry matters completed, they would return the same way, squishing more passion fruit, taking the same risk and making the same racket.

Fortunately for the reptiles, the combined tolerance level of our family members was rather high. Thatha couldn't care less and wouldn't have noticed if a *thalagoya* sat down to dinner with us. Amma grumbled and contemplated throwing kerosene oil at them, especially after a particularly troublesome exit and when the *thalagoya* succeeded in scaring the wits out of Maya, next-door Mrs. Vithanage's wisp-of-a-servant-girl.

One sleepy afternoon, Maya, who was only about eight years old, had been lured to our kitchen with the usual bait of cake and Bulto toffee, both items she loved with a passion. If cake were not available, Marie biscuits would do, and if Marie biscuits were unavailable, Maya could not be enticed. In return for the treats, she would wash the *chutty* pots in the outside sink, a messy task that Amma postponed for days sometimes.

Maya had wolfed down the piece of cake — or 'kehek' as she called it — and popped the Bulto in her mouth. She was sitting on her haunches on the concrete ledge and scraping the remnants of rice from a soot-encrusted pot with a coconut husk. The cascading water from the tap was washing away the debris.

She didn't hear the *thalagoya* that had smelled the food and nosed its way toward the pans. With a cry of terror, Maya fell onto the pots, two of which instantly broke into pieces. The hard clay dug into her knees. The lizard sensed that a quick getaway was required, but Maya could hardly walk away. When she found her voice, it was muffled because the Bulto, being treacle-based, had stuck her teeth together.

All in all, it was a scene out of a Charlie Chaplin film and drew a strong parallel to the Tikiri-liya nursery rhyme about a *kabaragoya* that scared a little girl at the well; but the servant girl didn't find it funny. She refused to wash our pots again unless Amma or I kept watch nearby.

After that hullabaloo, Amma took up the kerosene oil talk again, a known repellent that would hopefully make the monitors seek an alternative home. But on second thought, she refrained from this drastic measure. There was a chance that they would suffer, and as Buddhists, we would not harm or kill. She reasoned that they were doing us a service by ridding the place of unwanted creatures. According to her, the daily sight of an ungainly monitor lizard zigzagging its way to the undergrowth leaving a trail of destroyed passion fruit in its wake was preferable to having snakes such as *garandiyas* and *caravallas* lurking under flowerpots, rats hiding about the place, or snails curled around her crotons happily munching them into oblivion. As it was, in the mundane course of things, the scavenging monitors were confident of never being evicted and could have lived in their adopted habitat to ripe old age, if not for our tenants.

One side of our house had been extended and rented out to bring in extra income. The annex had only two bedrooms, but harbored a large family, which included my erstwhile friend Anura. Free to proceed through the roof from room to room in the house, a *thalagoya* had gone to the annex and let out a stream of urine that had trickled down through the ceiling, fitted by a cheap carpenter with shoddy workmanship, onto Anura's leg. It had seared and stunk.

Anura's family was annoyed at this and for the disturbance that the creatures caused every day. They plotted revenge — not on us, but on the lizards. Each time a *thalagoya* was spotted roaming about, they surreptitiously threw it a chunk of beef. Once the trust had been established and the creature was hooked on the easy food-line, the stage was set for its capture.

One day, I was drawn to a great commotion in the back garden that the two families shared.

"That's right, Aiya, get him, get him!"

"Tie the rope around his head, not his mouth–that's too difficult!"

"*Aaaaah!* Bring a gunny sack and hurry up!"

"It's slipping. *Eeeeek!* Hold tight!"

Further encouragement by Anura was dispensed from up the frangipani tree where he had hastily climbed when it appeared that his father and brothers were about to lose their grip on the lizard's tail. I seized my chance as Amma was not around. This was one of our favorite retreats in what seemed to be the days of yore. I climbed up. A double breach.

"Anura, why don't you talk to me anymore?" I regarded him woefully from among the foliage.

Anura's loyalties were divided equally. "Tamara, I can't. *Haaa*, get the fellow!"

"Why can't you?"

"Tamara, a few months ago, your brother called me aside and told me ..."

"What did Asoka Aiya tell you?"

"He told me to stop playing with you as you are grown up now and have other interests and studies to pursue. He insisted that I don't even talk to you, and that's why I have been minding my own business."

My mouth flew open and I almost fell down the tree, as startled as the big lizard that was now captured and inside a burlap sack that was securely tied at the mouth. I wished I could capture and remove the annoying customs of society as easily as Anura's father hurled his captive into the dickey of a taxi and shouted instructions to the driver to take him to the Diyawanna Oya, the waterway that served as the moat to the royal citadel in the ancient capital of Kotte.

***

The next day, the remaining members of the monitor family trooped out and crept into the undergrowth. They never returned. They may have watched the removal and shuddered with the knowledge that they might have been captured next. Or, maybe they found a more lucrative property to reside in and forage from. The one who got the ride must have been the patriarch. Perhaps they were now reunited and burrowing in the silty banks of the Diyawanna where they should rightfully burrow.

CHAPTER 9

THE PROPOSAL

As Nelson Uncle had predicted, Berty Uncle was bluffing about not wanting to see this new prospect. His holiday was proceeding without any real excitement, so with a few weak protestations to further assert his need to retain independence, he had agreed to visit on a Saturday afternoon. Olga Aunty had promptly sent word to the girl's parents through Sushila, requesting permission to visit. She had received a speedy reply in the affirmative, specifying a date and time. The girl's parents had previously compared their horoscopes, and they tallied reasonably well; thereby, all astrological barriers were clear.

On the appointed day, Olga Aunty announced her arrival at our doorstep with a tinkle of gold bangles that was more pronounced than the knock on the door. Amma admitted her inside. "Have to dress well, no men, they are related to the IGP," she said in response to Amma's wide-eyed admiration of her dazzling, mauve Benaris sari.

"Sit down, Sister, I'll be ready in a minute," Amma rushed back into her bedroom, and I followed. Olga Aunty's perfume was a tad too strong for my nose.

Amma needed all the extra time she could get; after all, she had to pass muster with the relatives of the Inspector General of Police. She looked at herself in the mirror, then wistfully opened her almirah drawer and took out the rolled-gold jewelry she had bought from a pavement hawker in

Pettah. Amma hoped nobody would notice, except for her sister who already knew. Behind the closed bedroom curtain, she sighed.

I had heard many times about the fate of her heavy gold choker necklace and bangles she received from her parents at marriage. It was so heavy that a friend had jokingly remarked that the choker might "choke her." Like all of Amma's items of jewelry, the choker had been in and out of the pawnbrokers until one day she found that the redeeming period had elapsed. They had not been able to raise the money in time.

Amma wiped away a tear. Then, pulling herself together and giving me a weak smile, she quickly walked out. I followed.

They both sparkled in the afternoon sun as they climbed inside Berty Uncle's mustard yellow Ford Capri.

Nelson Uncle, Olga Aunty and Amma, the trio of accompanying elders, made the stable family backdrop to Berty, whose parents were not alive. I was the odd member of the party, as Amma didn't want me to stay home by myself. Thatha was visiting a relative, and Asoka Aiya had his schedule full with an afternoon cricket match he was captaining. I didn't mind the excursion. In fact, I had a notebook and pen in my handbag to jot down any interesting observations.

Devoid of adornment as his gender decreed except for a shiny and prominent gold watch, Berty Uncle was neatly dressed in beige trousers and matching checked shirt. His only concern was his little balding patch, which he had begun to conceal by letting the locks around it grow longer than the rest of the hair. With the use of coconut oil, he had begun to train the longer hair on its special assignment, I observed from the back seat.

Berty Uncle had brought a tin of Mackintosh's Quality Street chocolates and toffees with its appropriate picture of the red-coated English Major and the demure Miss. The tin was from a now dwindling supply he brought from Saudi Arabia for such eventualities as these. Nelson Uncle had thrown in a Perera & Sons butter cake. If not for the IGP connection, Maliban Cheesebits would have sufficed. God knows how many tins of salted Cheesebits they had presented on such visits. At least until Berty Uncle married, the Maliban biscuit business would continue to flourish.

Nelson Uncle was the most conservative in a plain cream shirt and light brown trousers. He hated wearing gold, did not even consent to wearing his wedding ring and openly voiced his consternation about his brother's new penchant for the shiny stuff. He was battling an expanding paunch that occupied his attention every waking minute; even now, judging by his shoulder movement, I think he was practicing how to draw in his stomach and not look apoplectic at the same time. Apart from this temporary exercise under imminent social scrutiny, Olga Aunty often complained that he did not do much to control its expansion.

From the passenger seat, Nelson Uncle breathed out to join the conversation. The fact that Berty Uncle's horoscope matched with the girl's was in itself propitious. Olga Aunty was explaining why they were particularly well-matched: The male horoscope contained Mars in the Seventh House. The planet of passion, emotion and inner motivation was in the house depicting marriage, which meant that his partner could face a deadly calamity or marriage could lead to separation unless that same placing of Mars or another malefic was in that particular square in the girl's horoscope.

"Not only is her Mars in the Seventh House, but it's also aspected by a beneficial Jupiter in her horoscope, which negates ill effects," Olga Aunty explained.

No one could grow up in our extended family and profess ignorance to what Olga Aunty was talking about: horoscopes, aspects, malefics, dasa, and other assorted words connected to the Vedic astrology I had digested along with my first solid foods.

Vedic astrology, a mathematical science that originated in India, is the study of karma and the summary of one's past actions as shown by the placements of planets in signs and houses and the aspects – the interaction between these planets – in a person's horoscope. A birth chart, or a horoscope, is a symbolic map of the heavens at the moment of a person's birth.

A previous life's negative and positive energies are measured by considering the positions of the planets in the chart and their motion. While it is believed that past energies give us positive powers to be born as human beings, astrology also defines how they affect our current lives.

The Seventh House signifies partnerships and marriage, among other factors. Mars in the Seventh House, if unfavorable, indicate partnership conflicts, excess passion, and hasty decisions.

Olga Aunty and Amma looked meaningfully at Berty Uncle, or rather, at his bald spot in the back of his head, as though this was the last option left for his salvation. It was best for all that only I, as the other passenger in the backseat, saw their rueful look; it would have rankled Berty Uncle.

Olga Aunty did not reflect on the other facets of Berty Uncle's horoscope that the astrologer had cautioned very early in this process; that he was given to passionate or impulsive relationships, that it would be difficult to satisfy him sexually, and that an early marriage would have been the best for him. Olga Aunty chose to ignore the abstracts that she could not change and focused on the tangible issues like finding a suitable girl with a matching birth chart.

It was with some difficulty that we managed to find the house. There did not seem to be a number Fifty-Seven on Third Avenue. House number Fifty announced itself with a plastic nameplate but the houses next to them were too small and insignificant to be the address we sought. The lane, flanked by a woody hill, wound through until the next large residence, number Sixty-One.

Berty Uncle reversed the car and drove back slowly. Suddenly, a man who was perched on a flat rock by the side of the road jumped up and came toward the car. He peered into the vehicle and spoke in Sinhalese: "Are you the party that's going to Mr. Tilakarathne's house? Madam asked me to wait here for you as the house is not visible from the road."

He motioned toward a pathway that had an upturned board announcing "No 57" alongside an arrow. A wayside urchin had probably turned the board the other way, which was why "the party" did not spot it.

Berty Uncle drove down the circuitous lane, lined on one side by huge Jack trees bearing bulging, pockmarked fruit until we reached a clearing. There we saw a sprawling mansion with lattice-decorated verandahs on either side. More fruit trees — mango and cashew — were in bloom. House sparrows and mynahs enjoying the water in a spacious

78

birdbath fled upon our arrival. A cluster of enormous pink roses in a well-kept bed stirred their heads as if in approval. Through a clearing, we spotted a mahout feeding palm leaves to an elephant.

Berty Uncle stopped the car, visibly nervous. Nobody made a move to descend. "Get down," he urgently motioned his brother who, forgetting to hold his stomach in, obeyed the order like a startled colt. The roadside emissary who had followed us in a quick trot had by now reached the car and was staring at us curiously. I could barely contain my delight at what promised to unfold.

Only Olga Aunty maintained her composure. She disembarked in a queenly manner and mounted the steps leading to the house. Amma and I followed slowly. A pleasant-faced, elderly gentleman came out, placed his palms together in greeting and ushered his visitors inside.

"Hello, good afternoon, come in, come in. I am Martin. Please sit down and make yourselves comfortable."

The sitting room was furnished with Burma teak furniture with plush red cushioning. A vase filled with peacock feathers made a startling showpiece. Before anyone had time to absorb more, a tall, large-boned woman clad in a navy-blue Batik gown, obviously the lady of the house, swept in.

"How do you do? Did you find it easy to get here? It's easy to miss the road to our place so we always try to keep Sirisena outside." Even the peacock feathers seemed to droop obligingly in the background as the woman asserted herself in a stentorian voice. The long bell-sleeves on the gown helped her image even more.

"Good servants are hard to come by, but we can spare Sirisena for little things like that because we have a family of servants here. There's Sita, whose mother was my mother's maid. She was born here and is like a member of the family. There's Kamala, her sister, who's not as obliging as Sita but I'm trying to train her. Then there's Karuna, the youngest, who's not really a sister, but a cousin; she now takes care of the garden — did you see the roses before coming in? She says they grow well because of the eggshells and used tea leaves she throws into the soil every week. I don't entrust her with the cooking. I have trained the other two to be clean and methodical, but I have not been able to train Karuna. She goes to work in a nearby garment factory — planning for her future, don't you know."

Here she paused for breath and Olga Aunty jumped in. "I know *how* difficult it is to train servants. I had a few good ones too. But it seems that these days, there are countries that are hiring our Ceylonese women to work as maids. Just the other day, my domestic, Soma, was telling me her sister had gone and met this man in Colombo who is from an agency which sends maids abroad — I think it is to Dubai. Just imagine these women, they don't understand a word of English. How will they manage in a strange land?"

"They should be sent for classes in English first. You know, to understand the basic commands that a mistress will give to get work done."

"Also, it seems that in those countries people have money. They use electric machines even to cut vegetables!"

"Actually, we use a Kenwood chef with all the attachments. Martin brought it when he went to Singapore. Sita and Kamala know how to use them."

At the mention of his name, Martin cleared his throat and attempted to speak before his Amazonian wife could launch into another tirade, but it was useless.

"So, you're in the same staff as Sushila, at Samudra Devi. She has been telling me about you. What do you teach there? And is this your sister?"

"I also teach English, just like Sushila, but we have separate classes. And Blossom, my sister, is a teacher too. And this is her daughter, Tamara."

I smiled on cue appropriate to a thirteen-year-old.

"I'm told your brother-in-law works in Saudi Arabia. Interesting, going all that way for employment. Is it true that there are huge shopping centers there, just like in London, where you can buy everything under one roof?".

At least the question was addressed to Berty Uncle, I thought.

Berty Uncle, who looked less like a prospective bridegroom and more like an interloper every passing minute, adjusted his tie and began to stammer.

"Errr, yes, yes you get everything there."

She moved on quickly to the next question. "Is it true that women have to wear a black shawl to cover their whole face and body when they go out?"

"Yes, they can't reveal their faces to the outside world."

"And is it also true that women are not allowed to drive there?"

"Yes, they have to be driven around by their husbands or another male relative."

"My God. My Vinitha will not like to hear that," she told no one in particular in a disapproving tone.

Few men or women could be happy in the company of a strong woman, and this one was worse than anything we had encountered so far.

In the ensuing silence, Amma tucked her sari fold over the rolled-gold chain nervously. Olga Aunty adjusted her spectacles that kept slipping off. We wondered whether we would even catch sight of Vinitha.

Martin managed to get a word in. "Seela, why don't you arrange for some refreshments?"

Seela rose in a cloud of navy blue, excused herself and disappeared inside.

She reappeared all too soon, with a lanky, plain-faced girl bearing a cut-glass platter of rich cake. With her rustling sari and tinkling adornments, Vinitha moved about serving the cake. Berty Uncle dared not look up to her face when she stopped by him, so his gaze rested on rosy pink toes curled into a pair of open silver shoes. Before turning away, she looked toward him, I thought, with a hopeful look.

The cake had sultanas, chow-chow, and golden syrup. "How on earth did they manage to find these ingredients?" I wondered, as the rest of my family must.

Vinitha took her place in the drawing room. Berty Uncle studied the fruit cake for a while. Nelson Uncle found his voice and directed a question to the young woman. "I'm told you are working for the Ministry of Foreign Affairs. What do you do there?"

"I am one of the assistant secretaries of information, writing and coordinating the press releases sent to our embassies abroad. I also help organize press conferences that are addressed by the minister."

"That's a responsible job. How long have you held this post?"

"Four years. And before that, I was at the Ministry of Information, working along the same lines."

How pathetic! No wonder you didn't meet anyone interesting. All these administrative offices are full of poorly paid government servants in faded drill trousers and DSI sandals, carrying worn black satchels that contained their rice-and-curry-filled lunch boxes.

"Will you get a chance to work abroad?"

"I might, but first I have to pass the Ceylon Administrative Service exam. Then I can apply."

The interrogation concluded. Berty Uncle hadn't addressed a word to the girl. He wasn't expected to.

Next on the scene was a twenty-something young woman in a long, waisted poplin dress. She wheeled in a groaning tea trolley and then bolted off, but not before we could get a full glimpse of her youthful beauty. A long and luxurious plait of hair reminded me of a fairy tale character. This must be Karuna or Kamala. Or was it Cinderella?

The fine chinaware was lost on Berty Uncle. He kept stealing glances towards the doorway as if praying for her reappearance. He neglected to eat the thinly sliced ham sandwich he held in his hand. The others were noisily tucking into the cutlets, patties, cream horns, and milk toffees that were handed out by Vinitha's mother. Evidently, there were no food shortages in the IGP's sister's house.

To Berty Uncle, the unembellished servant girl must appear more delectable. Fortunately for him, the girl had forgotten the teaspoons and reappeared with them. I noticed

Berty Uncle studying her fair face and rosy cheeks. Thick black lashes fanned a beautiful pair of doe-like eyes.

In the minute that she was with us, he did not take his eyes off her. In the slight diversion, Vinitha, having played her expected role, murmured an excuse, and slipped away.

Presently, Seela made the tea and handed over teacups, all the while glancing toward Berty Uncle. I think she noticed his preoccupation. Even the blind would be aware of her servant girl's arresting beauty. If she wanted to marry off Vinitha, she should keep Cinderella in the kitchen where she belonged. She made such a contrast to the daughter.

As if reading our thoughts, Seela addressed Olga Aunty: "Karuna is going to be married soon to a carpenter who sometimes does work here," she said. "I knew that something was going on, but I didn't try to stop it as she cannot live here indefinitely like my other two servant girls. And also, she's getting a little salary now by working at Velona's."

Olga Aunty bit into her cream horn and winced. I felt empathy for her. Why did Seela insist on giving us all the details about her staff? Why not talk about Vinitha for a change? Had she already decided against the proposal?

***

"Vinitha brought the cake, but it's her mother who takes the cake!" Berty Uncle was all bravado once again and made the opening salvo as soon as we were back in the car and safely out of hearing. "It's mothers like these who spoil the chances for girls. How old is she – thirty-three? About to miss the bus, and it's clear why."

"Don't be ridiculous, the mother has nothing to do with her being unmarried. It happens to a lot of girls nowadays who don't throw themselves at men, who are quiet and reserved and wait patiently for the correct husband. You're not considering the mother, are you?" That was Olga Aunty's attempt to salvage the situation.

"Given a choice, I'd choose the servant girl; I'd take her away tomorrow."

"Yes, I saw you eyeing that girl. A pity she's not related to the IGP."

"I was reminded of the Cinderella story when I saw her," I volunteered to ease the tension. "The kitchen, the *ug* ... err plain daughter, the stern mother ... I'm sure Vinitha's prince will turn up soon since Cinderella already has her prince."

Berty Uncle appreciated my little joke. He looked my way and laughed. Of course, Olga Aunty wasn't amused.

There was no conversation for a time. The sisters exchanged wooden glances. Amma could never get used to crude comments and heated dialogue; her gentle sensibilities were easily offended.

Berty Uncle wasn't cross with Olga Aunty for long; it must have all been a game to him. These proposals came and went, one not much different from the other. It was rare for an attractive girl to have to resort to an arranged marriage. The pretty ones got hitched fast. The plain ones, like Vinitha, despite having everything that money could buy plus good connections that money couldn't buy, needed parental intervention and huge dowries. Well-to-do men have no need for more money or material possessions; they want beauty in their households. Until Olga Aunty nailed down a pretty young woman by chance, Nelson Uncle would continue to buy tins of biscuits, and Berty Uncle would obligingly play the part of "intended bridegroom."

Berty Uncle lapsed into a dreamy state. I think he was going over Karuna's features, taking a mental snapshot of them. On our way out I saw him looking intently at the rose bushes as if hoping to find her lurking among them. He must almost envy them for the constant tending they received at her hands.

I wondered if *her Mars* was in the Seventh House.

CHAPTER 10

APPROACHING CINDERELLA

Although Berty Uncle pooh-poohed the bossy mother and her plain-Jane daughter as another bad idea thrown in his path, he didn't deem the complete exercise as futile. He obviously could not get Karuna and her Cinderella setting out of his mind.

At the time, I didn't know how he approached Karuna. He didn't divulge anything to Thatha and it was impossible to follow Berty Uncle and trace his activities. I only had bits and pieces of information that Olga Aunty related to Amma after the episode ended. But years later, I managed to wrangle the story from Asoka Aiya who always knew more than he divulged. Asoka Aiya had friends who worked in the Velona garment factory, which was Karuna's place of employment.

I was overjoyed at the chance of being party to that formal drawing room visit. My notebook was filled with scribbles. But as entertaining as that visit was, the story that I cobbled together with Asoka Aiya's help, and with what I already knew, was even better.

One option that Berty Uncle must have considered was pretending to be interested in the proposal and returning to the home in the pretext of meeting Vinitha. But, thankfully, Berty Uncle didn't stoop that low. He had a regard for Olga Aunty, who was genuinely fond of him despite his madcap ways. Besides, it would be impossible to penetrate the kitchen fortress with that awful woman standing tall in the background.

He would have to marry Vinitha, and that was the one-before-the-last thing he wanted. (The last thing was getting Seela for a mother-in-law.)

On the other hand, Berty Uncle would have grappled with having to abide by society's decorum. When traditions threatened to hold him back, he usually had his own way. What if Karuna was the correct one for him? Did fate lead him to that house? Was he the wealthy Prince Charming who could turn around her life of rags to one of riches? Could he let her get away? The opportunity wouldn't come around twice. Ultimately, Berty Uncle must have fallen back on his bull-by-the horns approach to life.

Since Karuna was working at the Velona garment factory as the lady of the house had indicated, Berty Uncle decided to approach her there. I know that he had a close friend who held a senior position in the company.

The Velona factory is one of the biggest local garment businesses in Ceylon. Everybody wore cotton knitted T-shirts, undergarments and socks with their label, notwithstanding the sagging factor. Its underbelly was the labor of an army of poor, young women hired from the suburbs.

A matter of a phone call would have located Karuna. Although it's a common first name – he didn't have her last name and there may have been other Karunas in employment – employment records would indicate the area of residence. The girls worked in day and night shifts, and all he had to do was present himself at one shift or the other. To allay suspicion, he had cooked up a story that a colleague in Saudi Arabia was searching for the woman's whereabouts.

There had been three women named Karuna and Berty Uncle had been asked if he was looking for the beautiful

Karuna who was the talk of the office? Berty Uncle replied he had no idea what she looked like.

***

On Monday following the visit to the IGP's relative, Olga Aunty and Sushila had another staffroom tête á tête. Olga Aunty would have gushed about the "lovely" home and the quiet and refined young woman. She would have only stopped at calling her the perfect wife for her brother-in-law.

Sushila would have been keen to find out Berty Uncle's impression of the girl. Was he interested? What did he say?

The accepted tradition was for the male to express interest in the woman. If the female party did not want to proceed with the proposal, it would decline. That way, the boy's side would be rebuffed, but the girl's reputation would be unsullied.

Olga Aunty must have tight-roped her way around presenting Berty Uncle's response. In her favor, Berty Uncle was due back in Saudi Arabia in a week. She could have waited out the week and said his decision was postponed, buying time and temporarily worming her way out of the tricky situation.

Whatever it was, after their chat, during which time Olga Aunty would have even offered her a lemon puff, they parted amicably when the bell rang for the next class, and they went down the corridors to their respective classrooms.

***

Berty Uncle couldn't very well go into the Velona office and demand to meet the three Karunas sewing inside. Even if he summoned enough courage to do that and the three Karunas presented themselves, what then? He was confident that she would recognize him. But how free – or willing –

would she be to talk? Also, how could he talk to her in confidence?

Most of these young women hailed from poor suburban or village families and were ungrounded in etiquette and propriety. His obvious higher societal ranking would not help, apart from making him feel superior and, in turn, uncomfortable.

He had made plans to meet her after her shift ended.

***

During the week that followed, Olga Aunty wondered if Sushila was deliberately avoiding her company. A few times they had run into each other in between class periods, but each time, Sushila had rushed past, avoided looking her in the eye, or started a conversation with someone else. It was very odd. She thought back to the visit and asked Amma if she thought they had said something that could have been misconstrued. Amma drew a blank.

Nelson Uncle had asked Berty Uncle for the one last time about Vinitha and had been met with a derisive burst of laughter. If he was not interested in pursuing the proposal, there was nothing Nelson Uncle or Olga Aunty could do.

Olga Aunty racked her brains for a suitably diplomatic way out of the sticky situation. She had to talk to Sushila soon. If only her friend would stop acting strangely, she told Amma.

But Sushila had come up to her. Thankfully, no one else was in the staff room at the time.

"Do you know what your wonderful Berty has done?" she began.

"No, what has he done?"

"He has followed my sister-in-law's servant girl to her workplace and tried to be funny with her."

"Berty? Surely, he won't do such a thing. I think you're mistaken. Who told you this? *Cheeeeee!*"

"I'm not lying. There is evidence. The shameless fellow has given her some bright and silky dress material and the girl has told the other servants about it. You know how these girls are, jealous of one another. Anyway, it was a good thing that it was reported to Seela; otherwise, she wouldn't have known anything, and who knows what might have happened next? He had asked her if she can come with him to Saudi Arabia. He had even mentioned a secret marriage.

"He accosted her at the workplace just when she was getting off work. She was with others. He asked to talk to her on the pretext that someone in Saudi Arabia was looking for her and had sent her a parcel. This woman has nobody in Saudi Arabia. But she went and spoke to him in spite of ..."

Sushila would have continued with her tirade if the bell hadn't rung for the next period, not a minute too soon for poor Olga Aunty.

But the best part of this story came from Asoka Aiya. When Berty Uncle went to spy on Karuna the second time – the first time he had been unable to accomplish much as she was surrounded by her workmates – he had gone to the bus stand closest to her residence. There he spotted the comely Karuna descending from the bus, looking about her as if she was expecting to meet someone. Sirisena, the roadside messenger on the day of our visit, was waiting for her. As twilight rapidly gave way to a darkened evening, Berty Uncle watched, assuming he was unseen, from the vantage point of his car. They walked toward the lane, hand in hand. Didn't the lady of the house say the other day that she was engaged to be married to a carpenter?

I felt sorry for Berty Uncle when I heard this, although it served him right. If beauty and brains went rarely together, beauty and innocence were rarer.

Where would he find a beautiful young woman with good morals, equal social standing, and a matching horoscope in a short period? It seemed a hopeless quest. A man could get up to any mischief – that was accepted, even expected, in our society, but a woman ... well, that's a story for another time

CHAPTER 11

A BREADLINE ROMANCE

May 1974

Amma walked into Asoka Aiya's room, cleared a spot on the cluttered bedside table, and placed a cup of tea on it.

"Asoka, get up! It's time to go to the line. Get up, get up," she urged.

I followed her. I had been up since 4:30 a.m. studying for term tests, and it was time for a break.

"*Mmm* ..." Asoka Aiya clutched the pillow anew, turned around, and resumed snoring.

Amma shook off the thin cotton sheet covering him and sat on the edge of the bed, shaking him gently by the shoulder. "It's almost five o'clock; if it gets any later, you might not get the bread. I heard some of them going already."

Asoka Aiya muttered something unintelligible and turned his back to our mother.

It took another five minutes of coaxing before he could be persuaded to get up. He sipped the hot tea, rubbed the sleep from his eyes and started his customary grumble.

"What is this, Amma? You wake me every morning at this ungodly hour. Why can't Thatha go for once? Can't we do without bread for one day?"

"No Putha, we can't eat two meals of rice every day – the rations won't last."

Asoka Aiya took a cat wash and changed out of his sarong into shorts and a cotton shirt. Then he got on his bicycle and went his way.

Each morning, Asoka Aiya had to join the bread queue at the Malsara Bakery, a ten-minute bicycle ride from home. If he didn't go in time, the queue would snake along the pavement that bordered the drain and it wasn't a pretty sight or a good smell.

Bread had become a luxury. The year was 1974 and the country was four years into Sirimavo Bandaranaike's socialist government where farmers were urged to cultivate more rice, and the masses were encouraged to grow alternate crops. But so far, her policy of ceasing food imports to encourage cultivation and making the country self-sufficient had only resulted in shortages, substitutes, price hikes, and queues. Every household had a ration card on which was marked an allotted quota of one-and-a-half measures of rice per person, administered each month through a cooperative body. Although this amounted to about two pounds, it was barely enough to last the month. Rice was available in the black market, but most families could not afford the high prices demanded by unscrupulous traders.

With rice prices on the upward move, people switched over to bread and other staples prepared from flour, such as *roti*, *stringhoppers*, *hoppers*, and *pittu*. When faced with the hike in flour prices and also the soaring prices of coconuts used in most curries and sambols, people had returned to bread as an economical substitute.

But imported wheat flour was another restricted item, and bakeries were expected to manage with the limited quantities issued. Teatime favorites like the soft sugared buns and the

94

"crocodile" bread-rolls had all but disappeared, while butter cakes were exorbitantly priced and a luxury, if there were any to be had. Bread was baked during the small hours of the morning and made available for purchase by 7 a.m. By mid-morning it was sold out, so people had to come as early as possible to secure their allotted daily quota.

Bread lines were a great leveler, where the poor and the middle-class met by force of circumstance.

Asoka Aiya sometimes related stories that he gleaned from folk at the breadline. A woman customer at another bakery had complained loudly about the weevils and the fourteen-ounce baker's "pound" and had been unable to buy bread from the same bakery ever since. As soon as the baker saw her, he would declare, "No more bread!"

Romance bloomed even along the unsavory route bordering the drain adjoining the Malsara Bakery. Asoka Aiya told us about other people's relationships but never divulged anything about his own.

Bread lines often made newspaper headlines. By all reports, people were not always courteous or courting while waiting for their loaves. Queue jumping was frequently a cause for bickering; some accommodated their friends into the line while others forced themselves ahead with thuggery. Some households sent two members of the family to different bakeries hoping to secure more loaves and were sometimes found out by neighbors who dropped scathing remarks so that they would not dare repeat the performance. Emboldened by the circumstances, bakers assumed high status and audaciously sold underweight, poor quality bread.

The same situation applied to clothes; people had to stand in line in a cooperative store with the ration book to choose between the limited numbers of kerosene-smelling prints. Worse yet was that this same chintz would be turned into frocks by the whole town so that they would all be dressed like peasants in Mao Tse Tung's China.

About two hours after he left, Asoka Aiya would cycle back home, clutching to his breast with one hand the piping hot "pound" of white bread with its crusty top and soft center. It smelled heavenly. But by the time we sat down to dinner, it would be dry and hard.

***

A few weeks later, after a music lesson at which I had scaled the scales and stumbled through the sight-reading, Quaver asked me to inform my mother to meet her at the first opportunity.

"What could it be?" Amma reflected aloud as she hurriedly draped a voile sari around herself. "It isn't as if you have not been practicing for the forthcoming exam. And your fees are already paid for the month."

But it was not about me.

"Mrs. de Silva, I asked you to drop in to talk to you about something important. Tamara's doing better with her pieces, but she needs more practice to play at the exam. I have done the scales too, and she has learned them well."

"That's good," Amma beamed.

"But I want to talk to you about something else. You know, this is none of my business, but I thought of warning you all the same."

Amma looked alarmed and so was I. "What is it, Miss Norah?" she asked.

"You know how I take the dogs for their evening walk?"

"Yes?"

"Well, I have to tell you something."

"Oh, what is it?"

"Well, recently, I have been noticing that your, uh, son is seen outside ..."

I could tell that Amma was beginning to wish Quaver would come to the point. The fish was languishing in the kitchen sink and the coconut was unscraped. She did not have all afternoon to listen to this ramble.

"... I really don't want to get involved, but you know Malay girls. Well, I know how hard you work to keep your home fires burning; would you really like to have a daughter-in-law from a different ethnicity?"

"My son? And what Malay girl?"

"It's like this. When I go out walking with the dogs, I see your son with Izmin every day, you know, Mrs. Cassim's eldest daughter? They meet behind the parapet wall bordering the playground at dusk after the cricket matches are over. Don't even mention to anybody that I told you, but you know why I am telling this to you?"

Quaver sucked in her cheeks, stroked her throat, and rolled her eyes for good measure before continuing.

"I even saw them holding hands behind the parapet wall. I think you should put a stop to this affair. Before Malays marry boys from other races, the first thing they want is to change their religion. Would you like Asoka to become a Muslim and be alienated from you? I have seen it happen many times in several families. I don't want it to happen to you."

Asoka Aiya was not yet sixteen and here was Quaver marrying him off and banishing him off to the mosque, all in the course of one afternoon. Amma quivered her thanks, which was the least she could do. She must have felt both

97

affronted by and grateful to this spinster. She weaved her way out from among the quintet of cane chairs, clutching her starched sari fall.

As she opened the gate latch and let herself in, she saw me following her home and her face registered a vague surprise.

***

Lately, Asoka Aiya had not fussed about getting up early to go to the bread queue. Several times he had even woken up on his own and was already brushing his teeth when Amma took him his tea. She had taken it as a sign of maturity and understanding; I had heard her tell Thatha. But now, on second thought, maybe there was another reason for his eagerness. And he did seem to spend a longer time on his grooming early in the morning.

Around 6 p.m., Thatha walked in, looking bedraggled as usual from a day of boozing, working, and traveling in a bus packed like sardines. After a good cup of tea to revive him as much as he could be revived, Amma apprised him of the afternoon's happenings.

"Ha, a Malay girl! That's too bad when there are so many Sinhalese girls around. On the other hand, we can eat some good accharu. Just let him experience life. It won't last."

The Malay community makes a tasty pickle, and Thatha loved the side dish at lunch.

"But who knows what he will do? He's at a very vulnerable age," Amma continued.

"*Hmm*, we were all that age once. These things don't last. Just let him be."

And with that, he took up *The Daily News*, settled back his bony frame on the armchair and put his feet up on the footrest.

###

A Maiden's Prayer

The next day was Saturday. Thatha borrowed Asoka
Aiya's bicycle to go to the junction to get a haircut. Amma
asked him to get some vegetables from the market at the same
time.

I knew Amma was worried about Asoka Aiya and Thatha
offered no direction. Visions of Asoka Aiya eloping with this
girl crossed my mind from time to time. No, surely he had
more sense than that.

With a cane basket hanging on the handlebar, Thatha left
on his errands. Amma peeped in at the front room and
absorbed its condition in a leisurely manner. It looked as
though a cyclone had visited recently, with devastating results.
A dirt-encrusted cricket bat was propped against the
clotheshorse that was tottering dangerously and about to give
way. Shoes and socks lay scattered, with a trail of dried mud
and sand. Parts of a bicycle tire seemed to have had some
mechanical attention bestowed upon it beside the bed.

Books were everywhere but on the bookshelf. Asoka Aiya
was heavy on James Hadley Chase. Titles such as *The Guilty
Are Afraid*, *You've Got It Coming*, and *Lay Her Among The
Lilies* lay about and seemed to foreshadow the situation.

The keeper of the room himself was lying supinely on the
bed, engrossed in the latest Chase thriller in his possession. A
half-empty tin of condensed milk with a spoon inside was on
the windowsill, next to a spanner. A double trail of black ants
scurried to the tin and back from a crack in the wall. Amma
had forgotten to guard the condensed milk. Like the rest of
the family, Asoka Aiya relished sweets and would resort to
jam, sugar, jaggery or condensed milk when other, more
refined, goodies were unavailable. Amma's supplies were
usually locked in the safe but she had forgotten about the

99

condensed milk. Now she would have to buy another tin to make the milk toffees I wanted to take to school. And the price had recently gone up to two-twenty-five rupees from the usual one-twenty-five.

Asoka Aiya put down the dog-eared copy of *Tell It to the Birds* and looked up inquiringly. Amma sighed almost involuntarily and sat at the foot of the bed. It was useless to make comments about his room or ask him to clean up. Asoka Aiya cleaned his room when he got into his cleaning mood, which occurred about monsoon-ally. However tempted, Amma knew it was best to steer clear of all other inflammatory topics. She asked when the results of his advanced level exams were expected. She inquired about the forthcoming cricket match with the area teams. She asked about his friend, Vijaya, and whether he had found a job.

Then she came to the point.

"Putha, I want to talk to you about something very important. I understand that you are getting too close to some girl in the area. I want it to stop immediately. You should have more important things on your mind now than going after girls, and Malay girls at that."

"What girls are you talking about? I am not interested in any girl." Asoka Aiya wasn't good at lying and was visibly perturbed; I could see through the crack in the doorway.

"Now don't try to fool me. I'm your mother. I know you are meeting Izmin in the evenings after cricket. Don't think I'm not aware of what is going on. You must stop this nonsense immediately. After you qualify, you will have enough time to find a good girl."

"What nonsense! Who has been spying on me? I indeed met Izmin once or twice after a game, but there is nothing more to it than that. Her brother is one of my good friends."

Amma could have whacked him with his own bat, but Asoka Aiya was five feet, eight inches, and a whole head taller than she was.

"It's nonsense all right, but you are the one who is up to this nonsense. You must not bring any disgrace to the family. Remember what happened to Sirisoma Uncle? He had to live without his relatives when he took a Burgher wife. Take it into your head and just concentrate on your studies. Don't let me hear these things again. I have brought you up with lots of difficulties, not to have to face such a thing. I hope you will stop this."

"Don't be silly Amma, and please leave me in peace. I'd like to find out who has been telling tales. I think I have a fair idea. It was Quaver, wasn't it? I saw her snooping around the cricket grounds last week. I'll take care of her."

Amma walked out of Asoka Aiya's room on the trail of his threats, nearly in tears. After all, what could she do, except talk to him—or check his horoscope—which was the type of thing that was done during troubling times. She believed that if something drastic was to happen, the warning signals somehow lurked there.

CHAPTER 12

OF SUITORS AND BRIDES

February 1975

Ever since old Frisky died, I had been begging for another dog. Amma, as usual, had a thousand burdens on her shoulders and no time to look for a pet even if she wanted to please me. Thatha thought of it as "one more mouth to feed." Asoka Aiya was my only hope, but he had been unable to get one for the longest time.

So when Quaver asked around her circle of students if anyone would like to have a dog, I pricked up my ears. Someone known to her was looking for homes for six puppies.

The pup was delivered to me when she was only two months old, an adorable bundle of light brown fur through which shone a pair of bright, beady eyes. Attempts to cuddle her resulted in a splash of grateful licks from a soft pink tongue. I immediately responded to her heart-tugging display of affection and trust.

But she was less well-received by the others. They had wanted a male dog to guard the house. Besides, her breed was questionable – her tail was curled up; the ultimate giveaway. But who would give away purebred, male Alsatian puppies? They were expensive and there was never any money for things like that.

"What can we do with a bitch? She'll only cause trouble," Thatha admonished me when he returned home from work. "It's a Dachshund-cross? Looks like a pariah-dog to me."

I didn't understand how he could speak of her like this. Tikiri – I had already named her – had been ambling after me, her tummy nearly touching the floor after a good feed of bread dipped in milk.

"Tamara, you had better exchange her for a male pup. Surely they must have more – didn't you say there were six to be given away?"

"But Amma, just look at her, will you? She is so sweet. I want to keep her, pleeese?"

"What sort of guard dog will she be? I don't know; you better look after her when she's older." This was my brother, the dog lover, washing his hands of all responsibility.

I got my way. After the dust settled on the initial uproar, they too succumbed to her charms. Sometimes I think they objected just for the sake of having something to say.

In retrospect, I should have listened to them.

***

The trouble started a few days after my fourteenth birthday. Not yet two, our good-looking Tikiri had caught the "dog-eye." At first, I was amused when the neighborhood dogs found it particularly interesting to sniff about our lawn. They were gradually making it their bathroom. Then, things got worse. They darted inside the house, lifted a hind-leg near a piece of furniture, drenched it, sniffed around and cheekily sauntered out. Was this an appropriate code of conduct when seeking for a paw in marriage?

One lazy Saturday afternoon, when Amma and Thatha were taking a nap, I watched the dogs though the vantage point of the corner window. It was as if Tikiri had sent them a telegram to come by. Maybe she did send out a message of sorts that was conveyed by air, even though she was dozing in a corner.

The dogs came in all shapes and sizes. A black and white spotty hurried down the road and squeezed through the broken iron grill of the gate. He briskly circled our house as if on urgent business, lifted his hind leg, squirted a puddle of urine at the foot of the mango tree and sat down beneath its leafy shade. Next, a huge brown dog with the sweetest face leaped over the wall, growled at his companion, and sat beside him, paws crossed.

He was handsome, almost elegant. A browning mango leaf, set into circular motion by a breeze, dropped on his furry head. He flicked his ear and looked up, startled. From time to time, he would bark at his companion, but it was more like a conversation than an argument. Then, a fluffy white-turned-light-brown-with-dirt dog with a small, pointed face squeezed its body through the gate, boldly trotted into the others' view, uttered a hollow squeak, and settled down some distance away.

They were well behaved for dogs, almost as if they were preparing to take afternoon tea in our garden.

Then Tikiri woke up, stretched herself out lazily, licked her front paws and joined me at the window. She saw her admirers. The admirers saw her. All hell broke loose.

The party on the lawn made a mad dash toward the window. They scratched, howled, and hurled themselves toward her. Tikiri was equally responsive and ran to the door, sniffing madly through the gap. She looked at me eagerly and whined to be let out, so without further thinking, I opened the door.

What happened next took place so fast that I can hardly explain. Within minutes, the three dogs were fighting to jump on her and shake off the competition at the same time.

The black and white dog won the contest. While the other two growled and encircled Tikiri, the spotty mounted our poor dog. Her face took on an amazed look, and she began howling in pain.

Amma and Thatha woke up, rushed out of their bedroom to the scene of the crime. I could see Quaver peeping out of a window. Maya, Mrs. Vithanage's wisp-of-a-servant-girl who had been watering plants in their garden, came running to our gate and stood still with her bucket, staring as though a circus had unexpectedly arrived.

"Maya, Maya, give me that bucket," yelled Thatha. He ran to the outdoor tap, filled it with water and hurled it at the dogs. But they seemed to be stuck. More water was filled and flung, with the urgency brought about by a house on fire, but nothing could unlock them. Tikiri, who hated baths, was gasping, soaked to the bone, and protesting loudly at the dual injustice to her body.

Time seemed to stand still. It was so embarrassing, that I took refuge in my room. I knew they would blame me for letting her out. I never thought the dogs would pounce on her like that without getting to know her better and finding out if she was willing.

Some minutes later, I heard Tikiri whimpering. She bounded into my room and bolted under the bed. She did not come out even for dinner. I cleaned up the trail of blood and water that extended from the front doorstep to my bed.

Thatha was still yelling at the dogs.

***

In our English literature class, we read about Odysseus and his travels. While the Greek hero was delayed at sea after the Trojan Wars and not expected to return, his beautiful wife Penelope was being courted by a band of suitors. Homer wrote that they were fed with freshly baked bread, meat, and casks of wine.

In their constancy and stubbornness, Tikiri's band of suitors outdid those of Penelope's. But far from receiving freshly-baked bread – which was a scarcity at home, in any case – they were pelted with stones.

From time to time, our house was besieged by hordes of badly-behaved neighborhood hounds that thought nothing of tearing each other's ears on a daily basis. The immediate neighbors in our housing development were all too aware when our frisky young princess was having a period. I was glad that it occurred only once in six months. If it happened every month, we would have had to leave our home or get rid of Tikiri.

Each time, it seemed worse. Apart from our domestic peace, the neighborhood quiet was shattered. Gone were the silent lanes and bypaths, the stillness broken only by the kerosene oil cart and the occasional motorbike. Now there were yelping dogs beating a hasty retreat from missiles hurled by my family.

One day, Thatha had had enough. In the night, they had scratched and whined at our doors and windows: snarled, growled and fought. This was his third sleepless night.

"Bloody nuisance. Can't even open a door," he said. "Tamara, why don't you go and give Tikiri to Quaver? Ask her to keep her. She's the one who started all these problems."

Amma, who had been brushing/blowing away the ants that had crept inside the sugar bottle for the umpteenth time and was equally irritated by the dogs and the ants, agreed. "Yes, and now on Saturday, when Aranolis Kapuwa comes, how are we going to even hear ourselves talk with all this yowling outside?"

I had been thinking about that too but was reluctant to voice concerns just in case they decided to do something drastic.

"Why don't you postpone the visit and ask him to come the following weekend. By then, this will be over," I volunteered.

"How can I do that, Duwa? Can I ask Olga Aunty not to come here because the dog is having visitors? No, we'll have to manage somehow."

Aranolis Kapuwa was the matchmaker who brought proposals for Dirty Berty from time to time. He lived in Padukka, and whenever he wanted to introduce new prospects for Olga Aunty's inspection, he preferred to come to our place, as it was easier. He could only reach Olga Aunty's place by taking three buses. Besides, the matchmaker killed two birds with one stone; Another neighbor, who was keen on finding a partner for her daughter, was also on his list of clients. Amma had performed the introduction when I was present.

I disliked Aranolis Kapuwa for his habit of assessing all unmarried people – even children – as prospects. I bet he was making mental notes on me too, so that when the time came, he would already have a prepared list of my supposed accomplishments and suitable matches to boot. Thank you very much, but I didn't think I would need any help in that department. There were far too many boys interested in me, even now. I wished I could find a way to convey that message.

The more I thought of him, the more indignant I became. What right had this old man in his musty black coat to presume he could tie people's lives together? And earn his bread this way, too?

But there were good things about this too; his visits were entertaining, and although I was not expected to be in the audience, my help was often required. My notebook expanded accordingly. Besides, it was Dirty Berty's life he was dabbling with, and it provided a juicy story with which to regale my cousins.

Also, who could resist his comical appearance? Aranolis Kapuwa was an oldish man with an ancient hairstyle. The few long silver hairs that still clung to his head were scraped back and tied in a tiny knot at the back. A thick white soup-strainer mustache resembling a coconut husk curled stiffly around the upper lip. Bushy eyebrows matched his whiskers, and a tuft of hair sticking out of his ears matched them in turn.

Whatever the weather, Aranolis Kapuwa was dressed in a spotless white cotton sarong and black coat over a white poplin shirt. A thick leather belt firmly held the sarong in place. He never went anywhere without his black umbrella, considered the trademark of all marriage brokers. In fact, he was a walking advertisement for himself, a Ceylonese version of a Pied Piper trying to marry off the population to his tune.

***

The day before Aranolis Kapuwa's visit, a windowpane was cracked during a stone-throwing session that had backfired. The stone had bounced off the coconut tree. By now, our front door was giving off little wooden chips. Little wonder then that

Amma was in a bad mood as she hurriedly prepared the cutlets for frying, taking one by one the little balls of crumbled and spiced fish combined with kohila yam, dipping them in beaten egg with one hand and rolling them in breadcrumbs with the other.

"Duwa, collect those stones and put them inside the bedroom. Hurry up! Olga Aunty will be here soon," she admonished sharply from the kitchen.

I hastened to the mound of sticks and stones beside the door, but before I could do her bidding, the sound of the gate opening made me rush to the window. Aranolis Kapuwa was coming in. He was early.

Amma's fingers in each hand were covered with egg and breadcrumbs respectively and Asoka Aiya was not at home to give the stony treatment to the two hounds that had been "guarding" our entrance. Although by now, even the stones and the accompanying screams were not having any effect on the dogs; they refused to budge.

As it turned out, Aranolis Kapuwa was perfectly capable of handling the situation. When the dogs started growling, he simply unhooked the umbrella from its customary position hanging on his left forearm and swung it out at the nuisance. In doing so, his bag came crashing down for a minute, but that did not stop him. One dog howled in pain as he retreated.

The matchmaker picked up his bag, composed himself and knocked at the door. Stifling a giggle, I opened it and feigned surprise. He stepped in.

Unaware of our predicament with Tikiri, he raised his bushy eyebrows at the little pyramid of sticks and stones heaped inside. I offered no explanation but motioned for him to sit. He propped his umbrella in a corner of the wall and sat down on a settee. Amma was still in the kitchen, where I could hear her scraping off the breadcrumbs from her fingers under the running tap.

I didn't know how to make small conversation with this man. Olga Aunty had yet to arrive, I informed him, and Amma will be with you soon. With that, I left him to his own devices and went into my room and sat on the bed. I could keep an eye on him through the crack in the curtain usually reserved for Berty Uncle's capers.

The early afternoon sun was maddeningly hot, and Aranolis still perspired rivulets as a combined result of his arduous bus journey, walk to our house and the thick coat. He pulled out a large white hankerchief from his coat pocket and repeatedly wiped his sweat. I could have turned on the fan for him, but why waste precious electricity on this ridiculous person? Why couldn't he just take his coat off?

Sounds of sputtering oil were followed by the delicious aroma of deep-frying fish cutlets wafting into the hall. Aranolis sniffed appreciatively and brightened considerably.

For want of something to do, he began to restore his grooming. He first attended to his straying hair, which he ensured was pasted back on his sweaty skull by smoothing it repeatedly. He then made sure that the little knot of hair was secure. Then he grabbed the ends of his mustache with both hands and started curling them upwards. I hoped he would fiddle with the tuft of hair that was sticking out from his ears, but it defied gravity naturally and was unruffled by the journey and therefore left untouched.

Presently, the desired result achieved with his facial hair, he leaned back and pulled out a large folded pouch from its hiding place between his belly and belt. Inside the pouch was a wad of betel leaves wrapped in newspaper. He unwrapped the bundle and selected a plump one. After breaking the stem and the end of the leaf with great care and discarding them carelessly on our floor, he tore a piece from a withered tobacco leaf and placed it on the betel leaf. To this, he added a few wedges of dried areca-nuts, which have a mild stimulant effect like drinking a cup of coffee. Next, he took out a little ball of newspaper that contained some *chunam*, or slaked lime, from shells. He smeared a little of the white, chalky mixture onto the tobacco leaf with his forefinger and, never suspecting that he was being watched, smeared the extra *chunam* on the arm of our settee.

He then folded and popped the treat into his mouth, settled his sweaty person back and started chewing. Presently, the eyes closed in what must have been blissful enjoyment.

Thankfully, before he could do further damage to our chairs, Olga Aunty was heard coming down the garden path.

Meanwhile, the dogs had returned. I cautiously opened the door for Olga Aunty, and she gained admittance with the smallest opening her bulk would allow, in great competition with the dogs. The effort of this maneuver had a negative impact on her attire, as a corner of her sari caught on a wooden chip sticking out of the tattered door and tore off a few inches.

Smoothing the corner of her torn voile sari, Olga Aunty started complaining about Tikiri. "Why don't you get rid of her; see what a nuisance it is, having a female dog?"

I ignored her remark. She, too, was sweating profusely.

"Where's Amma? My, you are really growing tall, anney."

Amma finally made an appearance, hair disheveled and smelling of cutlets. By habit, she spoke to her sister in English

111

but switched to Sinhalese for the benefit of the matchmaker who, as far as we knew, spoke not a word of the former.

"Sit, sit. Duwa, put on the fan, will you? It's really hot, no? *Kohomada* Aranolis?"

Aranolis, who could not speak because betel juice was clogging his mouth, pointed to it with his index finger and made toward the door. Now that he was aware of the dog menace, he was cautious in his movements. But the dogs knew better than to bother the black coat. Standing on the bottom doorstep, he placed two trained fingers in a 'V' over his lips and expertly spat the red liquid over the fence into Mrs. Vithanage's garden.

"... had to wait a long time for the bus, men; even on Saturdays buses are so full, and I couldn't even get a seat until it was time for me to get off." Olga Aunty paused only to take deep swigs of the cool water that Amma had brought.

With only the betel bulge protruding from his cheek, Aranolis was free to join in the conversation.

"Oh, don't talk about buses," he said. "They never come on time. Just to make sure that I won't get late, I left one hour early today."

"*Ethin, kohomada*, Aranolis? What have you got for us today?"

Aranolis cleared his throat slowly and noisily in preparation for his great presentation. "In this bag, I have so many high-class girls that if I cannot find a match for Berty Mahattaya, I'm not Aranolis," he declared, threw his head back and guffawed showing a mouth that was a gold mine for a dentist.

Olga Aunty and Amma both looked at his black leather bag as if the maidens would pop out at any minute.

112

Aranolis opened it and pulled out a sheaf of papers. He then reached into his breast pocket and took out a pair of round, gold-rimmed spectacles, which he placed on his nose.

"I have two very good proposals for Berty Mahattaya this time, and both are from excellent Govibodu families," he announced, sorting through the pile of papers that turned out to have sketches of horoscope charts.

With the deliberation of a prosecutor during a significant lawsuit, Aranolis selected two folded sheets and opened the first one.

"This one belongs to Karagetihene Loku Mahattaya's older daughter. You must have heard of them. They are the ones who own half the area of Karagetihena in Homagama. With my help, the younger daughter recently got married to the Assistant Government Agent of Kurunegala.

"How old is the older daughter?"

"She's only 32. Due to *Kethu*'s bad influence, her marriage was delayed. Look," said Aranolis, pointing at the chart, "she has a malefic in the Seventh House. However, according to her *dasa kalaya*, this is a good time for marriage."

Aranolis transferred the bulging lump of betel chew from one cheek to the other and continued.

"I know that Berty Mahattaya is looking for an educated girl, and this one is really suited because she is a trained home science teacher. She's also very nice looking and has good character." He chuckled again.

"In spite of having servants, this girl does a lot of housework — she arranges flower vases, attends to the garden and much more."

"So, are there any other brothers and sisters in the family?"

113

"No, no, the Mahattaya has only two daughters. The mother protected the two of them like her own eyes."

At this point, he had to remove himself to the door and shoot another red stream over the fence. Mrs. Vithanage's garden was getting decorated.

"Right now, for the dowry, she is getting five acres of rubber and three lakhs of rupees. Not only that, one day these two girls will inherit all the wealth of the Loku Mahattaya."

Olga Aunty's eyes widened, and Amma looked at her in awe.

Aranolis handed over the horoscope chart to Olga Aunty and asked her to copy it so that it might be compared with that of Berty Uncle's.

This is where my services were required. By now I was accustomed to drawing charts and marking the positions of various planets. I set to the task without protest. The paper, in addition to the chart, contained details of the girl, her family and her dowry.

The next prospect was not as rich but drew a good income from presenting cake-making classes in a posh suburb of Colombo.

"I know her from a young age," Aranolis said. "They lost their father very early in life. The mother brought up the four children admirably; the three sons are all in good professions and two of them are abroad. The girl, Rohini, is the youngest and is now twenty-nine. Although she didn't do higher studies, she makes a lot of money from cake orders and classes. A very courageous girl who learned on her own and is now independent, moneywise."

"So, how much is she getting for the dowry?"

"*Umm*, I think she has collected about fifty thousand rupees on her own and the two brothers have promised another hundred thousand rupees. Especially when this girl is making such a good income, it's not bad at all," he pointed out.

"The only thing is, how can she make this income if she goes to Saudi Arabia?"

"*Aaah*, Berty Mahattaya is not going to be in Saudi Arabia forever. One day he will come back and settle down. And with this girl as his wife, the Mahattaya will not even have to work as she will make enough money."

Aranolis flashed a red-spittle smile at his audience and continued. "Not only that, two of the brothers are abroad. One is a doctor in a big hospital in England, and the other is a professor in an Amaarikan university. Some place, uh, like Cauliponia. The mother has told me that the brothers will sponsor Rohini after she gets married. What do you think of that prospect?"

Olga Aunty didn't waste any time. She almost snatched the chart from the man. "Here, Tamara," she called out to me, "this one too."

Amma excused herself, went into the kitchen and returned with a heaping plate of cutlets.

"Babee, please bring me some water," Aranolis asked.

With the glass of water in hand, Aranolis once again made a trip to the doorstep. He spat a lump of well-masticated betel on the ground and rinsed his mouth. Then he focused on the cutlets, which he devoured with a robust appetite. Bits of it stuck to his coconut-husk mustache.

"... so you'd better compare the horoscopes and let me know the results; I have already asked them to do the same."

I watched him take another cutlet from the plate, pop it in his mouth, chew it around and put his finger to remove what he thought was a hair.

Amma rushed to explain that it wasn't hair, but the fibrous parts of kohila root that she was forced to use, as potatoes were unavailable. And too expensive for us to afford even if they were available, I thought to myself.

To wash it down, Amma brought steaming hot cups of tea. I, for one, could never understand why they drank the hot brew in this broiling heat, but the visitors eagerly welcomed the beverage.

After drinking his rather noisily, Aranolis looked expectantly at Olga Aunty and started gathering up his things. "If everything is all right, we should go ahead and arrange meetings. I will come again the Saturday after next about the same time to find out. When did you say Berty Mahattaya is expected?"

"He will be here in time for the Sinhalese New Year. Let's see what happens," replied Olga Aunty opening her handbag and taking out two ten-rupee notes. "Oh Aranolis, you must finalize it this time, all my money and time is spent in finding proposals for this boy."

"Yes, yes, I think we can do it this time. So now I will take my leave. I must go to Daisy Missy's place now. I have several good ones for her daughter too."

Aranolis took off, shooing and raising his umbrella in a threatening manner at the three dogs that had crept to the door again.

Amma gathered up the teacups. "Aney, aney," she lamented. "You had to fork out twenty rupees again and he only gave two horoscopes. If these two don't match, what will happen?"

"Berty will come and go back for another six months. This is what happens over and over again."

"How much have you promised to give him if a marriage works out?"

"He is demanding a thousand ..."

"A thousand? Even my salary is only five-hundred rupees, and I have to teach for a whole month to get that."

"But it's not a steady income; he gets money only if he's successful, although he earns a sizable amount by showing horoscopes."

"Anyway, he only gave you two horoscopes this time. Why don't you contact more kapuwas?"

"No, I don't want to go through these people too much; some of them are real rogues. I've heard of kapuwas who take the same horoscope to every household with marriageable people. Remember Lewisa Nona. Several times she gave us horoscopes and we spent money to compare with Berty's, and nothing would come of them in the end. We didn't even go to see the girls — always she used to give some excuse not to proceed with those 'excellent' proposals."

"*Yeeess*, men, sometimes the young people are already married, and these kapuwas still use their horoscopes to earn money. That's why more and more people are relying on newspaper ads."

"Yes, like last time, I have told Nelson to place an advertisement in *The Sunday Observer*. You spend about twenty-five rupees and get at least sixty replies that way, although more than ninety percent are discarded and only a handful are worthy of consideration."

"Why don't you advertise in the *Silumina* too? The Sinhala paper has a bigger circulation and is read all over the country."

"Oh, Berty won't like girls from villages who don't speak English. He's very particular about that."

"But you know, parents are the ones who reply, but that does not mean that the children are not English-educated. I strongly recommend you advertise in the Sinhala paper, too."

"All right, I'll see what Nelson says."

***

That day, I accompanied Olga Aunty to her home because she was going to sew my school uniforms the next day. She was a good and quick seamstress, but she always wanted me to be around for the many fittings that the process required.

Olga Aunty and I were already on our way to the bus stand under her open black umbrella when Amma, who had stopped at the gate, shouted to attract our attention. She uttered little squeaky noises and flailed her arms in great agitation.

I ran back to her.

"Duwa, Duwa, ask Olga Aunty to come back. It's not good to go out after eating fried food at this time. I forgot ... ask her ... anney ... to come *baaack!*"

I ran back to Olga Aunty and explained Amma's reasoning. She turned back immediately.

Meanwhile, Amma had rushed into the storeroom and found a rusty nail. She wrapped it up in newspaper and gave it to her sister whose plump person was now breathless with so much exertion. No further explanation was necessary. She opened her straw bag and placed it at the bottom. The iron would protect us from greedy evil spirits if any would dare come after us. I doubted that very much.

Without a nail to protect him, I pictured Aranolis Kapuwa in the same predicament, brandishing his umbrella at the startled spirits and getting away unscathed in the same able manner he had tackled the dogs.

***

As for our frisky Tikiri, her single adventure produced results: a solitary, bonny pup, delivered and licked into shape under my bed. It took us all by surprise, but I think Tikiri was the most startled. Needless to say, being another female, she was quickly gifted to an unsuspecting person. I did not mind at all.

CHAPTER 13

THE ASTROLOGER

Olga Aunty didn't waste time. The copied horoscopes were in the bag. What did they portend? She had to find out. On our way back, we alighted from the bus at Rajagiriya junction and walked to astrologer Amarasena's house.

My aunt, I'm sure, had chosen a husband with less deliberation than an astrologer. Among qualities she sought after, she contended that the astrologer's reputation for accurate predictions must precede him. Word of mouth was the best way to learn about one, and usually, a good astrologer with a solid reputation was known and discussed for miles around. So she kept her ears open for conversation on the subject.

As Olga Aunty hated vagueness and vacillation in people, she wanted a direct and candid personality. However, a measure of diplomacy would suit the profession too. If, for example, a client who desperately wished to be married had no astral placing conducive to marriage, he should not be told that bluntly; instead, a parent or sibling was alerted. It wouldn't help if a client lost his mental balance. It was important for the astrologer to skillfully balance the indications of his head and heart.

Olga Aunty reasoned if an astrologer is advising others to better their lives, he should be able to use the knowledge to better his own life as well. If he could help others to reach lofty heights through calculating powerful nekath (auspicious times) and murthi (commencement times for various rites), he too, within reasonable limits, could achieve a better status in life.

Thus, she disdained poor astrologers. But those on the other end of the spectrum - who commanded big money from rich clients - she didn't trust them, either. She felt the acquired knowledge and the blessing of psychic ability should not be a commercial enterprise.

Furthermore, Olga Aunty divvied astrologers into two categories – those who saw the glass nearly empty and those who saw it more than half-full. Those in the former category were invariably born poor and bore a chip on their shoulder. These sadistic excuses of the profession scrutinized your chart and found disaster lurking in every trine. Even worse, they delivered the bad news with arrogant confidence and a happy air.

In Amarasena she found the latter; a kindly man who had perfected the art – or science – of presenting the negative in a positive light. The malefic or benefic disposition of each planet showed the way karma might tend to unfold throughout this lifetime. But I had heard Olga Aunty tell Amma several times that Amarasena wasn't fatalistic. He didn't shrug his shoulders or roll his eyes and dramatically attribute every negative thing to fate. He contended that a person can perform certain corrective actions and counterbalance negative karmic deeds. He thought quickly and offered solutions to every situation.

With Amarasena, hope reigned. He was the happy medium who possessed a good balance of each quality that she meticulously sought.

The astrologer lived in an old-fashioned Dutch-style dwelling with a tiled roof that was once red but was now blackish-brown, with varying degrees of fading reds, probably replacements.

The house had a broad, open verandah, which was particularly useful for his trade, as all his customers were expected to sit there and await their turn. But sadly, he didn't seem to care about his clients' comforts. The unfortunate thing about the seating was that those who remained after dusk were assailed by hordes of mosquitoes. If that wasn't enough, his rattan chairs harbored a considerable litter of bugs. The cushions on them were like pancakes, as people cringed and adjusted when they were bitten. It was far better to sit on the backless wooden benches.

With the increasing fame of Amarasena's accurate readings, the average waiting time had ballooned to several hours. Clients lined up at his gate at dawn and the last ones departed into the dark night. It being a Saturday afternoon, the verandah was rather crowded when we reached there. To avoid a bug attack, Olga Aunty took a newspaper from the teapoy, spread it out on the one vacant chair and sat down gingerly. She did not even place her straw bag on the chair but kept it on the ground. I fetched a stool for myself from inside the house.

Amarasena's office room was located on one side of the verandah, where he did his consultations secluded from the rest of the household. The only entrance to the room was through the verandah.

From the main double doors leading to the inner house, those on the verandah could observe the goings-on in the vestibule, which was another hubbub of commerce. Amarasena's two plain daughters were seamstresses and they were sewing at the dining table, on which there were two table-top sewing machines, yards of cloth, spools of thread, voile lining and various other tailoring trappings. Today, there was also a fair, comely woman working diligently alongside them.

When they tired of watching the happenings inside, the people looked at each other in a bored, yet curious manner. They stared at the person and belongings of whoever was looking the other way, but the moment they caught their eye, they looked away. Conversation was minimal, but from amongst the drone of the Singer machines and the mindless chatter of the tailoring women, Amarasena's deep voice could be heard dispensing astrological guidance.

"This child has a very bad period in store, which lasts for two years and during which time *Kethu* retrogrades, starting on January 20th. She has a *marakaya* at nine, which can be deadly. On her behalf, you must offer a puja with a blue cloth and seven baskets of flowers to God Vishnu at Vishnu Devalaya in the Bellanwila temple. Around her neck, you must place a talisman blessed with the *Rathana Suthra*. I advise you to send her away for at least one year to a relative's place where she could be separated from the immediate family. That way, the bad effects can be mitigated. Do you understand?"

A woman's voice could be heard quivering "yes."

"According to the horoscope, this child should not be under the same roof with her brother during this period."

"How soon do we have to do this?" questioned a male voice.

"Do all this by the first week of January. But if you can send her away before that, it's even better."

123

Amarasena was heard giving further instructions to the troubled parents. After a short pause, they came out of the room, followed by the astrologer.

He looked around at the expectant faces, acknowledged Olga Aunty, an established customer, with, "Ah, Nona, *kohomada?*" and without waiting for a reply, asked, "Who is next?"

An elderly man, who had been reading a newspaper in the far corner chair and had been bug-bitten, rose quickly, and scratching his behind, shuffled in after Amarasena. Everyone looked at his behind.

***

After a good two hours of eavesdropping on each and everybody's predicaments, malefic periods, and beneficial times, it was Olga Aunty's turn to entertain the others. By then, the sewing trio had decided to call it a day, so she had the undivided attention of the verandah listeners.

Olga Aunty took her seat on the opposite side of the large table where the man sat. I positioned myself beside her on the other chair.

"So, Mr. Amarasena, your daughters' sewing business is going so well that they have hired an extra hand?"

"Not at all, Nona; that is my son's wife. He got married recently, which made for a nice change around the home."

His voice dropped to a whisper: "Now if I can only get my daughters married as well, that'll be good. When their age was right and the time was astrologically correct, I tried to arrange marriages for them, but they were too choosy. Now it's too late. It's their karma, and even I can't help them."

Astrologers endeavor to uncover the correct times to undertake events for maximum effect, or to identify those

124

periods in which it might be better to avoid action in order to avert a negative outcome. To do that, they draw on mathematics and observations of astronomy, using these scientific tools to analyze and measure behavioral patterns over time, as well as forecast trends.

Amarasena had isolated the optimum time for his daughters' marriage according to their planetary placements and *dasas*, the planetary major period of their horoscopes, but they had not taken advantage of his knowledge.

Olga Aunty nodded understandingly. Here she was, saddled with the same predicament. Trying to marry off Berty Uncle was as easy as mastering the occult. If it were not for Berty Uncle's sister, who was equally bent on letting her brother be unmarried so they could continue to live on his property, Olga Aunty probably would not have bothered at all.

"I know how difficult it is to arrange marriages for people who are not willing to settle down. You can see the trouble I am having with my husband's brother. We are searching high and low for him, but always he has an excuse. Anyway, these are two new charts that I have, which are very good proposals. And here is my brother-in-law's *handahana*. Could you please check whether they tally?"

Horoscopes are generally kept hidden in a box or drawer in a home. The personal property is rarely seen by strangers, except for the family astrologer.

Amarasena clucked sympathetically as he expertly opened Berty Uncle's rolled up ola-leaf horoscope from its core.

It was one thing to offer sage advice and direction, but quite another for a client to follow it. Amarasena had been comparing horoscopes on Berty Uncle's behalf for more than five years. Often, he had found matching birth charts, but it had all come to naught. In that regard, Berty Uncle fit right in with his daughters.

A horoscope, or *handahana*, is a snapshot of the placing of planets at a person's birth moment, traditionally inscribed on an *ola* leaf, a type of palm leaf, after a birth. Astrologers can describe the characteristics of the person from this snapshot, outlined in a chart. It is also believed that a person is ruled by a succession of planets, the subsequent movements of which affect the individual's life. A good astrologer can interpret the movements and foretell the events in store. Marriage is just one aspect, but a universal one.

The exterior part of the *handahana* acts as a protective cover and is never unfastened during readings. It is secured in a slot on the outside of the roll with an incision to which two or three tiny decorative cutouts are added.

Accordingly, Amarasena flattened the intricately patterned spiral part that was about one-and-a-half yards long and looked at the fine calligraphic drawings of the twelve houses. He kept two paperweights on either side of the pertinent section to prevent it from curling.

Like many Sinhala horoscopes, the ola leaf also had incidental decorations on the inside; flourishes, tailpieces, ornamental borders, decorative squares and series of lines or waves linked the charts. The calligraphy that filled in the space between the edges of the ola leaf was rarely repeated and varied according to the inclination of the artist as well as the wishes and the pecuniary situation of the customer. Other sections contained long sentences in a few lines.

Olga Aunty was such a frequent customer that the astrologer only needed a brief perusal to remind himself of the planetary positions and aspects at the time of Berty Uncle's birth. But Olga Aunty and I looked blankly at the stylized lotus flowers, curly leaves, lattices, whorls, and plaids that were engraved; nothing made sense to us, including the long sentences.

The astrologer then opened the two sheets of ruled paper that she had handed him: my handiwork. "Let's see now," he said, and perused the unembellished charts, which nevertheless contained the essential details for the task. He wobbled his head mysteriously from side to side. For a diversion, he scratched his ear with the pencil that he retrieved from behind said appendage.

He next reached out to a dog-eared almanac and turned to a well-worn page. He went through a series of listings in the almanac and kept referring to the male and female horoscopes he had placed side by side. He muttered softly to himself: "*gothra* ... *hmmmm* ... good, *errrrr* ... *nadi* ... *hmmm*, excellent ... *yoni,* fair .... He penciled his findings on another piece of paper that had columns for the corresponding results.

I looked around. The astrologer's desk was cluttered with several dusty and tattered piles of almanacs. Some seemed as old as he was. A smaller table on one side contained a tray of betel leaves. Tradition dictated that the remuneration was not given to his hand but wrapped in betel leaves and placed on the tray.

This was a practice from ancient times, when esteemed people like *veda mahattayas* (village medicine men), Buddhist priests, and astrologers were greeted with a sheaf of betel leaves enclosing a cured tobacco leaf, the latter being omitted in the case of Buddhist priests. During the olden days, they were respected people of means who gave their service selflessly and freely and did not expect monetary compensation. They regarded their astrological prowess or medicinal abilities as a God-given gift and privilege that should not be bandied about for commercial gain.

Times had changed, however, and now, in addition to presenting betel leaves, it was accepted practice to pop a currency note inside, as these people were no longer wealthy and had few patrons to support them. I had heard Olga Aunty vent disdain and declare that she would never follow the new practice of replacing the tobacco leaf with a packet of cigarettes or a bundle of cigars, depending on the smoking habits of the astrologer.

I looked up at the wall behind the astrologer. Framed pictures of the members of the Hindu pantheon in vibrant garb stared back. The many outstretched hands of God Katharagama loomed above the astrologer's head in a protective stance. Attached to one side of the wall was a small shelf containing a statue of the Buddha, before which was a lighted brass lamp. The morning's stubs of sandalwood incense sticks still emanated their holy fragrance. The aroma of burnt camphor hung in the air.

I turned my face towards the shelves containing old books gathering dust. Their bindings had seen better days as loose, wormlike threads were poking out of the spines. I sneezed, almost involuntarily.

The astrologer looked up at Olga Aunty from above his glasses. "This one," he said, "matches Berty Mahattaya's horoscope very well. Sixteen out of the 20 *porondams,* or aspects, are excellent, two are fair and only two are bad. They go together like curd and honey. It will be a very satisfactory union for both parties."

It was the wealthy girl's chart.

"How about children? Would they be able to have children?"

"Oh, they will have at least one child from this marriage, but there's a possibility of two."

"And the other chart?"

"The other one is matching too, but not as well as this one. In this case, fourteen porondams match, but I am not happy about the Fourth House being aspected by Moon here," he pointed to the unsatisfactory square.

Amarasena handed over the papers. The age-old system had paired a man and a woman, psychologically linking them on the life-long journey of matrimony in fifteen minutes. Olga Aunty thanked the astrologer, surreptitiously took out a ten-rupee note, obtained a sheaf of betel leaves from the tray, placed the note on the top leaf and replaced it on the tray. This method was rather convenient. It was possible to leave him as much or as little payment as you wanted to, depending on your income and your satisfaction with the reading.

Clutching the findings, she led me out of the office room. The waiting brigade on the verandah, which had swelled again, looked up expectantly; they were now tackling the insect menace with sound and fury. The serial killing of mosquitoes would continue into the night.

The time was past six and dusk was rapidly setting in. A huge flock of crows cawed their way urgently overhead as if to convey the urgency of flying to the night's resting place. We had to reach home before it became too dark. By the gate, Olga Aunty removed her gold chain, placed it within a knot in her handkerchief, tucked it into her bosom and took my hand. We hurried to the bus halt.

CHAPTER 14

THE MARRIAGE ADVERTISEMENT

Olga Aunty was the type of person who believed in taking prompt action, but Nelson Uncle often dilly-dallied. This was the reason for a lot of their arguments. On him had rested the vital business of placing Berty Uncle's advertisement in the Sunday newspapers, but weeks after discussion, nothing had been accomplished.

The day after we visited the astrologer was a Sunday, and Nelson Uncle was happily engaged in breakfasting, alternately gorging himself on two regular offerings: sticky milk rice made by their servant, Soma, and the cartoon pages of *The Sunday Observer.* I was at the table tucking into the milk rice too, and we were laughing and sympathizing with Dagwood Bumstead, whose usual mode of leaving late for the office invariably resulted in crashing headlong into the postman, when Olga Aunty crashed into Nelson Uncle's repose in no less gentle a manner.

"So when are you hoping to go to Lake House?" the wife boomed. She was wearing a cotton housecoat, a flaming-orange, flowery affair, with a matching underskirt that was markedly longer than the outer garment. Amma and her sisters all wore this trademark housecoat with a rounded collar, buttoned in front, and with a little pocket at waist length that was a repository for almirah keys and coins. On days she had the sniffles, which was often, Amma's pocket also held a handkerchief and a small tin of a wintergreen balm, a whiff of which could overpower the whole room she happened to be in. The underskirt, usually white and sometimes matched in color to the housecoat, ended above the ankles in dainty trimming lace.

"Are you listening, Nelson?"

"*Hmmmm*?"

Nelson Uncle grunted and wrenched himself away from the pages. Like the Bumstead postman, I think he was also seeing stars. His eyes were watering. He drew in air through his teeth and made a hissing sound to indicate that his tongue was burning. Soma had made the onion *sambol,* a mixture of onions, chili powder, lemon juice, and salt that accompanied the milk rice, rather spicy. He reached for a ripe plantain to counteract the fiery chilies.

"Lake House? What for?" he asked after a significant pause.

"Why, to place an advertisement for Berty, what else?" Olga Aunty replied crossly, re-closing an errant button on her brilliant housecoat, which bore the danger of attracting a bee the moment she stepped outdoors. "I'm the only one who thinks about these things. I have to talk to neighbors, deal with *kapuwas*, consult astrologers (she ticked them off on her fingers) and do so many things, yet for you it's so difficult to place an advertisement. Do you expect me to go to Fort too? Is he my brother or yours?"

"All right, all right, don't scream. I'll see to it," promised Nelson Uncle after the soothing coolness of the banana had settled his burning tongue. "Can you tell Soma not to put so much chili into her dishes? This is a hell-of-a-hot *sambol,* no. Why don't you eat some and see? Have you written the ad?"

"Of course, of course I have written it," grumbled Olga Aunty. "That day itself I wrote it, but it's just an outline. It's sitting at your writing table this very minute awaiting your finishing touches."

Nelson Uncle sighed. He had no peace to enjoy a leisurely breakfast even on a Sunday morning. "Somaaa," he called out to the servant who was in the adjoining pantry, noisily stirring some half-dozen spoonfuls of sugar into an aluminum jug of tea. "Can you go to my writing table and bring the piece of paper that Nona is talking about?"

"How would Soma know; can she understand English? Wait, wait, Soma, you carry on with your work, I'll go and fetch it."

Olga Aunty bustled back with the paper and a pencil.

She had a long day ahead of her, sewing my school uniforms, and yet, she chose to argue with her husband as a start to the day.

Nelson Uncle pushed the newspapers aside to make room on the table, gave a lingering but conclusive lick to his fingers, wiped them on his sarong and started reading aloud.

Respectable Govi Buddhist elders seek pretty, educated girl with means for 34-year-old engineer brother, 5'8" tall, presently working in the Middle East and drawing a five-figure salary. Non-smoker. Apply with full family particulars. Mars in the Seventh House, malefic horoscopes only.

"Well, to begin with, it's too long. How much do you think it's going to cost us to say all this? About a hundred rupees?"

"All right, I told you this is only a rough copy. If you think you can cut it down, do it by all means."

"If you say he's working in the Middle East, it's automatically understood that he's drawing a good salary, so let's cut out the five-figure part. Is it necessary to say 'respectable?' When you're advertising in *The Sunday*

Observer, isn't it understood that you are from a decent, upright background?"

"Why? Can't scoundrels make use of the same service? Does Lake House refuse to sell ads to them?"

Soma abruptly stopped stirring the tea. I think she paused to listen to Nelson Uncle's reply. Although the official position the servant maintained was that she could not speak or understand English, during her eight-year tenure there, I was sure she had picked up sufficient lingo in this strictly English-speaking household to decipher much of the conversations.

She must have been disappointed this time because Nelson Uncle ignored the barb and went on. I heard her straining the tea into the cups.

"Why only with malefic horoscopes?"

"Can you remember, the last time we didn't state his Mars situation, and there were so many proposals which had no chance of a horoscope match. We wasted so much money too. This way, we can be sure that only those that have a chance of matching will apply, and it'll save us a lot of time too."

"Oh yes, you're right. Okay, how about this?" Nelson Uncle took a long, slurping sip of the hot tea now deposited in front of him and started scribbling at the bottom of the sheet.

He handed the new, economical wording to his wife. "I think this will do, no?"

Govi Buddhist elders seek pretty, educated girl with means for engineer brother, 34, 5'8" tall, working in Mid East. Mars in 7th House, malefic horoscopes only.

Olga nodded in agreement and reached for her teacup.

"I say," Nelson Uncle said, sitting upright suddenly as a thought occurred to him. "How about asking Oswald to place

the ad? He works in Fort, and it's easy for him to walk to Lake
House during lunch. We can just give him the wording and
the money when they come here today."

Nelson Uncle was allowed to bask in his bright idea for a
fraction of time.

"Oswald? He won't remember to do something if God
Kataragama arrived on his peacock and descended with a
request! I know the problems Blossom has with him. And
Tamara here, every year she's late with her school books
because Oswald promises to take the book list to Lake House
Bookshop and always delays."

I tried to look as if I wasn't there. There was some truth to
Olga Aunty's statement, but it sounded worse than it was.

"I can speak to him and see. I don't think he'll be that
careless because, after all, the favor is for Berty and he likes
the chap a lot," Nelson Uncle reasoned. "If he can do it for us,
all the better, no?"

Olga Aunty downed the remaining tea and nodded again,
albeit slightly. She had had far too many arguments and run-
ins with Thatha's thoughtlessness. Her low opinion of him was
not unfair. Amma was always short of money to manage the
monthly expenses and frequently borrowed money from her,
a few days before payday. Many times, Olga Aunty declined
the money when Amma returned it, but she wanted the fact
kept secret. I know that her pity for us was mixed with anger
towards Thatha, as he selfishly frittered away his earnings on
alcohol. If he found out that Olga Aunty was forking out
money to Amma, he would spend even less on the family.

***

That afternoon, when my parents came to Olga Aunty's
place to fetch me and my new school uniforms, Thatha

needed no cajoling to agree to place the ad. If the money was given to him, he foresaw no problem. "I will attend to it on Monday itself," he assured them, as he pocketed the cash.

But Monday was swiftly followed by Tuesday. Other, more pressing matters must have overshadowed his thoughts because the promised errand had escaped his attention until Wednesday evening when Amma inquired suddenly if he had placed the advertisement. She was alarmed when Thatha confessed he had spent more than half of the thirty rupees that Nelson Uncle had so trustfully handed over to him.

Never the type to worry unduly about anything, Thatha borrowed the necessary amount from Amma. He made his way to the newspaper office on Thursday afternoon, but the deadline for that week had passed, and Thatha could only insert the advertisement in the following week's newspapers.

"What's to be done? Just one more week, and who knows, there may be better proposals to come from the delay," he pacified Amma at the dinner table later that evening.

***

The following week, Olga Aunty opened the Sunday newspapers and searched high and low for the call to prospective brides. I wasn't around to witness her ire. Nelson Uncle must have had another disrupted breakfast.

***

When the advertisement finally made its appearance, followed by a thick bundle of replies, Olga Aunty forgot her rancor toward my father. She was taken aback by the response. Within two weeks after publishing, Lake House forwarded about a hundred replies in three lots. She scanned a few, but it was too much to go through carefully on her own.

135

She decided to get Amma's help to sort them since Nelson Uncle, as usual, was content to dump the task on her.

Amma promised to come on a weekday, but couldn't, and finally went on a Sunday morning with Thatha and me in tow. Although her anger about delaying the ad had subsided, Olga Aunty was not happy to see him and seemed uncharacteristically irritated with Amma. Olga Aunty often accused Thatha of crude commentary "from the gallery." I could see that the setting invited gallery behavior. (The gallery was the seating closest to the screen in a cinema hall and the cheapest. People had to lift their chins to see the screen, and it was uncomfortable on the neck. Generally, the folk who sat here made loud and disparaging comments and whistled and catcalled during appropriate moments in the film, such as the appearance of pretty damsels, love scenes and violence.)

After the initial pleasantries were exchanged, Olga Aunty led Amma from the sitting room to the kitchen table. I followed. The letters were on the table in neat piles with rubber bands around them. There was a writing pad and two pens to make notes, a little cardboard packet of paper clips and two files; a bright blue one marked "Excellent" and a dung-green one bearing the words "Under Consideration." A large cardboard box was on the floor. It didn't need a label; it was for the discards. Teachers did things in style.

Soma was asked to make tea.

They first opened the envelopes, removed the letters from them and pinned the astrological charts to the letters so that they would not get mixed up. Then they each took a stack of letters and began reading.

For some minutes there was only the rustle of paper. Then a low hiss emanated from the kettle on the stove. Through the open pantry door, I saw Soma pour boiling water into a teapot. While the tea steeped, glasses clinked. She was pouring Orange Barley into tumblers for the masters in the sitting room who had declined tea. I'm sure she, too, was looking forward to a morning of entertaining eavesdropping as she went about her work.

I had my notebook with me and had announced that I was working on an English essay for school. It was easy to fool them, but then again, it *was* part of my education.

Olga Aunty was the first to speak, but not before sliding her spectacles to that perfect spot on her nose. "Just imagine these people – I can't believe this!" She sounded cross.

"Believe what?" her sister asked.

"This mother writes a gushing recommendation about her thirty-one-year-old daughter and says last of all, *umm*, here, let me read it to you: '*We are looking for a gentleman of good standing. Dowry over two lakhs depending on the status of the proposal.*' As much as to say, the lower the standing of the man, the less he will receive."

"If he's a doctor, he will receive more and if he's a clerk, he will receive less. Shouldn't it be the other way around? Isn't a dowry given so that the couple may establish a comfortable life?"

"She makes it sound like a competition."

"Here, even this one is rather odd; the father says they are Catholics, but non-Christians are also considered provided they wish to become Catholic with parents' consent."

"Stuff and nonsense," declared Olga Aunty. "I can't understand why they should even waste the postage writing to Buddhist families. They should look around in their own church. Who will want to change their religion for a proposed marriage? Those things only happen with love marriages. As if there are no Buddhist girls around," she sniffed and adjusted her spectacles that were slipping again.

I saw Soma smiling into the jug of tea. She must be glad that her only daughter was happily married and a mother herself. None of this proposal business or visits with matchmakers to find a partner for her daughter – she had fallen in love with her neighbor's son in the village when she was barely eighteen.

I picked up a few letters from the discarded lot. Most of them were riddled with grammatical errors and that was one reason for Olga Aunty's disdain. Some were typed and some handwritten. They followed the same framework. A couple of paragraphs about their family background, their professions, employment and details of the various children, followed by the proposed daughter's information. The letters ended with a request to tally the horoscopes and contact them if they were found to match.

As for the girls, those who were employed were working in "a leading company in Colombo," while those who were not employed were well-versed in home science or housework. En masse, they were all "fair and pretty" or "pleasant looking," had "simple ways" or "excellent, unblemished characters." One was even "well disciplined."

When the daughters were well into their thirties, the parent wrote "looks younger" after their age. One was introduced as "a young girl of thirty-six." If the daughters had darker skins, they are described as being "tan in complexion." One had "a tan color complexion and a pleasant look." Another offered a "subsidiary dowry."

Some were so funny that I scribbled them down. One wrote: *"We are Karawa Sinhalese Buddhist family of three members and living in an own house at the above address. I am retired Vice Principal and my husband was late businessman (His own shop), but passed away."*

Another was particular about the infrastructure of the dowry: *"She is the youngest and the only daughter in the family. Free from family encumbrances, she will possess a furnished bungalow by the side of a trunk road with electricity, water supply and telephone facilities in 1 and ¼ acre block of land containing coconut and pepper with jewelry or one lakh cash and jewelry."*

This one was careless with commas: *"She is a teacher at a reputed school Nugegoda. Dowry provided is one million cash boutique room, paddyfield gold and jewelry. The house my son build at Nugegoda who migrated to Canada could be provided for living for long period as he has no intention of coming soon."*

"Here, do you think Berty will like this girl?" Amma had come across one with a photo enclosed.

Clad in a sari, the young woman sat on a red velvet throne-like, Kandyan-style couch. She had long, straight hair cascading down to her waist. Her features were not unattractive, but she looked seriously into the camera as though she was being photographed for the National Identity Card. I could answer for Berty Uncle: he had refused girls far more good looking than this one.

Her dowry included a block of land, an acre of cultivated coconut land and a reasonable amount of cash.

Olga Aunty looked thoughtful, said *"hmm"* and put the letter into the blue file.

If I had a choice, I would weed out the horoscopes and get them matched first, never mind the expense. After all, if everything hinged on that, what use are ten acres of paddy land, a rubber estate, or a strong grounding in Buddhist principles?

But no, for Olga Aunty, the external factors mattered most. They had to hail from somewhere important, bear exemplary lineage, carry distinct genes, have connections, be wealthy landowners and own a plantation or two to be worthy of consideration for Berty Uncle. She had little tolerance for black marks in a family – illegitimate children or low caste connections, inter-racial marriage or divorce were taboo.

Poor Berty Uncle. If only he could have heard the fun we had that day at his expense.

Presently, the "good" file contained a few hopeful proposals. But before it could get any fatter, the two husbands were seen heading towards us.

Thatha took one look at the scene around the kitchen dining table, which now looked like a post office, and exclaimed in mock horror: "*Omygod!*, are there *sooo* many desperate girls in this country?"

Olga Aunty looked visibly dismayed.

Amma offered a rational explanation as to why more was better than less. "Although there are lots of replies, only a fraction are worthwhile, and it takes time to sort these out and find the good ones," she said.

As though Thatha didn't know. They had been sifting the chaff from the grain for many seasons now. He grinned and took up a few letters.

"This is a very good one – a thirty-year-old girl who's an English trained teacher with a sizeable dowry," Amma commented.

"Don't you think there are enough English teachers in this family? If you throw a stone, you'll hit an English teacher. I think you should steer clear of them and try out another profession. How about finding a nurse *nona* for Berty? Then we can all use her services!"

Olga Aunty threw a freezing look at Thatha. Amma didn't notice. She went on.

"She also has a malefic in the seventh house, but it says here that they are Karawa Buddhists from a respectable family down South with Govi connections. What do you think, Sister?"

Amma had a hopeful note. Having fallen in love with Thatha, who is of the Karawa caste, how could she discriminate on caste grounds?

Karawa is a significant Ceylonese community that is considered secondary in caste to the Govigama Sinhalese and thought to be connected to fisherfolk or the military. When Amma had announced her decision to marry Thatha, there had been the usual protests and recriminations from the family on the low-caste issue. But she had prevailed.

"That's all right Sister, we can't look for everything, now that Berty is not young anymore. I think we should put it in the good file for the moment."

"I say! This is fantastic—ideal for Berty; she's only forty-five years old and has two children and a paddy field. Berty can have a readymade family!"

Olga Aunty sighed in exasperation and went back to her letters. Soma giggled and hastily turned it into a cough. I couldn't help bursting out, too.

"Did you notice how all the girls are 'pretty' or 'beautiful'? It seems like Ceylon doesn't have any ugly girls! Or maybe they are all married."

"In the world of matrimonial proposals, 'beautiful' means good looking, 'pretty' means passable and 'pleasant' means plain," Amma explained with a smile.

"A divorcee, innocent party," Nelson Uncle read aloud. "These divorcees are always innocent, aren't they? How do they get divorced if they are innocent? They are never the guilty party!"

Olga Aunty pounced triumphantly on her husband. "Nelson," she said firmly, "We are trying to do some constructive work here. Either you do this or you let us concentrate. Please don't disturb us."

CHAPTER 15

THATHA'S PAY DAY

Most Monday mornings, Thatha ignores the alarm clock until it has disturbed his sleep at least five times in three-minute intervals. Then he sits up groggily, more like a patient after surgery than a responsible bank clerk at the start of the workweek.

The house is by then mostly devoid of its inhabitants. Amma and Asoka Aiya set off for school at around six-fifteen while I leave to catch the school bus later, as our school begins at 8 a.m. Amma does not depart before placing the necessary offerings on the bedside table to placate Thatha's inevitable hangover – a glass of King Coconut water, two shriveling quarters of lime and a cup of bitter black coffee.

Thatha rinses his mouth in the bathroom, reaches for the sweet liquid and gulps it down quickly. Then he inhales the cold coffee and looks at the clock. Often, he does not pause to rub the lime quarters on his throbbing forehead. In fact, I'm surprised if he even has time to wash properly if he is to catch the seven-thirty bus that would get him there at the nick of time. It must be the accountant's disapproving face flashing before him that gives the impetus to splash cold water on his face and lather it with the shaving stick.

Thatha is ready and reasonably presentable in no time, thanks to the pristine white shirt and dark trousers that are pressed and ready for him on the ironing table and the polished shoes that await his departure in the shoe corner containing the matching, if threadbare, socks. Thatha snatches his wallet from the almirah, rushes to the kitchen to grab his sizeable lunch packet, and leaves.

It's a good thing that the postman doesn't arrive at our doorstep at this time like in the Bumstead cartoon; he comes at noon and deposits our letters in the little red postbox fixed to the gate.

I've been instructed to leave the house with Thatha, but that would have made me miss school for most of the year. The only school bus from the area dedicated to Bishop's College passes Battaramulla at around seven.

On the days that Thatha is on time, we leave together, walking rapidly, ignoring the drizzles and avoiding the muddy puddles on the uneven pavement. The main bus stand is twenty-minutes away. We've made acquaintance with a few others who have equally sloppy morning ablutions, including a sari-clad, always-late neighbor who rushes past, treating us to a good whiff of yesterday's sweat.

The bus depot teems with people. Thatha snakes his way through the narrow passages of the corrugated stall where the No. 171 bus to The Fort commences. In the cool morning hour, the conductor is easygoing, even joking, as he stands by the steps of the bus and cranks out tickets from his little hand-held machine. By evening, the tropical humidity and the heat will take its toll, and this very same conductor will transform into a weary and irritable being, barking commands to the commuters like an impatient army officer dealing with his subordinates.

On the rare days that Thatha has the luxury of time, he occupies a position toward the beginning of the line and awaits the next bus to get a seat. Mondays are generally worse than other days. Thatha often grumbles that it seems as if "the world and its grandmother were going to work on Mondays."

We part our ways, and I board my school bus, which has seats available at this point of the journey. Even if there weren't any, I don't mind standing, as it's filled only with schoolgirls and our teachers. No lewd men with long fingernails or groping hands lurk here like in public buses—or rotund market women with their huge baskets of brinjals and carrots, pushing their way through grumbling office crowds from one end of the bus to the other.

The bus that Thatha boards is packed like sardines in a tin, and the conductor waves at the other "fish" to await the next "can." Most often, Thatha is still at the back and has a fifteen-minute wait until the next bus lumbers up. After he shows his season pass to the conductor and climbs in, he makes his way into the furthest corner of the vehicle and curls his skinny frame around a steel pole to safeguard against sudden lurches. The earliest he can expect a seat is in Borella, which is about a twenty-minute ride.

After Thatha arrives at the imposing granite stairs of the bank's staff entrance, the first objective is signing the register before it's taken to the accountant's office. Mysteriously, no one signs after eight-thirty, he says. In that office, as in many others, the minutes between eight-thirty and eight forty-five don't seem to exist.

The chief clerk comes in with the red pen to draw the line at eight-thirty and the peon hovers about to take the register to the accountant's office, Thatha says, but he always manages to scratch his name and enter eight-thirty before it's too late. The time showing on his wristwatch is a different matter. All those who arrive simultaneously at eight-thirty are invisible.

145

Thatha's job entails entering in the ledger checks to be returned. But he can never settle into the day's work until he visits his favorite haunt. Even a drag on a Player's Navy Cut, his favorite cigarette, can't help him here. The Fortune Bar opens precisely at 9 a.m. each weekday in anticipation of regulars such as my father. A misfortune for many, theirs is one of the many bars flourishing in The Fort, Colombo's commercial heart, catering exclusively to an office clientele. Business is so good that it is never kept open after six p.m. and remains shut on weekends.

Thatha patronizes the Fortune for its proximity as well as its cleverly designed entrance. Once inside, you can have a drink without being seen from outside and yet without going into the seating area.

It's essentially a flying visit, this first one: a shot of coconut arrack downed in a couple of gulps standing, no doubt, with his left leg raised in the curious manner I've seen him drink at home when he's in a hurry and wants to conceal it from Amma. It's all he needs to jumpstart his "engine" on a Monday, he explained once to Berty Uncle.

***

But his engine apparently needs constant tending, as do the engines of several of his colleagues. Theirs is an unspoken language. Around 10 a.m., Thatha and his colleagues are back with Gune, The Fortune bartender-turned-friend. The wad of checks at their desks can wait.

Without much delay they return to their respective workstations but make another quick trip before noon. As the clock marks the hours, Thatha must increasingly come to life with the help of the spirits that course through his body.

Sometimes, Thatha is forced to borrow money from a colleague. Not that they have much to spare either. His best bet hinges on the unmarried and, in his opinion, unburdened, younger clerks who don't yet have "hungry mouths to feed," to use one of Thatha's oft-repeated envy-tinged remarks about bachelors. The oldies are more difficult to tackle. But it is tough to persuade even the unmarrieds to part with a "tenner" or even a "fiver" when the monthly payday is still weeks away. That's why Thatha returns home more intoxicated just before – and after – payday when wallets are more inclined to be loosened.

By all accounts, at lunchtime the atmosphere of the bar reaches its noisy and hectic climax. Apart from the back-slapping office groups, there are other regulars about. I heard Thatha describing to Berty Uncle the different types of lunchtime bar frequenters: The solitary drinker with worries, the serious drinker who sat behind a newspaper taking short sips and who was generally harmless to others as well as to himself, the chronic alcoholic who needed hour-by-hour fortification, the quarrelsome type who suffered from a complex and needed Dutch courage to give vent to feelings, the scrounger who went from bar to bar and table to table striking up conversations with strangers, armed with a winning smile and little else: they were all assembled and active at this hour.

For his lunchtime tot, Thatha heads upstairs to the very bowels of the restaurant, where the aroma of spices competes with cigarette smoke. Here, in the club atmosphere, the younger crowd lunches with abandon.

Pre-1970s, lunch packets at The Fortune were legendary — enormous affairs of steaming hot rice with beef or a huge chunk of fish spiced with chilies, two vegetable curries swaddled by coconut milk, and brinjals, deep-fried and then sautéed with onions and mango chutney. All this for seventy cents for heavy appetites, and half-packets for forty. Now, the rice packets were leaner, emaciated versions; casualties of food rationing and controls on supplies.

"Only the prices remain the same," Thatha grumbles.

On Mondays, the restaurant is prohibited from serving rice at all, the government's way of reducing dependence on rice imports and promoting locally grown other staples. The high point of the lunch menu then is cutlets made from sweet potatoes and leeks. Cutlets are generally savory meat or fish balls breaded and deep-fried. Until austerity dictated, vegetables were seldom used as a base for them.

I guess it doesn't really matter to Thatha that he can't afford to eat lunch often at The Fortune. Amma is a good cook who can make even ordinary fare taste wonderful. She often wraps his rice-and-curry in a browned banana leaf to add to its fragrance and flavor.

***

One payday Monday afternoon, Thatha made his way to the cashier's counter and stood in line to receive his monthly salary. With the deduction of two-hundred rupees he had taken as a salary advance two weeks ago, he received a little more than three-hundred-and sixty rupees. I pictured his exuberance: at home he sometimes held up and then kissed the crisp one hundred-rupee notes from his pay, still smelling of printing paint. He must have thanked the cashier profusely before returning to his desk.

The next task that day was to pay back the loans he had taken from his young colleagues, making him forty-five rupees poorer.

At five-fifteen p.m. sharp, with the day's work completed, Thatha emerged from the staff entrance to face a throng of loan sharks waiting to gather the booty of their trade. At least seven regulars worked the banking area. Thatha avoided looking at the middle-aged woman with the black umbrella with whom he had a rift; she was one of the prime lenders but could get nasty and use her loud mouth to good effect should you miss payment by even a day. A peon from a nearby government office who made an extra income this way – who could be spotted yards away by his khaki shirt and white sarong, if not his betel-stained smile – also had a tough guy reputation.

Loan sharks conscientiously arrived at The Fort each working day and hung around office doors, corridors, and passages. They were bred by social necessity and thrived on the skyrocketing living costs of the day. Many skulked around bars where the pickings were excellent. Office workers in dire straits, especially those who had whittled away on drink the money meant for vegetables or the electricity bill, would resort to using their services.

Bank staffers, ranging from the lowly cleaner to the officer, were at the mercy of money lenders to meet the month's expenses. The lenders, who made it their business to find out the payday schedule, never failed to surround the staff exit by 3 p.m. and stayed there until their clients appeared. Although some attempted to shake them off by remaining inside the office until about 8 p.m. pretending to be working overtime, the "miscreants" would be caught the next day. The lenders knew the importance of collecting on salary day; the difference of a day could be disastrous to their business. The interest rate was pegged to the personality of the borrower; the meek ones were rewarded with a five percent interest, while the rate could hit twenty percent for troublesome retrievals.

Thatha had his favorite loan shark, a retired peon-turned-Shylock with a Uriah Heap smile. I'm not sure what princely sum of money Thatha owed him that day.

The next debit was at the sweep ticket stall.

"*Ganna, ganna, mahajanasampathadinaganna.*" The ticket seller's intonation into the loudspeaker in his nasal, public voice that was supposed to attract attention got Thatha's attention for sure.

The Mahajana Sampatha lottery draw took place on Thursdays, and the first prize was one lakh rupees. Like The Fortune barman, the sweep ticket seller was on a first-name basis with Thatha, who needed little encouragement to buy into luck and hope. The second and third prizes were forty-thousand and ten-thousand rupees respectively, and there were a hundred consolation prizes of six-hundred and ninety-nine rupees, each waiting to be won.

Thatha bought three tickets. He was a firm believer that one day he would stand to gain a hefty profit from the National Lotteries Board, which he supported with a diligence that he lacked in other more important areas of life. Amma, who only believed in hard work and didn't share his enthusiasm for lotteries, often rebuked him when she came across the two or three sweep tickets he bought each week. "What a waste of money," she would scold. "If you had collected all those one-rupee coins that you spend on sweep tickets, you would already have your first prize!"

150

A Maiden's Prayer

***

When Thatha boarded a bus to return home that day, it was nearly 7 p.m. By now, with the celebratory drinks that were part of every payday coursing through his veins, he was nodding and half asleep in the lurching bus. Hanging on to a leather strap that made a monkey of him, he swayed back and forth to the dictates of the still heavy evening traffic. The bus was not too full, but there were plenty of others standing around him so that when he became dimly aware of someone brushing against him from the back, and then forcing a path for himself towards the back exit, Thatha said he didn't take particular notice.

Fifteen minutes into the journey, he thankfully sank into a vacant seat and resumed his snooze but kept waking up as he was subconsciously trying not to miss his stop. If he missed getting off at the Battaramulla junction, the bus would next stop at the main bus halt, which would mean a longer walk.

Half an hour later, Thatha alighted and started his trudge home, stopping only to buy cigarettes. He then noticed that his wallet, which he generally kept inside the right back pocket, was missing. He panicked and searched all his pockets but the wallet — and his money — were gone. He was wide-awake now and remembered taking it out before boarding the bus to retrieve the bus pass. He shivered, and his thoughts went over the dismal prospect of breaking the news to us: his pocket had been picked. Every payday, Amma begged him not to stay late drinking. She had warned him countless times that the light-fingered gentry were most active on such days.

Thatha walked home, dejected. He usually listened to his favorite radio play on Monday nights, which invariably began before he reached home. Almost every house was tuned into the long-running drama, *Muwan Palessa*, set in a rural village with characters that every Sri Lankan knew, such as the foolhardy Kadira, the coy damsels Gomari, Komali, and Namali Naga and the pompous and bumbling Korale Mahattaya, whose authority disintegrated in the company of his scornful wife, Menike. When the dialogue emitting from one home faded, the radio in the next home restored it.

But today, he didn't hear a single line. The last and final debit of the day was totally unsettling.

Back home, Thatha told us his long and sad story. He showed us his three lottery tickets, which were spared, as he had put them in his shirt pocket. Instead of the month's wages, he had hope.

CHAPTER 16

A BURGLAR WREAKS HAVOC

June 1975

Tikiri was unwell. I missed her boisterous homecoming welcome; the wet kisses, joyous growls, and tugs at my arms were replaced by a lethargic and half-hearted thumping of her tail on the floor under the dining table, my bed or whatever place she happened to be resting with her face in between her paws.

I first mistook it for maturity, an indication that she was learning that I, as well as the others in the family, had to be away from the house periodically each day and could not spend all our time dancing attendance on her. But as the days passed and I looked closer, I knew that she was suffering from some physical discomfort because I saw her throwing up her food. Her appetite was gone too, and a sniffing and a half-hearted lick around the plate replaced her customary ravenousness at mealtimes.

Tikiri was now a robust three-year-old who had never warranted a visit to the vet except for a trip to be wormed and to administer rabies and distemper injections, which were compulsory municipal regulations. She wore two silver coins attached to her collar proclaiming that she was immunized against these terrible diseases.

She would need to go to the vet again, but where would the money come from? I was only too aware of the state of the family kitty. Recently, Asoka Aiya had been complaining that

153

his shoes were flapping at the sole. Another day, after a bath, he had flung his frayed towel on the ground in a temper and suggested that it be torn into bandage strips and donated to a wounded beggar.

"Duwa, how can we take her to a vet? I don't know how much money it will cost. As things are, I need money for Asoka's shoes, and your music fees are due soon." Amma's reaction was all too predictable.

Then one day, Tikiri rushed out the gate, ambled off by herself, and returned panting with a triumphant look on her face. Amma said she had probably eaten *bala-thana*, a type of grass, to cure herself, as dogs often do. For a whole month thereafter, she seemed to have taken matters into her hands, first displaying symptoms of illness, then rushing out of the gate and returning breathless. When I examined her mouth, there were bits of grass stuck in its folds. I slipped some sliced ginger into her food to coax back her appetite. It seemed to work.

* * *

One day after school, I was in the garden engrossed in a Nancy Drew book, shaded from the mid-afternoon heat by the sweeping boughs of the frangipani tree. Tikiri, as usual, was out on a ramble. "*Bothaal, pathraiii*," the familiar, harsh voice of the bottle collector rang out. Amma, who was supposed to be resting, called out through the window, "Duwa, Duwa, ask him to stop by."

I clapped my hands and beckoned the dark-skinned man who obligingly came into our premises. Calling the bottle-man on a school day could only mean one thing; money was so scarce that Amma had to resort to selling old stuff to make ends meet. But was it possible to make up Thatha's stolen salary by selling bottles and newspapers?

The man lifted his burlap sack off his head and deposited it under the mango tree. He sat down at our doorstep and wiped his sweaty forehead with the dirty cloth wrapped around his head. Soon I could hear Asoka Aiya wading into the recesses of the storeroom, noisily fishing out things that could be converted to cash. I dropped my book with a sigh. Unless I was deaf — and blind — there was no way that I could continue to read in peace. It was time for high drama, much more than the eighteen-year-old American fictional detective could ever provide.

Amma started bringing the bottles out to the front door and motioned me to keep an eye on him in case he pinched something when no one was looking. The man began to inspect the bottles with his grubby fingers, holding them up one by one to find any signs of damage. He smirked from time to time to indicate his disdain, in the hope of lowering the price.

"These Marketing Department bottles are not in demand nowadays because of the strike. Now if you have more arrack bottles, those are always easily disposable, and I can give you a very good price." He grinned, displaying his loose front teeth.

Already, an impressive collection of empty arrack bottles was forming, nearly two month's usage of my father. The man was arranging them in neat, three-deep rows on the upper step for easy counting. This would fetch a fortune – at least four whole meals.

Amma couldn't resist the evidence. "Look at these bottles," she said to no one in particular. "Just imagine the money your father has spent on his drinking. If I were given that money, how much more I could have done for all of us? Look at Nelson Uncle and Dinesh Uncle. They don't waste their money like this. Only your father is irresponsible and careless."

"Not only this, every day he must be spending at least another twenty rupees drinking in the bar. If not for my salary, you'd go hungry."

Amma's diatribe would've lasted longer if she hadn't caught sight of the man casting aside the Marketing Department bottles.

"Why are you doing that?" she shrilled. "You were quite happy to buy the MD bottles the last time. How can things change in two months? Take them and try to get your price."

"But Nona, how can I do that? Due to the drought and electricity cuts, most of the sorting shops in Colombo Pettah are closed. I might have to store these somewhere until the rains come." He started counting the bottles in Tamil: *onnu, rendu, moonu...*

"How much are you paying for newspapers today?" Asoka Aiya emerged with a stack of newspapers that seemed about to topple. I rushed to his aid.

"I'm paying fifteen cents a pound."

"Fifteen cents!" Amma cried in exaggerated dismay. "But that's not enough; you paid a lot more last month."

"Fifteen cents, Nona, and not a cent more."

Amma looked despairingly at Asoka Aiya.

"Twenty," he said firmly, and the bottle-man didn't say anything. He took out a little weighing scale from his burlap sack, examined its dial and pulled the hook back and forth.

"Now, now let me see that before you weigh," said Amma, holding her hand out in a pointedly suspicious manner. These bottle-men were famous for their doctored weighing scales; it was common knowledge that they had one scale to buy the newspapers and another to sell them.

The bottle-man did some further adjustment to the scale before handing it over. Amma checked to ensure that the indicator was at the zero mark and not above. "Now don't adjust it anymore," she warned.

The bottle-man tied the huge stack of newspapers with string. Then he adjusted the weighing scale once again, ignoring Amma's cries, and with strength belying his looks, lifted the bundle by inserting the hook under the string.

"Twenty-four pounds," he declared.

"Let me see!" Amma pounced.

"That's not twenty-four; it's nearly twenty-six! Remove your finger from there! And it's showing twenty-six because you adjusted the needle after I looked at the scale. Weigh again properly without cheating," she demanded. "There must be at least thirty pounds."

I slid out of the front sitting room and went to my room. The haggling would continue until Amma was satisfied. I couldn't decide whose plight was more pathetic—the bottle-man's or Amma's.

Imagine having to go from house to house with a burlap sack on your head and a cheating scale hooked to your waist and enduring the wrath of housewives to make a living? And imagine having to extricate every possible cent out of this poor man so that we could have food on the table when Thatha spent so much money on liquor?

***

157

The usual southwest monsoons that drench the Western Province from May to September were late this year. It was nearly July and it hadn't rained in months. Power cuts, as well as water cuts, were in effect. "Close that tap, switch off that light" screamed the *Daily News*, which was full of dire warnings about the consequences of having low levels of water in the Labugama and Kalatuwawa reservoirs; the drought had caused water levels to drop thirty-six feet below spill level.

The choice was either being in the dark or not having enough water. I was also unsure how we were supposed to conserve water when the service was only available for a few hours each morning. In that limited period, we hastened to collect the precious liquid in every conceivable vessel available.

The kitchen table looked like the base for a modern art exhibition, with its rows of bottles, jugs and earthenware pots containing water for cooking. The bathroom was equally interesting, with assorted buckets and basins full to the brim.

At least, they were full until my brother went in. Asoka Aiya's idea of conserving water was calling off Tikiri's bath. He was inside for ages, splashing himself liberally, all the while singing *Oblahdee, Oblahdaah* in his best voice, unperturbed by the limited supply and unconcerned about keeping enough for the others.

Generally, Thatha wasn't overly keen on bathing, so he was quite content to forego the hassle and only splashed a little here and there, judging by the little-depleted levels when he emerged after a wash. Amma's biggest woe was that her beloved crotons were withered and sad because she had stopped watering them. Tikiri became increasingly dusty and dirty, with mud-caked paws that I tried to "dry-clean."

Everyone was irritable at twilight when they switched on a light switch and didn't receive the welcome illumination. Thankfully, there were fewer mosquitoes about. Every week, Amma bought a twenty-five-pack of tall white candles and each evening, we lit a few and stuck them on empty, upturned tins placed on the hall table. The kitchen had a kerosene oil lamp that attracted a whole village's worth of gnats and flies.

Seated at the hall table with his back to the wall, Asoka Aiya pretended to study for his school exams. I say pretend because I had noticed the comic book regularly slipped in between the pages of his bulky chemistry textbook. For all his bravado adopted from the likes of *Butch Cassidy and the Sundance Kid, Billy the Kid* and *Jessie James,* Asoka Aiya never stayed in his room after nightfall since the power cuts. His head was full of *Count Dracula, The Headless Horseman,* and others of similar ilk. Even when he had to collect a book or some stationary from his writing table, he asked me to accompany him to the room. I obliged without complaint because I also required occasional escorting, since his fear had transferred to me as well, even without reading these comics.

One day, after our evening wash, we had settled down at the hall table for our homework and general bickering. In the background, Thatha lounged in his easy chair with his first glass of arrack for the evening. By dinner time, he would have finished at least four glasses and fallen asleep with his feet up until Amma awakened him with the call to dinner. Some days he didn't even have dinner.

Asoka Aiya's last report card with its liberal sprinkling of zeros was still fresh on Amma's mind and she had given him a piece of her mind before retiring to the kitchen to prepare dinner. The zeros even had a dot in the middle representing exactly what, I couldn't understand. His teachers had written a series of caustic remarks for each subject, mostly to the tune of "good brains, lazy work" and "clever, but careless."

For a time, there was peace and work in progress, the only sounds from the movement of the seconds hand in the hall clock, the scratch of my fountain pen and the occasional rustle of a page. Asoka Aiya could work with intense concentration for short periods, and today he really studied. But these bouts were inevitably followed by playful interludes.

"*Thunai Potta* Meeyo*! Three Blind Mice!*" he sang out suddenly to the tune of the nursery rhyme. "*Ballanna Duwana Heti? See How They Run?*"

I must have looked exasperated, because he grinned and continued reading, but not before declaring: "*Take Durol with Ironnnn. Makes you feel like a Lionnnn,*" the "ns" stretched out like the radio commercial.

When the next break came, Asoka Aiya began to play with the candle wax. He took out the compass from his battered mathematical instrument box (which, being metal, also served as a drum in class, I was told), scratched his head with it and scraped some tallow from the now stubby candles. He sniffed at it and spread it thinly on the table. He scraped more wax and looked about for a more interesting place to rub it and caught sight of Tikiri, gazing with doggy solidarity at our labors.

Without hesitation, Asoka Aiya rubbed the wax on Tikiri's wet nose. She jumped up, startled by the heat, and tried to remove it with her mud-caked paw. I shouted in protest and lifted her on her hind legs and examined whether her snout was burnt, by bringing a candle close to her. Tikiri backed off from the flame in alarm, uttering a howl of protest that questioned if the humans around her had suddenly gone mad.

Amma came running up the kitchen steps, missed one and fell sideways towards the wall.

***

They say it never rains but pours. That night, a burglar came.

In the silence of darkness, I awoke to the sound of screaming. It was a low, guttural noise that came from the back of a throat, as if someone was trying to say something, but no words were coming out, just a long-drawn moan. Then a thump of quick footsteps—someone wearing rubber slippers was running out the front door.

It was Amma's voice. Within moments, Asoka Aiya tumbled out of bed, followed by Thatha, both simultaneously trying to shake off their stupor and make sense of the situation.

"It's a thief, it's a thief! Tamara, Tamara! See if she's all right." Their first thoughts were to ensure my safety.

I froze on my bed, too scared to budge in case an accomplice was lurking about. Asoka Aiya and Thatha rushed into my room and checked on me, before charging out of the house and into the road.

But of course, the thief had gotten away.

***

We didn't take long to figure out what was missing. He had collected some money from Thatha's wallet and the few valuables that were within easy reach, like Thatha's and Asoka Aiya's wristwatches, a pair of Amma's ear studs that were on the bedside table, some shirts and saris. Clothes were strewn here and there as if he had been sorting through them.

161

Fortunately, most of Amma's jewelry was at the pawn shop, and my gold bangles and matching earrings were hidden under the false bottom in Amma's almirah, so the thief could not get to them.

Tikiri was under my bed and it was her growling that had woken up Amma. But she had kept quiet when the burglar had pried open the iron grill in Asoka Aiya's open bedroom window with a crowbar, and practically jumped over his sleeping body to gain free access into our home. He had first opened the front door and several of our long windows, ensuring an easy getaway. He was combing through the contents of Amma's almirah drawer, which he had removed from the bedroom and set on the dining table, when Amma had woken and parted the door curtain.

***

At daybreak, Thatha went to the local police station in our tenant's car to report the burglary. He was also under instruction to call Olga Aunty, always the first to know of our fortunes and misfortunes, though there were more of the latter than of the former. Amma had asked Asoka Aiya to remain home in case there were further problems, but she need not have worried along the lines of security.

Word spread quickly, and the whole neighborhood began trooping in. Our tenants in the annex were the first to arrive. Anura, with his new-found height worn awkwardly, stood about with folded arms. I scarcely recognized him now. He spoke in a funny voice too, and his Adam's apple was rather wobbly. I wanted him to stay as much as I wanted him to leave, but his visit was brief because he had to get ready for school. I found that I couldn't look him in the eye properly, and he seemed to have the same difficulty.

Maya, Mrs. Vithanage's wisp-of-a-servant-girl, had heard the hubbub during the night. In the early morning, the little monkey had clambered on to a tree limb, put her head over the fence and shouted to Amma who had been making tea in the kitchen. Amma opened the kitchen door and satisfied her curiosity (For once Amma didn't need cake or Bulto to get her attention.). The Vithanage couple was here, the mister, still in his morning sarong and stubble. They were both retired from their professions and in no hurry to leave.

Quaver's elderly driver, who slept in the garage, had woken up too but dared not venture outside until calm descended. He had alerted Quaver, who came with Anoma, both of whom seldom hobnobbed with neighbors.

At 10 a.m. when the dung green police jeep with its contingent of constables drove up to our gate in a cloud of dust, there were a dozen more people gathered there than was our regular household.

The inspector alighted, handsome in his sand-colored shirt and trousers. He doffed his black peaked cap with its double strand of golden chords and adjusted his flattened hair, all the while glancing around in a professional manner. He looked like Amitabh Bachchan, the Indian film superstar who was a constant topic at school these days. His gaze took in the assembly quickly and came to rest on my father. "I hope you didn't move anything," he said. "We will be taking fingerprints, and if you have touched the drawer or the almirah after the thief left, we won't be able to get accurate prints."

Fortunately, Amma had had better sense and indeed had warned me against moving anything. Everything was still in disarray on the table and the ground. Tikiri had been picked up and carried away from the scene of the crime and was tied to a tree in one corner of the property where she could do little more than bark in protest for everyone within miles to hear.

While the inspector talked, pointing with his baton for added emphasis, his subordinates circled the house looking for clues. Tikiri, so gentle on the housebreaker, was barking ferociously at the law-enforcement.

"Your dog—was it ill recently?" The inspector's questioning caught my attention suddenly. "Sometimes, when a burglary like this is planned, they first try to kill the dog by throwing it poisoned meat, causing indigestion and very often death. It has happened in many instances."

We explained that the dog had indeed been unwell, but she had recovered without much assistance from us.

Our neighbors, still standing about the front door, parted like a wave to allow the constables to come inside the house, where they proceeded to look for fingerprints, squinting through an ancient-looking magnifying glass at some powder they sprinkled on the window handles, almirah drawer and dining table.

There had been a spate of break-ins in the area lately, but this was the first to occur when everybody was home. The others had taken place during the day when the occupants were out. "Eighty percent of housebreaking occurs due to your negligence," the inspector said, looking even more like Amitabh in his role as an honest police inspector in *Zanjeer*. "Doors must be locked, windows must be closed." And we hadn't even told him that Asoka Aiya had left his bedroom window open. "Ordinary thieves open doors and come in.

Professional thieves break open windows or make holes in the walls."

Would Amma be able to come to the police station and look through a file of photographs to try and identify the thief?

Amma, who had never been inside a police station, looked nervously at Thatha before nodding her agreement. Quaver, who had been listening intently, offered to lend her car and driver to Amma. Anoma nodded her head vigorously in sympathetic agreement.

At that very moment, we heard another car stopping at our gate. Wearing Adidas shorts and a navy-blue t-shirt, Bertie Uncle came running in with Olga Aunty close at his heels. "Nelson could not get away from work, but I didn't go to school today, and we came as fast as we could," she explained to everybody, including the police inspector, in her breathless manner. "What happened?"

Thatha wrung his hands at her and looked up at the ceiling. Amma took her aside and started to cry.

After a few more words were exchanged and promises were made to try and catch the culprit and retrieve the stolen goods, the police party piled back into their jeep and departed in another billowing cloud of dust.

Now that there were relatives present, the neighbors thought it best to move on. In twos and threes, they shuffled out, murmuring sympathies, and extending all manner of help. Mrs. Vithanage promised to send us dinner. Bertie Uncle stared at Anoma as if he had seen a vision. She and Quaver reiterated the offer of the chauffer-driven car.

"No, no, that's all right," Bertie Uncle jumped in, taking another long look at Anoma. "I will take her to the police station in my car."

"Please let us know if you need to go anywhere else," Quaver said. "Our car will always be available to you."

I couldn't help thinking that if thieves came more often, we would have a car to go about. Not that we had any money to buy petrol with.

***

Olga Aunty quickly took matters in hand. She sent Asoka Aiya to Mrs. Vithanage's well with instructions to fill as many buckets with water as he could. Amid the calamity, we had forgotten to collect the day's supply.

We hadn't eaten anything for the day, and it was already past noon. She declared that hunger made everything worse and took us all into the kitchen. While we sat around the kitchen table, she made copious amounts of tea. She washed and sifted some rice to remove stones, placed it in a pot with water and kept the pot on the stove. Then she asked me to scrape the coconut. She made a coconut *sambol* and a dhal curry so that we had something inside us and did not feel so bad. Amma nursed her injured arm; in addition to the shock of the morning, she was enduring pain.

Bertie Uncle, who had begun his vacation just four days ago, was all kindness too, consoling us and promising to replace our losses when he next came from Saudi Arabia. I had no doubt he would do so in his generous manner, but how could we live on others' generosity for the rest of our lives? When were things going to improve for us, and who was responsible for making things better?

Were the planets that Amma and Olga Aunty constantly talked about, responsible for all the misfortunes that happened to us on this earth? I had read that more than six thousand years ago, sages who had extraordinary powers started

166

noticing a relationship between the life cycle of human beings and the movements of the planets. How could these astral bodies rotating millions and millions of miles away influence our day-to-day lives?

Did these planets really cause our suffering due to past sins? Who gave them the authority to control our lives, making us dance like puppets on a string? It seemed crazy that predictions by astrologers could come true and yet, thinking back, even this loss had been foretold.

Individuals face difficulties due to the malevolent effects of a particular planet. When the planets move, they impact human lives. When people pass through a bad period, which they call a "*graha apala*," astrologers advise them to perform certain rituals and practices to avert the mal effects of that planet. This involves more than a visit to a temple and engaging in religious activities.

Months ago, Amarasena had warned Amma about a possible loss of possessions during this time. He had asked Amma to propitiate a certain goddess with fruit and other gifts but Amma had neither the time nor the money to carry out his advice.

CHAPTER 17

ANOMA

We never recovered our stolen goods. The inspector came around again to ask more questions about that awful night. Amma visited the police station and went through the scrapbook of burglar photographs but could not recognize "our thief." Little else happened. Everybody blamed the inept police force and hinted that nothing would be done unless we "oiled their palms."

This was the first time that I had heard this delightful expression. I had a fleeting vision of Olga Aunty rubbing coconut oil on the handsome inspector's outstretched palm before understanding what it meant. Given the pecuniary situation at home, "oiling" could not take place, and soon, our file went under and was thought of no more. Berty Uncle, who had friends in high places, offered to contact some higher-ups in the police, but Thatha declined the offer since, as he put it, "this was no great train robbery and we were still intact."

After much talking, lamenting and casting blame on each other as it often happens in these cases (Why did Asoka Aiya sleep with his window open? Why didn't we investigate Tikiri's sickness? and so on.), we tried to put it behind us. The thinking changed after a few weeks. After all, he had stolen our belongings because he had even less. "Let the bugger be happy with our things," Thatha declared in his customary cannot-be-bothered manner. We agreed although Amma's emotions went deeper.

The neighborhood didn't let us forget. Everyone, from the sewing lady to the kerosene oil-cart man, took a vicarious pleasure in digging for details. For months after, people pointed at our house and said things like "that's the house that was burgled recently," and shrugged their shoulders as if to distance themselves from the experience and express relief that they were not the ones affected.

But something unexpected and long-lasting did happen as a result of that fateful day: Berty Uncle began to take an interest in Anoma.

***

Since the burglary, Berty Uncle had been in and out of our house. Even without a burglar, he was received like ice cream on a hot day. His presence these days was an added strength to poor Amma who still woke up screaming in the middle of the night. But so far, only I knew that Berty Uncle had something other than thieves on his mind. A few days after the break-in, Berty Uncle had cornered me in the garden, where I was reading under the frangipani tree, and asked a barrage of questions about Anoma. Who was she, and why was she living in the unmarried music teacher's house? Where were her parents? What did she do to pass the time? Where was she schooled? Did she go to work? Does she have friends?

The questions were so unexpected that I didn't know what to say. I looked at Berty Uncle's brown leather sandals and then studied the yellow-streaked white blooms above us. A string of black ants climbed the tree trunk and was heading towards the flowers.

After all those other girls, was he interested in Anoma as well?

Then I remembered Asoka Aiya's comment about Berty Uncle and buried my face in the book to surpress the giggles.

He noticed my shaking shoulders. "Why, why, why are you laughing?" he asked.

"Uncle, Asoka Aiya says that you have too many girlfriends." I dared to say it aloud.

But Berty Uncle didn't find it funny or care about what his nephew thought. He wanted a path to Anoma, rather like those black ants pressing on to the flowers.

I was in a quandary. He expected my help to find the answers. As chatty as we were, I had never questioned Anoma about her circumstances. How did her parents die? Was Quaver the only living relative she had? Why wasn't she allowed to go anywhere on her own? Quaver spent most of her hours at the piano and Anoma spent hers in the bedroom, her outings limited mostly to cookery lessons that she followed in another part of the city. They seldom went out for anything, so I guessed there were no secret boyfriends in their lives. Occasionally the old uncle visited them, but the only frequenters were music pupils, and I knew them all.

To me, Anoma existed rather than lived and was fussed around much less than Quaver's prized belongings. She didn't cause ripples in the music teacher's structured life. She conformed to her surroundings, dissolved even. Or was she made to dissolve?

But of course, I could hardly give voice to my inner musings, so I hemmed and hawed and told Berty Uncle that "She lives there because she has nowhere else to go and because it appears that Quaver is her only relative."

I also volunteered rather carelessly to find out more. I had no idea how to pose these questions to her suddenly, but Berty Uncle looked so earnest. Besides, I thought that I owed him that much, especially because he had given a fair amount of money to Amma through Olga Aunty to make up for the ordeal she was going through. I knew some of that lavishness would benefit me. It was working almost like an oiling of the palm.

***

At the next music lesson, I looked for an opportunity to talk to Anoma. My wish was fulfilled rather easily as she came out of her bedroom with squeaking rubber slippers, smelling of sandalwood soap and toweling the long, wet tresses hanging around her face.

She asked if there were any developments regarding the police handling of the burglary. Quaver had given me some theory questions to answer and had disappeared into the kitchen from whence came the unmistakable clink of teacup on saucer. I answered Anoma's question and seized the chance to apprise her of the other development.

"Berty Uncle was asking about you," I said, taking care to drop my voice. "He was asking me lots of questions."

"What did he want to know?" She stopped toweling the hair.

"He wanted to know everything about you, but I said I didn't know much. He also asked for your phone number."

"Did you give it?"

"Yes."

"*Anney* ... what will happen if he calls when Aunty is home?" A fair hand covering her mouth in dismay, her voice a whisper, Anoma was a beauty even with furrowed brows.

171

"Don't worry, I'll tell him to call around 6 p.m. when Aunty is out taking the dogs walking. She's always out at that time, no?" I ventured what I imagined to be a bright, optimistic smile.

"Yes, but I don't have anything to ..."

Just then, I looked out of the window because I heard a car approaching and stopping at our gate. Sure enough, it was Berty Uncle visiting us for the umpteenth time with more than the burglary on his mind.

"There he is again," I pointed. Anoma looked out of the window and blushed when Berty Uncle, as if on cue, looked towards us.

Why were some people drawn to others? I remembered an interesting sermon by the temple monk the last Poya day. He was talking about relationships and how we were instinctively drawn to some people while we shunned certain others. This is because we have known them, liked them, and nurtured our associations with them over time during numerous past births, he said.

The monk had cast his hand around the large, mostly white-clad audience and said: "You were all together in the same place another time, drawn by Buddhism, as you are all together now." The people had looked around at each other and exchanged weak smiles.

Was that why Berty Uncle was drawn to Anoma? Did he sense a bond, and would she react in the same way?

Maybe there was some connection between them, waiting to be renewed.

***

Like Young Lochinvar, Berty Uncle leapt into action. The next time I talked to Anoma, he had not only phoned her a few times, but they had also managed to meet.

"He came to meet me after my cookery class," she whispered demurely. "I didn't know what to say, but he's very nice. He told me that he's returning to his job soon and kept asking if he could write to me. You know how difficult that will be. Aunty will kill me if she finds out. How can I ask him to send letters here?"

"Why don't you tell Aunty?"

"No, I can't do that. She'll never understand. I told him to talk to her, but he wants to get to know me better before talking to her."

"Don't you have a friend who can help? That way Aunty won't know," I suggested.

"No. There's nobody I meet regularly that I trust who can pass letters to me."

She hesitated. "Berty suggested sending them to your place. He thinks that you won't mind doing that job."

"How can I do that? Amma will skin me alive if she finds out!"

Anoma looked sad. I must have been her only hope. I tried to comfort her by saying that if I knew my resourceful Uncle, he would find a way.

***

Berty Uncle always left for Saudi Arabia on a Thursday. That way he could get his home cleaned on Friday, which was the weekly holiday in the Islamic Middle East and begin the workweek on Saturday. The evening before his flight, he visited us again.

He was, as usual, received like ice cream, even with a little jelly on top. Thatha had not yet returned from work, but Amma was around and made her customary fuss. She made him sit on our most comfortable chair in the sitting room, bid me put the fan on and ran to the kitchen to make a cool drink. Berty Uncle was one of the few Ceylonese I knew who did not drink tea.

The man in love seized the opportunity to ask me if I could receive his letters to Anoma and deliver them on the sly.

"*Aiyoo*, Uncle, how can I do that?" My dismay was genuine. "Amma would scold me if she found out a thing like that. Also, she gets home before me and on most days, she's the one who collects letters from the box."

Amma then appeared with a tall glass of deep yellow passiona. I couldn't suppress a giggle—as if Berty Uncle needed more passion in his life.

"Duwa," she said, misreading my interest in the drink, "There's more in the kitchen; go and get some." Recently, the passion fruit vine had run wild along the kitchen fence, its mature tendrils clinging to every nearby surface and yielding dozens of the green speckled fruit with its seedy yellow pulp. But I didn't want any.

Berty Uncle took a sip of the yellow drink, closed his eyes and winced. Amma must have heaped sugar into it, on the premise that the number of spoons of sugar is a measure of love.

When Thatha came, Berty Uncle was still nursing the drink, perhaps in a vain hope that the sugar would crystallize or something. Being a Wednesday, Thatha had his mid-week arrack bottle secure under his arm.

174

"*Haaaa*, Berty, when did you come? What are you drinking, men? You're like a woman, no, drinking passiona at this time? Wait, wait, I'll take a wash and come back. We must have a drink."

"Why do you have to start drinking now, why don't you first have your tea? Berty can wait for dinner. You can have your drink before dinner," Amma suggested feebly.

"Before dinner, after dinner, we drink. What difference does it make?" Thatha winked at Berty Uncle who smiled back diplomatically at both.

Amma quickly made a cup of tea and had it ready by the time Thatha was out of the bathroom, in a vain attempt to postpone the drinking. She had her own covert methods to reduce the amount of alcohol that Thatha ingested. One was to throw out some of the liquid and refill the bottle to the same level with water. Sometimes Thatha grumbled that "he didn't get a proper kick" and blamed the distillers for making "substandard stuff."

***

A little while after they had settled down with their filled glasses, I could make out a conversation that gradually diminished to a whisper. Amma disappeared into the kitchen again; judging by the noises and smells coming from there, she was cooking industriously.

"Berty, what are you saying?" Thatha blurted into the darkness. "Are you trying to make us leave this place? Do you know that that woman is half-mad and will scream till the roof comes down?"

As far as I could make out, it was Thatha who was screaming until the roof collapsed. He was so taken aback with this latest development under his nose. It was a wonder that

175

Amma didn't hear, but she had just started frying something that crackled.

"For god's sake, leave that poor girl alone. She has no parents even; why don't you find someone else for your fun?"

I couldn't hear Berty Uncle's reply.

"If you're so serious, why don't you speak to the old lady directly? You're a grown-up man. Besides, she's looking into proposals for Anoma too. The old lady uses one of the matchmakers that Olga once used for you."

"*Shhh!*" Berty Uncle said. Amma emerged from the kitchen with a plate bearing two fried eggs smothered in chili sauce. After she returned to the kitchen, I could not hear the rest of the conversation from the dining table where I was doing my candle-lit homework. The voices continued in a softer tone.

***

It was nearly 10 p.m. by the time we sat for dinner. Though we were all hungry, Berty Uncle was not in his typical carefree, jocular mood and didn't do justice to his end-of-holiday dinner. Amma had made a rich fried rice with vegetables, sultanas, and cashew nuts. A delicious chicken curry, daal, sautéed beans, homemade mango chutney and papadom were the accompaniments.

"So Berty, what's bothering you today? Don't tell me you're feeling sad about leaving us?" Amma noticed his mood. "Your flight is so late at night this time. If it was during the evening, we could have come to the airport like last time."

But Berty Uncle just smiled and brushed off her questions without giving a direct reply. I don't think he would have liked us to come to the airport this time, knowing about the row that had erupted the last time during the return journey, when

Thatha had wanted to stop at a bar with the other males, and the wives had vociferously objected.

After dinner, we sat in the front sitting room, while Amma returned to the kitchen to cube a papaw.

Thatha got up abruptly and gruffly patted Uncle Berty on his back. "Okay, okay, let's see what we can do. Don't worry, *isaay*! But don't play the fool this time."

"No, no, I'm not playing the fool, Os."

"You never play the fool, but you end up putting everyone in trouble."

***

Two weeks later, the first letter came. Amma retrieved it from the letter box and saw the address: To Anoma Fernando c/o Oswald de Silva.

Holding it up, she said: "What's this? Now what's happening? Berty Uncle sending a letter to our next-door Anoma? Duwa, do you know anything about this?"

I shook my head. Thatha would have to settle this one.

Later, at the dinner table, bluffing came easily to Thatha; he tried to make it sound a casual, everyday thing: "Oh, Berty, don't you know, he wants to write a letter to Anoma, and I said it's okay to send it here."

"But why is he writing to her? Is he trying to play the fool with her too? They are our neighbors, and you know how Quaver is."

"What are you worried about? They are both looking for partners. What's wrong with helping to bring two nice people together?"

"Bring together? You think he's serious? Remember what happened last time? Sushila still doesn't talk to Olga after he ran after that servant girl. Just return that letter to Berty when he comes next time. Don't encourage these things. However good he is to us, we can't help him with his madcap ways. Now I know what you two were whispering about that last day!"

"How can I give it back to him? Now, don't be silly. Just send it through Tamara. I promised to send it."

"Tamara! You're trying to get this child also involved in this nonsense."

All of Amma's protestations came to no avail. After the dust had settled, Thatha had his way, as usual. Amma had to give in, but she declared firmly that she wouldn't let this happen without letting Olga Aunty know.

The next afternoon, Amma promptly sent Asoka Aiya to the post office to telephone Olga Aunty and ask her to come this way as soon as possible. Asoka Aiya reported that Olga Aunty's first question, jokingly, was whether another robbery had occurred. I grinned to myself because, in a way, another robbery *was* taking place.

The very next day, Olga Aunty took a bus from her school to our place without going home. My music lesson was due to start just after she arrived, so I couldn't witness the full brunt of her anger. When Amma told her about Anoma and the letter, she shrieked as though a gecko from the ceiling had fallen onto her lap.

"The rascal! Here we are going round in circles looking for a girl for him and once again, he does things behind our very backs. He's behaving like a teenager. Let him call home next time; I'll give him a piece of my mind. I won't let him step into my house again."

"And what's wrong with Oswald? Doesn't he have more sense than to encourage this reckless behavior? He has a grown-up daughter himself and this is how he is bahaving? Berty is not at an age when he can just play around and get away with it. All these things leave their marks on his character; especially in your neighborhood, it won't look good for you at all."

"That is what my fear is too," Amma said. "These things tend to come out sooner or later and how can we face Miss Nora?"

Olga Aunt continued with her oral bombardment. "I'm going to ask Nelson to call Berty tonight and give him a piece of his mind. This man is behaving like a reckless teenager."

I was in my room listing to their conversation, but it was really the time to go for the music lesson. I came out of the room but lingered for a few more minutes.

Amma saw me and shooed me away.

When I returned one hour later, they both pounced on me. "Duwa, where is the letter?"

It was too late. I had already made my first delivery. If Olga Aunty had been less emotional, she would have been able to prevent it while I still had the letter tucked inside the cover of my music book. Even Amma had forgotten that that was the day I was going to deliver the first letter from Berty Uncle to Anoma.

***

Even though both Olga Aunty and Nelson Uncle had screamed at Berty Uncle when he phoned next, things were progressing like a house on fire, judging by the post. After that first letter, which was a thin aerogram, bigger ones arrived enclosed in scented, pink envelopes on a sweetheart theme. Some were like little cushions and still others had small enclosures, like sticks of chewing gum. I didn't open them, but

Anoma kept me informed. She had nobody else to confide in, and I was the sole link to her budding love.

I didn't tell her about the uproar at home.

I was just the postman.

CHAPTER 18

MONSOONS

July was well on its way before we saw any sign of rain. After the inordinate delay, the monsoons came with a vengeance. Preparation for the deluge was out of the question. As luck would have it, I was at Quaver's place practicing my music when the downpour began. I cut short my practice and ran home, but it was impossible to avoid the raindrops that speared like needles.

I could see people hurrying home beneath large umbrellas. Some had pieces of transparent plastic draped about them while others only had *habarala* leaves for cover. Irrespective of the device, they were all dripping wet. We could not hear ourselves speak for the thunderous noise. The winds did all the talking. Tikiri took refuge under my bed and did not emerge for her meals one entire day. I shoved food and water under the bed as though she was a prisoner in a cell.

It was impossible to concentrate on anything else for two whole days. The pages of my books clung together as though I had pasted them. When the earth could drink no more, the deluge stopped, only to start again.

"If this goes on any longer, we'll have to buy a boat," Thatha joked into the damp air.

As it turned out, this became more of a sensible suggestion than a sarcastic remark. It rained so hard that the water came up to our lower step. We were marooned. Subterranean insects with multiple legs and antennae I had never seen

181

floated on the surface and climbed the walls. Ants, beetles, bugs, and grasshoppers scuttled about; they all needed air and apparently had never taken swimming lessons. Cats screeched and climbed the trees. Maya, Mrs. Vithanage's wisp-of-a-servant-girl, screamed in terror and pointed to a snake-like creature that had materialized from nowhere and went swimming past her, "wagging its tail."

Humble dwellings collapsed in places and resourceful residents used the material to build makeshift rafts. People waded through the water with their clothes and other precious belongings held over their heads. Vagabond boys soaped themselves out in the open and jumped into the drains with cries of glee. Asoka Aiya took a walk, wading waist-deep in fetid water "just for the fun of it," amidst Amma's shrieks.

Three more inches of rain and the water would have been in our sitting room. When the surroundings were adequately flooded and the people were given enough trouble, the rain decided to go away. More than a week passed before normalcy was restored.

***

About three weeks later, Olga Aunty and Nelson Uncle were agitated once again. Due to the monsoons, everything was still in disarray, and we had not met them for some time. Nelson Uncle had called Thatha at his office and told him that Berty Uncle had phoned from Saudi Arabia. But for once, the problem was not his affair; it had to do with Nelson Uncle and Berty Uncle's sister, Elisa Aunty.

I heard Thatha telling Amma about it.

"You know the latest? Nelson's sister has written to Berty telling him about how the rains have damaged the house. You remember that huge mango tree in the backyard, the one

182

Asoka fell off trying to pluck mangoes? A branch fell in the winds, and a side of their kitchen roof is badly damaged."

"What does she want him to do?

"She has written asking for money to replace the roof; she wants five-thousand."

"Five-thousand rupees? It's a joke, no? They are living in the house and Berty has to pay for its repairs? Olga must be hopping mad."

"All this time they were not bothered about doing anything, even though the house is falling apart; when something drastic like this happens, they want an easy way out."

"So is Berty going to give the money?"

"Berty is asking Nelson whether to pay and he, too, doesn't know what to say. I told them to hold off on the decision until we can discuss it at Martin's place next week."

CHAPTER 19

A SPEND-THE-DAY

A dults, children and servants alike, we all looked forward to our monthly spend-the-days in one of the four sister's homes. In an atmosphere of hilarity and warmth, we admired new clothes, played games, cooked mountains of food, exchanged news, and discussed problems.

This month, it was Beaula Aunty's turn to host, and the day was chosen to coincide with her daughter Jasmine's seventeenth birthday. Everything was good; the only problem was the hassle to get to their home.

Martin Uncle and Beaula Aunty lived in a highly congested commercial quarter of Colombo in a hundred-something-year-old house they had inherited from Martin Uncle's father. To access it, there was an extremely narrow lane lined with tiny, impossible dwellings that had blatantly encroached on the roadway over the years. It was even trickier to enter the lane, as one had to pass through a bustling vegetable market where the hawkers spilled their produce all about the street with total disregard for its effect on traffic.

We started early from home. Asoka Aiya grumbled that we were the only ones who didn't have a car while all the others, meaning our cousins, had cars to go about. Amma looked down sadly. Thatha pretended not to hear.

The bus stopped right in the heart of the vegetable market, and we alighted onto a bed of rotting lettuce leaves, narrowly missing the drain that emitted a terrible pong. The market was in full swing. The rains had liquefied the dust into a chocolaty mud, but undeterred by the setting, the vendors were raucously pitching their produce. Several beckoned, mistaking us for a family of vegetable shoppers.

"*Mahattaya, mahattaya*," a man called out wearing a dirty white cap and sitting astride the drain with the help of a wooden plank. Didn't he have a nose? He dangled his Bata-slippered feet dangerously close to the clogged muck below him and pointed hopefully at his puny carrots before catching sight of me and winking his appreciation. His partner sat behind a pyramid of limes and repeatedly entreated people to use the citrus "to chase away the devils."

A driver tooted the horn stridently as if that could clear the traffic. Two rotund women sitting behind reed baskets that were partially blocking the road smiled at us. A small transistor radio beside them belted out a Hindi song. To this tune, one waved a flywhisk over her basket of mango and pineapple pieces. Adding to the general mayhem, a bullock cart loaded with firewood materialized from a side road, and the bulls were jolted when they stumbled into a mud-filled pothole on their moonlight stroll. But the customers only had eyes for the vegetables; they leisurely sifted through produce and bargained with traders, as if their very lives depended on the state of the vegetables.

We picked our way precariously, in single file, mindful of the slippery vegetable matter underfoot, the drains on one side, the pulsating humanity and the numerous buses, cars, and scooters tooting their horns in cacophonous abandon on the other.

Our next task was to pass through the lane that had ceased its main function of being a means of transport and evolved into an untidy campground. Washed clothing was on view, including an unabashed female's home-stitched underwear spread about in what passed for a garden. The drain continued here as well, further limiting the width of the passage and adding to the smell.

The dwelling just opposite Martin Uncle's gate extended a tiny parlor of commerce catering to the market crowd, providing such necessities as betel chews, steaming hot tea in tumblers and *beedis*, the impoverished cousin of the cigarette. No harm in that, except for the infernal radio that blared music, news, views, obituaries, or whatever else Radio Ceylon chose to transmit at its highest volume throughout the day. It was hard to deduce the thinking of the shopkeeper; was he trying to provide entertainment to the nearby market? Was he trying to make a statement to the community? Was he simply hard of hearing? Did the volume button get stuck at maximum, and did he not bother to repair it?

As usual, the radio that hardly slept made a terrible racket as we treaded vigilantly, avoiding the drying supportive garments, the stray cats and dogs that surely must be deaf by now, and the odd paraphernalia strewn about. From their positions within and without their homes, the scantily clad children and the loitering adults feasted their eyes on us, staring as though we had alighted from Mars. I felt at least two-dozen pairs of eyes directed at my bell-bottoms and me. I felt sorry for Renuka and Jasmine who had to undergo this intense scrutiny each time they came out of their gate. Whenever they had to use a bus to visit us, Renuka and Jasmine would wear skirts for the journey. They carried their bell-bottoms in a bag and changed at our place to lessen just a tad of those staring eyes.

If pedestrians had trouble reaching them, those arriving in vehicles didn't have it any easier. Drivers came to a virtual standstill with their noses almost pressed to the windscreen as though steering through a violent storm, to get through the vegetable market without running over someone's limb or basket of woodapples. Once through, the bottlenecked lane provided an equal challenge because it only accommodated one vehicle at a time. If by chance two vehicles were approaching from either side, the inner car had to reverse several hundred yards until the lane broadened and both vehicles could pass. During this process, I'm sure vehicles often went over that poor woman's underwear. I couldn't even imagine their state under those circumstances.

Thatha opened the iron gates and we entered with visible relief, like travelers that had maneuvered the Khyber Pass. My first task was to remove the muck off my platform shoes by wiping them on the manicured front lawn.

A distinct feature of Martin Uncle's house was the large open porch with its decorated front wall. On this wall, was a prominently sculpted cutout of a capital D and its geometrical reflection. When they were small, my cousins Renuka and Jasmine would climb inside the Ds and wrap themselves along its contours. Now, at eighteen and seventeen, they were less willing to adapt themselves to their home or its neighborhood conditions.

They often clamored for a newer house in a more residential part of the city, but their father would have none of it. When they grumbled that they couldn't invite friends there, he jokingly offered to fly them over by helicopter and land them in the backyard. Recently, Martin Uncle had reinstated the parapet wall around the house, building it taller to keep out the dreariness and the prying eyes. But nothing could filter out the music.

"We have our own neighborhood rooster," he once proclaimed in mock pride. "It wakes us promptly at five forty-five in the morning with *pirith* chanting, and rocks us to sleep at midnight with the national anthem. Which other neighborhood boasts of this free service?"

In response to the doorbell, Martin Uncle opened one of the heavy double doors dressed in a longish pair of olive-green shorts and strode onto the verandah with a welcoming grin.

Martin Uncle was tall and robust and always in a good mood.

"The electricity cuts were a blessing in disguise," he said, speaking loudly to be heard above the din. "For a long time, I didn't have to bribe the shopkeeper to keep the radio switched off! I was beginning to become poor from doling out my rupees."

In this vein, he made us forget our tiresome journey and took us inside, through the ancient sitting room with its walls covered with black and white portraits of mustachioed relatives, beyond the curtained-off bedrooms and past the staid grandfather clock that stood guard over the heavily carved dining table, and into the back of the house to the center of activity. Thanks to the sheer length of the house, the noise faded into the distance and we had relative peace here.

The back of the house featured an elongated verandah that opened to the outdoors on one side and led to the kitchen and further assorted rooms on the other. The bathrooms were at the far end and separate from the main house. Everybody had arrived and made themselves comfortable in various corners. Jasmine leaned against one of the sculpted columns in the back verandah, looking pretty in pink crimplene bells that flowed gracefully about her ankles. I had never owned a pair – they were too expensive. Mine were either made of drill that was too stiff or poplin that was too droopy.

Amma quickly changed into the green and yellow polka dotted cotton housecoat she had brought with her and joined her three sisters in the kitchen. Like the others, she left intact her hairstyle, the hair in a little bun worn at the nape of her neck. She slipped on the bangles and chain she had carried in her handbag during the journey; even though they were rolled-gold and valueless, she didn't want to tempt any jewelry snatchers who may be about. However, Thatha often pointed out that thieves knew the real thing from the false and wouldn't touch her adornments with a bargepole. It's all very well for Thatha to talk when his thoughtlessness was the reason for her jewelry to be in the pawnshop in the first place.

Although there were four servants about – the two at Martin Uncle's place, Mary Aunty's servant and Olga Aunty's servant Soma – the sisters preferred to take more than a supervisory role in the cooking. The food was not everyday fare and the curries were going to be cooked in special ways; spicier, thicker and more flavorful.

I glanced into the happy hive that was the kitchen. The aromas mingled just like the family.

At the large table in the center, Olga Aunty and Malkanthi were peeling a mound of garlic and discarding the skins on a newspaper. Olga Aunty was famous for her pungent garlic curry, of which I would have none. Oh no, I had spent far too many nights with garlic bulbs stuck inside my ears as a panacea for earache, my constant childhood companion. Those days, when I woke up in the morning, my pillow reeked of it. I hated the taste of cloves, too, because they were placed in my mouth to alleviate toothache, another constant childhood bugbear.

Mary Aunty was at the kerosene stove, overseeing a servant who was tempering boiled fish to make cutlets, a staple at any Ceylonese event. She dropped finely minced onion, garlic, and curry leaves into the hot oil, which hissed and sputtered before emanating a delicious smell after the spices took hold. Instead of potatoes, which must not be available again, she mixed the boiled kohila root vegetable into the tempered fish. Next, she balled the paste in a circular motion, and with the help of her sister, coated them with egg white and then with breadcrumbs. The servants would be entrusted with deep frying the cutlets in an enormous vat of coconut oil.

In a corner of the large room, Beaula Aunty stood in front of a huge Pyrex bowl, whipping pink-colored ice cream with a rotary eggbeater. It reminded me of Asoka Aiya's bicycle wheels – turning the handle affixed to the spokes began the beating motion. Dhamith was imitating the circular action, only faster, urging her to make haste. He worried on behalf of us all that the ice cream wouldn't set in time for dessert. Beaula Aunty patiently explained that she was beating it to hasten the setting, and that it had been in the freezer since morning.

Seated, Soma scraped the coconut while straddling a low stool containing a serrated steel blade protruding from the front. The shreds fell into a basin underneath the blade. Jasmine's white Pomeranian kept a watchful eye nearby, ready to dart at any stray coconut shreds. Her immediate surroundings on the floor looked clean. Soma had already shredded three coconuts, and was on to the fourth, the shells neatly stacked on the table nearby.

If the traditional Ceylonese coconut scraper sounds like a recipe for disaster, the servants' method of cutting vegetables was worse. Amma always warned me against getting near them when they sat on their haunches on the ground with a sharp knife, blade up and handle secured between the big and second toes. With the foot securing the knife, both hands were free, and the vegetables were pared beautifully. It seemed that a cut was just one slip away, but I never witnessed any bloodied fingers.

I walked into the adjoining room, where two household domestics were wiping the crockery. A stack of plates, curry dishes, and rice and salad platters had been removed from the display cabinet in the formal area and washed at the kitchen sink. They were wiping them with a serviette and, as usual, making a great noise when restacking. Beaula Aunty always scolded servants when they handle the crockery, saying they didn't understand its value and warned them to take extra care when handling it. I often wondered why she wouldn't do it herself and save her grief for the Royal Doulton China that had originally belonged to her parents and imported to Ceylon from England during British colonial times. The china was a dainty shade of blue with a border of tiny bluebells in stalks with pink ribbons connecting the flowers and a larger poesy in the middle. Martin Uncle believed in living "a good life," and that included using the best china for family gatherings. But I tried to avoid serving chicken curry on the bluebells because they were too pretty to cover up with food.

The next room contained a cavernous cement structure holding a wood fireplace, made with three stacks of bricks kept together like the prongs of a ceiling fan. The fire, fuelled by firewood and coconut husks placed in the middle, was waning, and Mary Aunty's young servant girl blew through a plastic pipe to bestir it. With a crackle and a display of sparks, the flare leapt through the husks to cook what smelled like samba rice inside the huge clay pot.

I had little time to pause and chat with anyone as the cricket game was being organized. If played parallel to the house, the yard was large enough to host a modified version of a match, and it was an integral part of our day. Martin Uncle had already set up the two wickets with sets of three wooden stumps and was marking the creases by drawing a strong line on the ground with a stick.

The girls, except Malkanthi, hurried to change into shorts. Malkanthi, who was of a sickly constitution, had something or the other wrong with her at any given time and was supposed to be suffering from some ailment, as usual. She volunteered to be the umpire. They all shouted her down. Dinesh Uncle, her father, personally escorted her to a mid-on fielding position.

The four brothers-in-law were generally on one side, while the children made up the opposing team. The numbers did not match, as the game is usually played by two teams of eleven players each, but no one complained because the emphasis was on fun. The adults maintained the spirit of the game with the help of the spirits that were sipped at frequent intervals. The wicketkeeper kept uttering cries of exaggerated "*howzaat?*" appeals to an imagined umpire and Asoka Aiya, our star player, kept hitting the ball over the parapet wall. As the game progressed, it became progressively more boisterous and toward the end, there was more horseplay than cricket.

Lunch was an unhurried affair. There was much food to get through: yellow rice and curries with plenty of chilies for the adults and milder, turmeric-flavored, coconut milk-based preparations for the children. Martin Uncle was a privileged government employee who often received gifts in kind, so the food shortages did not affect him too much. We couldn't all sit at the table, so the children sat wherever there were chairs.

As I had expected, Berty Uncle's latest affair and his sister's request were high points of conversation during the meal. I gathered that both Olga Aunty and Nelson Uncle had been somewhat pacified when Berty Uncle had indicated over the phone that he was serious about marrying Anoma.

"But my question is, if he is serious, why is he waiting so long to talk to Quaver?" Nelson Uncle asked, helping himself to another cutlet. "It's not nice to let this go on under her nose for too long."

"This is what makes me suspicious; he doesn't seem at all keen to talk to Quaver," Olga Aunty furthered the point. "When she finds out, she might think we had something to do with it."

"Oh, give the boy a chance; just let things take their course. How can he talk to Quaver so soon?" If no one else, Berty Uncle could always rely on Thatha's support.

"The other thing is, Olga says this should not be allowed to proceed without checking horoscopes," Nelson Uncle said. "But when we suggested it to him, he just brushed it off."

"Well, if he wants our blessings, and if he knows what's good for him, he should allow you to check the horoscopes," Beaula Aunty declared.

"What horoscopes, men? If they want to marry, let them get married!" Thatha broke in again waving a chicken bone. "Can you remember how much your father objected to our affair? Everyone told Blossom and me not to marry when our horoscopes didn't match, but now see, is there anything wrong with our lives? It's all just nonsense!"

Amma looked at Olga Aunty in a meaningful manner. Her lower lip quivered.

"True, true. You don't check horoscopes when it's a love affair," Martin Uncle agreed, shaking his head up and down.

"I think you should try and obtain the girl's chart and get it matched," Mary Aunty insisted. She was feeding eleven-year-old Dhamith who was the baby of the family and still finicky with his rice and vegetables. He didn't need coaxing when it came to dessert. "Ask Berty to get the horoscope before they go any further. This boy has been through so much already, he must be happy when he gets married."

"We can do that, but then it's pointless asking Anoma to post it to him and then wait for him to post it back here. It's better if we tell him to ask Anoma to give it to us."

"How about getting it from your former *kapuwa*?"

Everybody spoke at once and drowned Mary Aunty's suggestion. Olga Aunty's voice was the loudest. Over the years, Olga Aunty had run through half-a-dozen *kapuwas* and one was no better than the other.

"...Lewisa Nona will take all the credit if they get married and ask for payment as well. No, no, we have to leave her out of this. These *kapuwas* are all the same."

"What happened to the so-called 'good' proposals that Aranolis Kapuwa brought last time?"

"Berty went and saw both girls and he didn't like them at all. He asked us once again not to waste his time. Remember the Karagetihene Loku Mahattaya's older daughter who is inheriting all that wealth? She turned out to be an odd case. She kept twisting her hanky this way and that way, and I even saw her picking her nose in broad daylight. Not at all like the rosy picture that Aranolis painted. No wonder she's unmarried. And her brother-in-law wore such a broad belt around his waist, he looked like a real thug. What's the use of money if you have to put up with people of that caliber?"

"And as for the other girl, she wasn't that bad looking, but she wore a black skirt instead of a sari. Now if you don't want to wear a sari when a prospective bridegroom comes home and you want to wear a skirt instead, at least you must choose something that's a pleasing color."

"But the worst part was how the lights went out when we were there. Just after the electricity got cut off, a gecko cried mournfully into the dark. That decided it for me then and there—too many bad omens."

"We have decided not to entertain Aranolis Kapuwa again. He's just wasting our time. The newspaper offers a better way of doing this."

I was relieved to hear this. It was obvious, even to a baby, that he was taking everyone on a wild goose chase. Why had they taken so long to realize this? In any case, I think these Kapuwas were on their way out; I would certainly not need one, and neither would my cousins and friends in school. It was a much more interesting prospect to be chased by a boy and fall in love.

Toward the end of the meal, it was decided that Anoma should send us her birth chart and let us do the honors. But the next problem was more difficult to resolve: should Berty Uncle give the money that his sister asked for?

"If she's living in that house, why can't she do the repairs herself? After all, as things are, there's no guarantee that Berty

195

will even get it later on, is there? Why should he spend money on it now? Let them open umbrellas inside the kitchen!"

Opening umbrellas indoors was said to invite bad luck, but Olga Aunty's indignant outburst was only to be expected.

"I'm trying to convince Olga that if my sister expects Berty to provide money for repairs, it's asserting his ownership of the house. I think by giving it, he has a greater hold on it," Nelson Uncle said.

"She's so thick-skinned that she can just take the money, repair the roof and conveniently forget about it," Olga Aunty scoffed. "After all, we hardly visit them now. Even Berty makes only one trip just to show his face; he never stays there."

"Doesn't the husband have any money?" Martin Uncle wanted to know.

"What difference does that make? They want to have their cake and eat it too," Thatha butted in. "I know how these buggers are. Stingy devils ... so sick ..." Everyone looked at Thatha who muttered something more, but no one could make sense of his speech. The alcohol and the rich food were taking their toll.

"All because Berty doesn't want to settle down and have children. People think that those who don't have children don't need anything. They think they have to give away their properties like King Wessanthara and mope in a corner because they don't have children." Olga Aunty sniffed. "But actually, they need to collect as much as possible because they don't have children to look after them when they're old. Their security in old age is money." She looked mournfully at the generous servings of fruit salad and ice cream that the servants had deposited on the table.

"Why don't you tell Berty to ask them to repair the roof with their own money? Surely the husband must have some means?" Martin Uncle deftly took charge of the flow that had strayed somewhat.

Nelson Uncle shook his head. "Whatever they had has been frittered away on living expenses."

"Why don't you ask Berty to give it as a loan?" Mary Aunty asked. "After all, they are not paying him any rent, are they?"

"What rent! They have been living there for donkey's years and have not paid a cent. But what's the idea of giving it as a loan?" Nelson Uncle asked the question on everybody's lips.

"There's no point in giving loans to people like them. Such loans never get repaid," Dinesh Uncle observed quietly with the air of a man who knew what he was talking about.

"People think you're stingy if you're amassing wealth when you don't have children. They ask if you're planning to take it to the grave." Olga Aunty continued on the self-destructive path she took sometimes. Martin Uncle reined things in once again.

"Look, there's really no way to come to a firm settlement on this issue. Either Berty gives the money and forgets about it, or he doesn't. Either way, you've got to take the consequences." The adults nodded their heads and gradually spoke of other things.

After lunch, things quieted down. The afternoon heat invited slumber. The servants cleared the table and started washing up. Even for the four of them, it would take quite a while to wash the dishes, tidy the kitchen and put away everything. The four sisters, meanwhile, retired into Beaula Aunty's bedroom and lay sideways on the large bed, sharing

197

pillows and reminiscing about the times "when we were young."

"Can you remember how we discovered the B-O-M-B?" Olga Aunty asked with a laugh.

When they were in school, my mother, Blossom, and aunts, Olga, Mary and Beaula, whose names' first letters spelled out B-O-M-B, were collectively known as The Bomb Sisters. No appellation could be more unsuitable for these four mild-mannered women with Victorian sensibilities. The "O" was somewhat fiery, but a single "O" did not a bomb make.

Their husbands, who were known to be more explosive, were smoking quietly, lapsed about the various corners of the sitting room like pythons that had swallowed gazelles.

Asoka Aiya suggested a game of three-nought-four and the card regulars brightened. Malkanthi, who hated physical exertion, played cards with a passion. She rummaged for the card pack in her bag from among her pills and potions. The other diehards were her brother Tilak, Asoka Aiya and me. Brother-sister partnerships were disastrous; ending in fights all too often, so we avoided such pairings. My partner was Tilak, who had invented devious ways to reveal the trump to me, like lodging a trump card in between his toes and stretching it towards me from under the table. Once Dhamith, who had been lurking about, had spotted the card and gave him away. The results had been chaotic. Another mode he employed was to touch his heart, scratch his chin, finger his earlobe, or pull his hair, denoting hearts, diamonds, spades, and clubs, respectively. The other two were equally well-versed in the art of cheating and were particularly prone to analyzing at length the just-concluded game if they happened to lose, hoping that we would forget to claim the winning cards. You could say we were well-matched.

Toward early evening, Beaula Aunty produced the birthday cake. The pink rosettes on the cake were lost on Thatha, who, by then, had reached his saturation point and dozed on Martin Uncle's armchair. When we started singing 'Happy Birthday,' he woke up with a start and flailed his arms about him wildly as if fending off someone. Everyone laughed, except Amma.

Fortunately, our return journey was much easier, as Dinesh Uncle gave us a lift home. In any case, Thatha was in no condition to board a bus.

Thatha always declared that despite the difficulties of getting there, spend-the-days at Martin Uncle's place were the jolliest.

If only that radio broke down ... and we had a helicopter.

CHAPTER 20

LEAPS AND BOUNDS

Something was missing in our neighborhood. No one could quite explain it.

Dimly aware of an absence, we mulled over our evening cups of soup. We pondered even as we scolded the butcher for including so much offal with the meat. We puzzled over our weevil-infested loaves of bread.

During the day, everything was familiar and disturbances were predictable. The postman rang his bicycle bell outside the gates and handed important-looking letters in brown covers with government seals to servant girls. The kerosene oil-man trundled down the road in his bullock cart and was stopped at almost every gate with requests to disburse the smelly liquid. The odd job man shouted his availability into the sunshine like an insistent mynah bird.

While house sparrows twittered during warm afternoons, Quaver's students sailed in and out of her home. Depending on the player, harmonious or discordant tones rang out, scales thundered down octaves, semitones were lowered or raised, and lazy minims were lengthened to even more languid semibreves.

At twilight, mosquitoes continued to rise from their hiding places among the coconut husks and embark on their stinging missions. Neighbors continued to close their windows in unison against this murmuring menace. Quaver continued to emerge with the hounds in her white calico dress with the brown border and cascading hair like a local Diana, Goddess of the Hunt.

It took me a while to realize that the sunset rendering of *A Maiden's Prayer*, the immediate precursor to Quaver's dusky ramble, had ceased. In its place, silence reigned: an unusual hush that whispered from the rafters, and at times, hollered from the rooftops.

True enough, the maiden's prayer had been answered. A young man – well, not so young, yet a man, and a good man – had responded. And the maiden had accepted with a loving heart. But they still had barriers to overcome. Anoma, being an uncomplicated young woman, didn't make a conscious attempt to conceal the change that came over her. She harbored the new delight within, dreaming of delicious possibilities, pondering the prospect, and lapsing into reverie.

Thus, the music teacher had found her one evening as she was about to leave for her walk: sitting at the piano and gazing at the ivory keys, a smile playing on her lips but the fingers idle.

"What is this child; why are you looking at the keyboard without playing?" Quaver had asked, half in concern.

Anoma had turned around startled, mumbled something, and started fumbling for her music sheets on top of the piano. When she resettled herself and started playing, she had stumbled on the notes.

Quaver had let that pass but made a mental note to keep a closer tab. Usually, Anoma played the piano for a good forty-five minutes, almost for the duration of her aunt's walk, and we could hear the final arpeggio of the *Teddy Bear's Picnic* or the denouement of *The Robin's Return* as Quaver neared home. Besides, Anoma's piano playing was Quaver's best advertisement – passers-by heard her heart and soul in her play. It was much like a clever restaurant owner bringing the kitchen to the front of the premises; all people needed was a whiff from the saucepans to entice them inside.

On subsequent days, Anoma sat with a book and pretended to read.

Anoma told me that she had arranged for Berty Uncle to call during Quaver's absence. This was the only time she could speak with her beau unhampered. At first, he had promised to call every two weeks, but as the weeks passed it had become more frequent. Now it was more like daily. They had so much to talk about. Berty Uncle had usurped not only *A Maiden's Prayer* but also *Für Elise* and *The Entertainer.* He had effectively robbed the neighborhood of its dulcet musical treat.

***

Under Berty Uncle's bidding, Anoma handed over a copy of her horoscope to me, concealed in a brown envelope, which in turn, was inserted inside the cover of my music book for the duration of my crossing the lane and going home – a full twenty-yards-long journey.

When Olga Aunty received it, she was reanimated. She had something to do again, a role to play in the drama that was Berty Uncle's marriage. For the past few weeks, she had been waiting in the wings with only a vague sense of the rapidly unfolding events. Now she could hurtle along with them.

A glance at the chart told her that Anoma also had malefic placings in the appropriate square – the Seventh House – which explained why she was long unmarried. She rushed to astrologer Amarasena's house. I can imagine Olga Aunty smiling and nodding around at her fellow sufferers, this time oblivious to the bugs and the mosquitoes.

However, once the consultation began, Olga's thespian exuberance had evaporated along with the camphor that burned on the brazier.

***

Following the reading, Olga Aunty felt an urgent need to be at Amma's sympathetic ear. She came round to our place and repeated the conversation between the astrologer and herself:

"Nona, although there are two malefic planets in the house representing marriage in this horoscope, I don't like the Saturn-Moon yoga in the eighth house," Amarasena had said. "It empowers Saturn while Moon's benevolent influence is weakened.

"As you know, Saturn is responsible for most problems that befall us humans – like sicknesses, job losses, money losses, and personal tragedies. Besides, Saturn and Moon are astral enemies. This girl is under Saturn's maha dasa (major rule) now. Very soon, she is going to enter her Moon sub-rule and with this particular placing, a *maraka apalaya* – a deadly calamity – can take place in the future if these two parties unite."

Olga Aunty was stunned. "Are you saying that you won't recommend marriage between these two?" she had asked, nay whispered.

"I'm afraid I won't condone it," he had replied. "Berty Mahattaya has a complicated horoscope, and it's not easy to match his with another's. On the surface, you might think that these two match, but when you examine it thoroughly you find a severe situation looming ahead. There is a very bad influence from the boy's planetary positions on the girl."

"Is there anything, anything at all that we can do?" Olga Aunty had asked, faintly.

Amarasena had turned the charts this way and that. He had thought long and hard before speaking again. "Their current time is not beneficial either. But if they are willing to wait for at least five years, if she can pass the Moon sub-rule and then get married, say for instance, during the beneficial Jupiter sub-rule, they will have a much better chance to build a successful life together. But even then," he had paused doubtfully, "they will have to make a vow, perform many pujas at God Vishnu's temple, and release a cow awaiting death in the abattoir and take a vow never to eat beef again, among other things. I could write you a list of the appeasements they would have to fulfill before marriage."

***

Amma's face fell when she heard the disheartening recommendations and realized the gravity of the situation. Berty had to be warned before it was too late, she said. He was like a car going pell-mell down a road without headlights. They discussed and pondered at length. But like many of life's problems, this one lacked a ready solution at the outset.

"Why don't we ask him to take the advice of the astrologer and wait five years before he gets married?" Amma suggested. "If he's adamant about this girl, surely he can wait?"

"When Berty is hungry he can't even wait until the rice is boiled. Do you think he'll agree to wait five years to get married now that he has finally found someone he likes? And especially when we have been nagging him so much to get married? We are talking about a person who has been hedging all the proposals that came to him over several years. Besides, anything can happen in five years; that's a far too long period in anybody's life, at any age."

They both silently conceded the hopelessness of the situation. Thatha, upon returning home, took one look at their gloomy faces, heard their story, and laughed his disbelief of the "claptrap" associated with revolving astral bodies.

"What nonsense, horoscopes," he scorned. "Let that fellow marry whom he pleases. You must be happy that he is willing to get married at all! I think this Anoma is a good girl and will look after this man. He needs looking after."

With her gentle personality, Anoma made a kindly impression on people. Amma liked and trusted her, and Olga Aunty, whose opinion of the young woman living opposite her sister's house was shaped more from Amma's view than Berty Uncle's actions, held nothing against her. All the same, the astrological results were unsettling, and no virtue could make up for mismatched horoscopes when it came to the lifelong institution of marriage.

***

The next day, Amma was having one of her "a woman's work is never done (sniff)," days, when we had another unannounced visitor. Amma had just sprinkled coconut refuse on the muddy hall floor and, broom in hand, was about to rub it when the doorbell rang.

Quaver barged into the house, wailing like a banshee, and brandishing a letter that she had found directed to Anoma and bearing the address of our house. With a little snooping on her part, she had managed to unearth Berty Uncle's latest billet-doux to Anoma and read its tender wooing. It didn't take her long to confront Anoma and uncover the story.

"How can you let these things happen under my nose? Why have you been helping them and not telling me anything? Sending letters through Tamara! You're a teacher, and you're using your own child for underhanded activities!"

"Oh Miss Norah," Amma began, "I don't know what to say about this. We had no hand in bringing Berty and Anoma together, but when he insisted on us passing the letters to her, we didn't know how to refuse. I was telling my sister ..."

"After all I did for you when your son was carrying on with that Malay girl ... didn't you feel obligated to tell me about all this? I could've stayed quiet too!"

Amma hated violent outbursts and tried her best to soothe the music teacher with quiet negotiation. But Asoka Aiya, who was in his bedroom, heard the ruckus and the reference to him and came out like a charging bull. His episode with Izmin was now history, and his new interest lived down another lane, but he had a score to settle. And when young men settled scores, they could get rather unruly.

"Do you expect everybody to go round telling tales like you? Besides, what's wrong with Berty Uncle? You think he's not good enough for Anoma?" Asoka Aiya demanded in a high-pitched voice.

"Asoka, don't interfere in adult's affairs, go back to your room," Amma shrieked.

Quaver went one octave higher: "Don't you understand that that man is too old and he is ..."

"Old? If Anoma goes on like a prisoner in your house any longer, she'll be too old too!" he continued, ignoring Amma.

"How dare you talk to me like that? All the males in this family are up to no good. This Berty, I know about his character, flirting with every skirt. People around here talk about him. His reputation is well known."

"As if people don't talk about you! Berty Uncle is too good for your family. If he has any idea what he's getting into ..."

"Asoka," admonished our mother, "what business do you have to talk like this? For heaven's sake, go to your room. I will look after this."

Asoka Aiya grudgingly walked away. Apart from throwing an occasional stone to break a few flowerpots, and rattling her gate at night, he had not done much to get even with the music teacher. He had once contemplated out loud stuffing mice into her postbox, but his aversion to handling such creatures had changed his mind, and I had refused to help him.

Amma looked Quaver squarely in the eye. "There was nothing we could do, Miss Norah. These things sometimes happen because they are destined to happen. We have no power to change people's karma. And after all, they are both adults and should know what they are doing."

"Of course, Berty knows what he's doing, fooling this innocent girl whom I have been protecting like my own two eyes. If I knew at the beginning, I would have nipped this in the bud. Believe me, I won't allow this!"

Without much success, Amma tried to reason with the enraged woman. After giving further vent to her emotions, Quaver stormed out.

"What could have been broken off with a nail now needs an axe," Amma shook her head from side to side and told no one in particular. "If the horoscopes don't match, they should never get married."

She took up the broom and continued: "On the other hand, if we manage to convince Berty to give up Anoma, this woman will think Berty *was* playing the fool and we are going to be in trouble. How can we go on living here with this madwoman in the front house? How can Tamara go there for music? It's all my fault. I should have asked Berty to get the horoscope the very day I found out."

Amma continued her soliloquy like a Shakespearean actress, turning things this way and that way while she continued to rub coconut refuse on the muddy stains. It was insightful, how she found a reason to blame herself for the situation.

***

That same evening, unaware of Quaver's outburst, Olga Aunty and Nelson Uncle sat down at the table and composed a perfectly reasonable letter to Berty Uncle explaining the astrologer's recommendations. They did not attempt to dissuade him from marrying Anoma. They underplayed the elaborate pujas and offerings he would have to undertake at the end of the five years and concentrated on communicating the necessity of the wait.

***

Berty Uncle phoned after receiving the letter and laughingly dismissed their notions, asking them not to believe everything concocted by the "Master of Horror Scopes." "If he's so clever with astrology, why are his own daughters unmarried?" he had asked.

"What can an astrologer do if his daughters didn't want to marry when their stars pointed to marriage? He's not a magician," Olga Aunty had replied.

Berty Uncle didn't want to dwell on the matter and instead spoke of his impending holiday and sounded impatient to be

208

back in Ceylon. But at the insistence of Nelson Uncle who emphasized that it was Anoma's decision as well and that he couldn't decide for her, Berty Uncle promised to let Anoma know.

***

Quaver suspected that Berty Uncle was phoning Anoma when she was out walking the dogs. Dhanawathi had reluctantly nodded her head in the affirmative when she was questioned. So, the next day, Quaver did not put on the white calico dress after her last pupil departed; she dispatched the dogs with Dhanawathi.

But the servant woman returned panting in a few minutes. She had only been as far as the nearest lamppost; she was unable to control the dogs; they didn't accord her the same respect they did their mistress. Perhaps they knew on which side their bread was buttered.

When the phone rang, Quaver crossed the room in two strides in her high heels and picked up the receiver. She raised her cosmetically enhanced eyebrows and spoke sternly. "Is this Berty? Why are you calling here? What business do you have here?"

Anoma said she tried to look unruffled and went into her room and sat on the bed, feeling like a criminal on the verge of discovery. She listened to her Aunt, her heart pumping more blood with each high-pitched cry.

"What do you need to talk about with me? I have nothing to say to you. All I want is for you to stop calling Anoma."

"Problem? Don't you know what the problem is? Don't think you can fool me. I know your reputation, leave this girl alone."

209

Anoma said she could not remain in her bedroom. She returned to the sitting room. The argument had merited a local audience; Dhanawathi came from the kitchen and stood with her hands on her hips, and the taciturn driver left his garage habitat and peeped through the window.

"How long did you think you could go on with ..." Quaver was saying, when she caught sight of the driver hanging onto the window bars like a chimp at the zoo. She looked about for a missile, picked up the writing pad near the telephone, and flung it at the driver who promptly retreated.

Dhanawathi took the cue and disappeared from her mistress's immediate view. She stood behind the door curtain at the entrance to the kitchen instead.

After nearly fifteen minutes of arguing, Quaver slammed the phone down and went charging into Anoma's room, where she had taken refuge once again, to continue the rest of the quarrel.

Anoma tried to be defensive for a long time, but in the end, unable to contain her dismay she burst out: "You're not even my mother. Why are you so worried about me? It's my decision, and I must decide with whom I'm going to spend the rest of my life!"

"Is this how you talk? Don't try to talk back to me. Haven't I been both mother and father to you, ever since you were two eggplant seeds tall? How can you say that?" Quaver lamented, genuinely upset.

Anoma felt that in spite of Berty Uncle's declaration that he wanted to marry her, Quaver didn't believe he was sincere. She lingered defensively on the warpath, extra protective of her charge. Her objections were superficial, like their age gap.

210

"I don't think you could stop us unless Anoma wants to stop this," Berty Uncle had told her.

***

The next morning, Quaver had looked away when Berty Uncle called again and spoke to Anoma. The previous day's call had ended without resolution, but her Aunt had sounded less hostile toward the end, Berty Uncle said, especially after he mentioned the word "marriage."

"Don't take notice of her harsh words," Berty Uncle comforted Anoma. "I will see her in four weeks, and by that time she'll be calmer."

So Berty Uncle had already formally committed himself by speaking to Quaver when the letter came from Nelson Uncle urging him to wait five years before he got married. Not that it made any difference to Berty Uncle. And fortunately for him, Anoma had no interest, knowledge, or belief in astrology either.

It had been an eventful week. Anoma had tears in her eyes when she related its happenings to me.

***

After a week or so, Quaver had a more composed chat with Anoma, and gradually realized that he was not a bad catch at all. She indicated that they should compare the horoscopes if they were both genuinely interested in each other. By that time, Anoma knew about the horoscope reading, and imparted its negative results. As was to be expected, this brought forth another spate of protestations. Anoma asked her aunt to get an independent reading from another astrologer.

Quaver resumed her walks. If she was troubled, she did not show it.

CHAPTER 21

THE VOW

E ven though Berty Uncle brushed aside the astrological implications of his future marriage, Olga Aunty and Nelson Uncle were worried. As much as they wanted him to settle down, they didn't want him to marry into trouble. As usual, he behaved in his characteristic, irresponsible manner, hurtling through courtship like the *Udarata Menike* on the Kandy railroad. So, Olga Aunty took it upon herself to safeguard their future. Besides the marriage, they had to produce children. She decided to supplicate to a Hindu god and make a vow on their behalf.

With its emphasis on self-reliance for salvation, Buddhism does not endorse praying to a god to receive blessings or favors, material or spiritual. Buddha himself was not a god, but a human being aware of his own limitations, who exhorted his disciples that prayers and symbolic veneration were secondary to seeking the Noble Truths leading to the ultimate liberation from an endless cycle of births and deaths.

Life's tribulations, however, often beg external support. Humans need a crutch to lean on, and it is only natural to solicit help from a superior being when in trouble. On this fertile premise, Hindu deities had won their way into the Buddhist heart, home, and temple, as early as during the reign of Ceylonese kings. These kings secured Indian consorts who brought their retinue from across the Indian Ocean, who, in turn, brought their beliefs and faiths that quickly spread among the Buddhist population. The rulers found that the support of such beliefs was conducive to the social cohesiveness essential for political stability.

To this day, in every Buddhist temple, several *devalayas*, or shrines, are dedicated to various Hindu deities. Incumbent monks encourage their presence because they generate income, a concept alien to temple-goers who were not, as a rule, expected to drop more than a few cents into the coin box when they worshipped. The *kapu mahattayas*, the link between ordinary mortals and the deities who supplicate on their behalf and receive a generous currency note in return, man these *devalayas*. Each deity specializes in areas such as wealth, learning, matrimony, progeny, reunion and even revenge.

But Olga Aunty didn't want to make the vow at the *devalaya* of her neighborhood temple. She wanted to make the promise on sacred ground; at the foot of the Sri Maha Bodiya, one of the most hallowed Buddhist shrines in Ceylon, located in the equally sacred city of Anuradhapura.

This ensured both anonymity and maximum efficacy.

***

When Olga Aunty spelled out her plan, Mary Aunty and her family were interested in joining in the journey, as they had never been to Anuradhapura, which is about a hundred and fifty miles northeast of Colombo. Amma said that we could go, too, and reminded everyone that our railway warrants – the free annual passes issued to government workers – lapsed unused year after year. The excitement caught on, but Olga Aunty sounded doubtful.

"I don't know, Sister, this is not a picnic, this is a religious undertaking. You have to be sober. Do you think Oswald will stand one day without ... liquor?" Her voice trailed off, but Amma was now sold on the idea, especially because of the extra money she was getting next month.

This was the money from the staffroom *seettu,* a type of lottery where nobody lost money. Amma and eleven other teachers had enrolled in the *seettu* and pledged a fixed amount of money to the teacher who had drawn that month. The next month's booty was hers to splurge if you could describe Amma's never-ending expenses as splurging. Looking back, I don't think Amma realized then that it was her own savings – without interest – that she was "splurging."

It was decided that we should apply for warrants and travel by train. Mary Aunty and Amma wrote a letter to a distant relative announcing our arrival during the upcoming April school holidays.

***

Two weeks after school closed, Thatha, Amma and I took a pre-dawn bus ride to the Colombo Fort train station. Asoka Aiya had pleaded exams and wormed his way out of the trip. He had tried to stay at home alone, but Amma wouldn't hear of it, and he was packed off to stay with Nelson Uncle; clothes, textbooks, cricket bat and all. Tikiri was deposited at Mrs. Vithanage's place. They were not exactly dog lovers, but not averse to them either. Maya, Mrs. Vithanage's wisp-of-a-servant-girl, had been suitably bribed and entrusted the tasks of feeding and playing with Tikiri.

The morning was cold and moist as we set off finally, after a mad scramble during which Amma had panicked more than twice that "the train will leave without us." The air smelled of wet earth. We walked to the Battaramulla junction, each carrying a bag in silent meditation. Thatha had the added responsibility of carrying the kit bag containing food for the journey, as well as the *thala guli*, *kolikuttu* plantains and *kithul* jaggery that we were taking to some relatives I had never seen or heard about until recently.

"Bloody nuisance men, this bag is so heavy, I wish Asoka had come too so that he could've carried some of this." Thatha suddenly broke the march and grumbled at Amma, changing his grip from one hand to the other. "That rascal knows how to escape from these things."

"But the boy is studying, no? I'm glad he seems to be taking things seriously now. I hope Nelson will keep an eye on him, and see that he isn't up to any hanky-panky," Amma reasoned.

"I thought he had finished his fling with that girl? Just let him be, men. If he can't have some fun at this age, when can he?"

Amma did not reply because she was really mad at Thatha's relaxed attitude.

It was always one rule for the girl and another rule for the boy. They watched me like a hawk; I was delivered like a parcel to classes, accompanied everywhere except when I got into the school bus and kept under surveillance at home in case I got friendly with a boy. *One-law-for the-girl, another law-for the-boy*, I chanted to myself as I walked to its beastly rhythm.

It was strange seeing the junction at this time of day. It was not yet 5 a.m. and the streetlights were still on. Beggars stirred sleepily on strips of cardboard under shop awnings. A crack of light showed through the vertical planks of a small boutique, announcing another early riser already up and about preparing for the day's commerce. A scraggly cat sprang out of nowhere and went screeching down a path, startled at our sudden, suitcase-burdened appearance – it may have been previously attacked by a carrier of illicit cargo. From inside a hut came the unmistakable sound of someone making tea.

Presently, the bus clanged and swooshed into sight, nearly empty for once. We climbed in thankfully and deposited the loads at our feet. At this hour, bus drivers were almost human. This one even smiled at us, and the conductor took his time to issue us tickets without the usual rude call to buy them—as if we would travel without tickets. We had the road nearly to ourselves, and the driver did not have to toot the horn or intimidate smaller vehicles that he wanted to pass until we reached our destination.

We were to meet the others at the Fort Railway Station, which was rather crowded even this early. Thatha showed the warrants at the counter and received tickets, which we used to gain admittance through the guarded barrier. It wasn't long before we spotted Dinesh Uncle's tall frame and balding head bobbing up from among the other travelers. He latched on to Dhamith's hand so he did not get lost. Mary Aunty and Malkanthi were considerably shorter, so it was some moments before they could be made out. Olga Aunty, who had spent the night at their place, was with them.

The *Yal Devi* seemed rested and anxious to set off, judging by the quivers and hisses it discharged. We piled in, found a near-empty compartment, placed our bags on the overhead racks and settled down. Malkanthi was seven years older than I was, and Dhamith was too young to be anything but a nuisance, so they supplied less-than-ideal companionship for a long trip, but as Amma always said, "What cannot be cured has to be endured."

I resolved to endure Malkanthi's heavy breathing all along the four-hour trip to Anuradhapura. As usual, she was prepared for any health emergency and carried in her bag an assortment of pills, potions, and lotions that emitted an *ayurvedic* smell. This hodgepodge of medication went with her everywhere, just in case. The family joke was that they went even when she did not go anywhere.

Suddenly, there was a blaring announcement over the public address system which I could not decipher, and with a blast and a whistle, we were off. The platform throbbing of humanity was soon a memory. The roaring pistons ensured that conversation was reduced to nods and grimaces, but the constantly changing landscape of sights and sounds compensated for the loss of speech. Unlike in a bus ride, there was something enjoyable in the rhythmic sway.

Dawn streaked through fast and the rosy glow soon gave way to first light, revealing muddy ponds with pink water lilies, leafless trees dotted in white by resting storks and little *dagabas*, or Buddhist shrines, with their domes stark white against green paddy fields. Narrow-stemmed coconut trees, straight and delicate like a class of ballet dancers, supplanted groves of mist-covered banana trees. Dogs scratched themselves behind their ears with hind legs, and crows perched on lazy buffalo. The flora was yet to move, awaiting the wind. The world was at rest, and we were in motion.

After half an hour from blastoff, we came to a grinding halt. My body pivoted back for a few seconds. First stop, Veyangoda. An army of food vendors embarked along with more passengers. *Wadai* sellers flaunted little mountains of *isso wadais* on rattan baskets, sprinkled with green chilies shining with oil. Gram sellers had paper-cones filled with the savory boiled brown pulses, while the sweetmeat vendor touted *thala guli* and honey-filled sweetmeat rings. To further entice prospective customers, he would bring down the enamel basin he had perched on top of his head and display the neatly arranged fare inside. But our group was averse to contaminated food, and Olga Aunty looked away with disdain writ large on her face.

In the next station, a pineapple seller was busy cutting up his fruit, which emitted a tangy aroma. Before wrapping up the slices in paper, he would sprinkle some salt and chili powder for added zest. Here, the main import was a bare-chested boy who came around selling pink and green sweep tickets with his deep-throated incantation: *sweeeeep tickaaaat*, wearing a pleading look of poverty in addition to his shorts. (Thatha, of course, had to buy a ticket. They were germ-proof.)

Then there were the other passengers to observe, especially those harried families who would scramble in at the last moment and rush to place their luggage on the overhead racks and whose children's faces registered disappointment when they failed to secure a window seat.

Hence, for the most part, I found that I was neglecting my Somerset Maugham in this less-than-library-quiet atmosphere. Enveloping this seething mass of humanity was the rhythmic clatter of the diesel-powered wheels. As if that weren't enough, the announcers at every station platform intruded upon my concentration, monotonously booming the various stops through the loudspeakers, first in Sinhala and then in Tamil, until I could recite the route by memory.

Following an unvoiced agreement, Thatha and Dinesh Uncle suddenly nodded to each other and walked off toward the cafeteria carrying a parcel wrapped in brown paper. I wanted to buy some *wadai* with those fried prawns on top, but my request was turned down by Olga Aunty who made discouraging statements like the food was not clean, how did we know whether the person who prepared it had washed her hands, and there could be a hundred varieties of germs in them. Dhamith gazed longingly at other passengers who evidently had no similar qualms. Thatha and Dinesh Uncle returned soon, fortified by one swig or the other, judging by the smell and the pleased looks on their faces. Olga Aunty pouted and suddenly became keenly interested in the scenery outside. What cannot be cured must be endured.

As it turned out, I didn't need to watch the food sellers, beggar boys, or the formidable-looking squad of uniformed ticket checkers to pass the time. After the passing scene became monotonous, I had something new with which to occupy myself for much of the journey afterward and indulge in pleasant dreaming for the rest. At Polgahawela, a kindly-looking peasant woman walked into our compartment looking for vacant seats. Behind her was a young boy clutching a cricket bat, likely her grandson.

There was just enough space in the opposite seats for them to squeeze in, so they sat in front of us. The boy was about thirteen, but with none of that fidgety impatience associated with a boy of that age. Instead, he had a faraway, melancholy look about him, as if half the world's burdens lay on his young shoulders, so unlike my Asoka Aiya at that age or even now.

I couldn't take my eyes off him. He wore a pair of cream drill shorts, a short-sleeved, light brown, checked shirt and a pair of black Bata slippers that were wasted with use. His longish hair was oiled and combed neatly to one side. He had such depth to his eyes, framed by thick lashes shading an innocent face. To me, he was as fresh as a new pail of milk. I wanted to touch him, to see if he was warm.

I followed his every move; the flicker of his long eyelashes, each twitch of the finely shaped nose. But he never once looked at me. His attention was equally divided between the flashing scenery outside and the cricket bat that he had placed upright in between his feet. From time to time, he fingered its black, rubber-covered handle, ran his index finger down its spine and looked down at it fondly as if seeing it for the first time. Like most village urchins, did he until then fashion a bat from a branch of a coconut tree? Was it the first time that he had owned a bat made in a factory?

I willed him to look at me with his deep, black eyes. What was he thinking about? The matches that he would play in his village, the poses and the strokes that he would perfect? I imagined being married to him, this country boy with the long face. He would be kind-hearted and gentle-natured. Never would a cross word pass between us. It would be the perfect marriage.

The back room of our village home would be the storage for sacks and sacks of pungent cloves, cardamoms, cinnamon and nutmeg. This would bring part of our income, yielded from his inherited acres of land. The other part of the income would be the harvest from the rice paddies.

A rude elbow jab jolted my reverie. Malkanthi was wheezing heavily and passing *seeni sambol* sandwiches.

***

Hours after the country boy and his grandmother had hurriedly alighted from Maho Junction and disappeared into the crowd – thereby ending my future plans – we arrived in the Buddhist city of Anuradhapura, a capital of ancient Ceylon from the fourth century B.C. until the beginning of the eleventh century A.D.

Although the railway station had an impressive building, it was near desolate. There wasn't anything to signify past glory.

Although Thatha's kit bag was considerably lighter now that we had eaten the food, he suggested hiring a car. Dinesh Uncle readily agreed. The address was produced and a hiring car procured. The driver looked doubtfully at us. The problem was: how to squeeze four bags and eight humans of assorted sizes (none of them trapeze artists) into an Austin Cambridge. After we managed to pack ourselves in, I was left inhaling the driver's Bryl-Kreem because of my elevated perch on Amma's lap. Malkanthi's wheeze became louder with every passing minute inside the vehicle. Only Dinesh Uncle was relatively comfortable since he was in the front passenger seat with Dhamith, but he had the biggest bag on his lap.

Thankfully, the journey was short, and we arrived, crumpled but intact, at a modest house. Dinesh Uncle rang the doorbell, and a woman in a floral cotton shift opened the door. She had a puzzled expression on her face as she scanned the sea of expectant faces and pieces of baggage deposited at her doorstep. She evidently was not expecting us and thought this was some mistake. We must have looked like a herd of cows patiently waiting to be milked.

"Yes?" she asked. "Are you looking for someone?"

"Is this Simon De Silva's place? We are his relatives and we wrote to him informing him of our arrival. Is he there?" Olga Aunty, ever the brave one, piped up.

These were tense moments. I had an urge to conceal myself beneath one of those enormous *habarala* leaves, each larger than an elephant ear, that were growing profusely in their garden. But I would probably end up with an itch that would spoil the trip even more than the accommodation problem.

A girl of about five years came out and joined in the questioning. "Who are you and why did you come?" she asked pointedly, to be brushed aside by her mother.

"I'm not sure if he received a letter, what are your names? He's at work, but I can call him and ask."

"Tell him that Dinesh and Mary Subasinghe, Olga Rajakaruna, and also Oswald and Blossom De Silva are here. We are hoping to stay with you for a few days."

"Come in and take a seat. I will call him," said the lady of the house before disappearing inside.

We trooped in and seated ourselves the best we could on the open verandah that was not set up for an invasion of luggage-laden relatives.

After what seemed like half-an-hour, the woman returned with a more inviting look on her face. "Yes, my husband is happy to hear that you have come and welcomes you, but he did not get any letter. He'll leave the office early and be here soon. Let me bring you some cool drinks."

I saw relief registering on everyone's faces. Malkanthi, who had been whispering the dreaded possibility of having to get back on the noisy train and return home, sighed and reached for one of her pill pouches, a sure sign of normalcy restored.

***

While Dottie Aunty – that was her name – bustled about getting rooms ready for us with the help of her domestic, which also meant bundling up the bedclothes and paraphernalia of her daughter and installing her in another part of the house, we sipped the lime drinks with relish.

Within an hour, the master of the house returned.

"My god, after how many years later am I seeing you! Sit, sit, what brings you this way all of a sudden, and how did you get my address?"

Everybody started talking at the same time. "Oh, I got it from your sister; I met her at a wedding recently."

"Didn't you get the letter?"

"You have changed quite a bit. I wouldn't have recognized you if we had met on the road."

"When did you get transferred here? Where are you working now and what is the department?"

Only we cousins didn't "yap." We were meeting this person for the first time and were not yet sure whether we liked him or not.

"Dottie, did you offer them some tea? Are the rooms ready?" Without waiting for a reply, he turned again toward Dinesh Uncle and said, "You're a hell-of-a-fellow, no? Why didn't you tell me that you all were coming?"

"It's funny that you didn't receive the letter. I gave it to the office peon, but maybe the fellow threw the letter away and bought cigarettes with the stamp money."

"I would've booked the office Jeep for the weekend. Now it may be too late. I'll try tomorrow anyway."

As it turned out, there was another daughter who had been away at a tuition lesson when we arrived. I was happy to see Tanya, who sauntered in through the door and didn't seem quite as ruffled as the rest of the family to see us. She seemed to be more mature than her fourteen years and was quite a beauty.

It didn't take long for me to realize that Tanya's singular interest in life was boys, and she must have been sorry to note there weren't any in our party in her age group. She seemed to be writing letters to quite a few of them, and her twice-weekly tuition classes were an opportunity for her to meet whoever caught her fancy at that time. Her frequent visits to the pool in their housing complex also presented golden opportunities to look for more prey.

She didn't warm to me and seemed distant much of the time. The only information she volunteered was centered on her favorite topic. She might have seen me as a competitor. But boy oh boy, was she interested in my glossy bronze lipstick! (One of only two I possessed and something that I wouldn't have given to her had she pleaded on bended knees.)

She even sent her younger sister to steal it from our bedroom. The five-year-old had free access to our room and one morning, I came out of the bathroom just in time to catch her rummaging in my suitcase with all the innocence of a trained thief.

"Aney, give it to my sister, will you?" she pleaded when I quickly closed my suitcase and snapped it shut.

***

Early next evening, we piled into Simon Uncle's car with Dinesh Uncle at the wheel. Olga Aunty wanted business out of the way before pleasure, so we were headed for the hallowed shrine of the Sri Maha Bodhiya. On the way, however, we got lost on the unfamiliar roads which led to some bickering unworthy of a pilgrimage inside the limited confines of the Volkswagen. Each remembered a smattering of a road's name, a turnoff, or a pointer that Simon Uncle had given us, but collectively they did not lead us to the destination.

225

Finally, Olga Aunty, who by then had assumed charge of the group since we were on *her* pilgrimage, insisted Dinesh Uncle ask a woman at a wayside king coconut stall. Sighting a sea of expectant faces and sensing a fair bit of commerce, the woman presiding over bunches of the bright orange fruit sprang up. She re-tied her chintz cloth around her waist with an expert tuck and flashed a smile from a dental advertisement at our approaching Uncle, while her husband hastily seized a bunch of choice king coconuts and started breaking them off their grooved stems.

Unfazed by his real intent and dispensing the requested information with a directional wave of her hand, the woman tried her best to "quench our thirst" with a refreshing king coconut. But Olga Aunty nodded a stern "no" at Dinesh Uncle who parted with a fifty-cent appeasement and lamely withdrew in the face of acute disappointment.

Once on the correct path, peace reigned. It was impossible to squabble on the tranquil avenue of trees that led to the venerated site. We parked in the allotted parking area, removed our shoes, alighted barefoot from the vehicle, and walked towards the imposing main gate. A notice board severely warned us not to step on the grass barefoot, for a prickly weed of a plant would invariably sting us for our callousness.

One of the oldest trees in the world, the Sri Maha Bodhi was grown from a sapling of the Bodhi tree under which Siddhartha attained enlightenment in the North Indian city of Gaya more than two-thousand five-hundred years ago. The esathu tree was called "the tree of wisdom" by people of the Indus Valley even before the time of Buddhism. It became known as the bodhi tree after the ascetic Siddhartha reached the highest intellectual state called Nirvana, or bodhi, which released him from all desires and bonds of the human world as he meditated underneath its leafy boughs.

I tried to locate the sacred tree and Thatha helped by pointing out the saffron draperies wrapped around the base of its trunk. As bodhi trees go, this tree is small despite its age. Dinesh Uncle told us that its leaves didn't fall in season with other bodhi trees, but either before or after.

The sacred tree is cordoned off on its elevated perch within the inner precinct by a golden fence. There are many other bodhi trees at lower elevations, whose vast canopies are spread in all directions and their heart-shaped leaves shimmering and swaying in the wind seem to salute the sacred one.

In the gathering dusk, a mild breeze rustled the leaves of the Sri Maha Bodhi as we, along with dozens of other worshippers, gazed up with reverence and offered our prayers.

The tree's history of about 2,250 years is written in the Mahavamsa chronicles, which records the story of Lanka. That makes it the oldest documented tree in human history.

In the third century B.C., during the reign of King Devanampiyatissa, my country received Buddhism from emperor Dharmashoka of India. The emperor's son, Arahant Mahinda Maha Thero, brought the doctrine of the Buddha to the island. The logical philosophy of Buddhism so appealed to King Devanampiyatissa, who embraced it and made it the state religion, that he thereby named the Sinhalese people of the island "Sinhala Buddhists."

Following Buddhism, the southern branch of the Sri Maha Bodhi tree in India was brought ceremonially to

Anuradhapura by Arahant Sangamitta Maha Theri, the daughter of emperor Dharmashoka.

The maternal tree in India was destroyed during Dharmashoka's reign by a queen of a different faith. The bodhi tree in Budh Gaya, India is a fourth-generation tree grown from the original. But the tree from its sapling endured in our soil. It's considered a rare living world heritage.

***

Olga Aunty had come prepared for her mission. She had with her a basket of flowers, a bottle of coconut oil, homemade cloth wicks, a box of joss sticks and a book of *gathas*, or prayers. We all followed her to the main shrine room, located to the east of the Sri Maha Bodhi. She proceeded to offer flowers to the Buddha statues, one of which is of the Buddha in a rarely carved posture of "*bhumi sparsha*," where his fingers touch the ground.

Outside, we lit a series of oil lamps and burnt some joss sticks that emanated a heady fragrance. She then sat on the sandy ground, leaning against the outer wall of the second promontory, and took out her book of prayers, which she started to recite in the faint light. We mingled about, the crunch-crunch of our feet on the sand seemingly loud in the tranquil atmosphere, assisting her when possible and keeping a distance when she needed the space. During one unguarded moment, however, Thatha caught the three sisters seated in a half-circle, palms together in front of their chests, deep in conversation, not with a god, but with each other, about a rash that afflicted Malkanthi.

Presently, it was time to meet one of the Villidura people of the Bodhahara caste who functioned as the *kapu mahattayas* here. The Villidura people were brought to the country by Arahant Sangamitta Maha Theri, along with various classes of artisans who would serve as guardians of the tree and the Buddhist culture that would establish with it.

The Villidura people were not difficult to spot with their white, long-sleeved, kurta-style shirts and sarongs and trademark white shawls around their necks. The one we approached had his hair tied in a little knot at the back of his head. Olga Aunty whispered the nature of her concern to him and he nodded at intervals, all the while fingering his chin thoughtfully. He led us to a shrine, where Olga Aunty untied a knot in her handkerchief and took out a copper penny wrapped in a rag and a ten-rupee note that she placed on a betel leaf conveniently left lying about. The man nodded his approval, took the proffered penny with both hands and invoked the blessings of the Buddha and the Dhamma on the whole party. He next propitiated loudly to the god in a language I hoped the god would understand, because none of us could.

Olga Aunty received the *pandura,* tied in a knot, from the man. In return for blessing Berty Uncle's marriage and praying for the birth of an heir, Olga Aunty pledged seven baskets of fruit, seven baskets of vegetables and a host of other items to be donated to a temple in her neighborhood. She also promised to release a cow from the abattoir and place it in a dairy farm.

Everybody sighed, some not so secretly, when Olga Aunty's mission was accomplished to her satisfaction. The sacred Bodhi tree is but one of eight places of Buddhist historical significance, or *atamasthana,* in Anuradhapura. However daunting it must have been to construct the great *stupas* and palaces of the other seven sites during the reigns of various Sinhalese kings, I felt that satisfying Olga Aunty was nearly as great a challenge.

We spent the next few days touring the historic sites of Anuradhapura, a testament to the physical and intellectual development of the great city before and after the establishment of Buddhism.

Now in picturesque ruins, the sites included huge, bell-shaped stupas, some more than a thousand feet in circumference and built of small sun-dried bricks; temples, sculptures, palaces, monastic buildings; and ancient drinking-water reservoirs.

In the fourth century B.C., King Pandukabhaya established the enclosed city of Anuradhapura with four guardian gates, water and sanitation, and hospitals and amenities for its residents.

For more than one-thousand, three-hundred years, the city became a political and religious capital that flourished in the number of its inhabitants, and in the splendor of its shrines and public buildings, ranking alongside Babylon in its colossal proportions – its four walls, each sixteen miles long, enclosing an area of two-hundred and fifty-six square miles.

Historical records kept alive the memory of the city which outlived the reign of 113 kings. King Devanampiyatissa's Thuparamaya is shaped for a heap of paddy and considered the first dagaba built after the introduction of Buddhism; it enshrines the Buddha's collarbone. King Dutugemunu built the magnificent, pristine white Ruwanweli Maha Seya and Mirisawetiya Stupa after defeating the Tamil king Elara. The Ruwanweli Maha Seya compound is supported by stone elephants and the surrounding wall is decorated with nearly two-thousand elephant figures.

A Maiden's Prayer

Lovamahapaya is also known as the Brazen Palace for the bronze-tiled roof it once had. King Dutugemunu created the nine-story monastic building with forty rows of stone pillars, each row consisting of forty stone pillars that took six years to build. Its ruins consist of the foundation and pillars.

King Walagamba's Lankaramaya is another stupa enclosed by rows of stone pillars that may have been from an edifice built to encircle it. The king enshrined relics of the Buddha in the figure of a bull made of gold in the Abhayagiriya Dagaba. It once had an adjoining temple that housed a large library for monks. The *dagaba* was covered with greenery.

King Mahasen built the Jetavanarama, the largest stupa in Ceylon, and possibly in the whole world, with a height of four hundred feet. The doorpost to the shrine is twenty-seven feet high and is a foot underground. A part of a sash tied by the Buddha is believed to be enshrined here.

I had spent many hours studying about the two-thousand years of the Golden Age of Ceylon's history, and it was awe-inspiring to see some of it with my own eyes. Even centuries later, their dignity and grandeur didn't fail to strike me.

CHAPTER 22

BERTY UNCLE COMES ON HOLIDAY

May 1976

That year, Anoma said, Christmas came to their household in May. The day after returning from Saudi Arabia, Berty Uncle visited our place with his usual heap of gifts.

As soon as he had presented them to us – saris for Amma, shirt and trouser lengths for Thatha and Asoka Aiya and fabric for me, in addition to an assortment of edible goodies – Berty Uncle ignored Thatha's teasing and made a beeline to his sweetheart's house across the road.

But not before taking out two bulging bags from the Capri.

I could see something of the unfolding events through our front windows. He lacked only the red costume and the reindeer sleigh when he deposited himself at the doorstep laden with the bags. I saw Dhanawathi open the door and make as if to close the door in his face – she probably thought he was a traveling salesman peddling plastic toys.

Then, Anoma, who probably had had her ears tuned to the sound of the doorbell, hurried to the door, and broke into a wide smile. She was wearing her princess line navy blue dress with the tiny red roses, which brings out her fair skin color to its best effect. Dhanawathi waddled away, probably to inform her mistress of the brazen new development.

Berty Uncle lugged in the suitcases, executing a little dance among the cane chair quintet. That's all I could see, but I can picture Quaver's eyes growing bigger and bigger as Berty Uncle unpacked the gifts.

Later, Anoma told me that there were two of each. It was as if Berty Uncle was wooing two people: Anoma, who in a matter of a few months had completely capitulated to Berty Uncle's charms, and her doubtful Aunt, who had softened like a slab of butter placed in direct sunlight.

Flimsy georgette saris in pastel shades, crimplene trouser lengths in cherry, beige, dark green and the more refined navy blue, fabric prints capturing Utopian visions of flora and fauna, cotton blouses with ruched sleeves, cosmetic sets made in Paris, enormous bottles of 4711 Eau de Cologne, shampoo and hairspray, hair ornaments and silken scarves took up most of the room that was not renowned for its size. Tins of Rowntree Mackintosh toffees, Danish Butter Cookies, boxes of KitKat, slabs of Galaxy chocolate, packets of Kraft cheese, and Wrigley's chewing gum spilled out next, but there was even more.

Dhanawathi and the taciturn driver were not left out; they, too, received lengths of cloth, and boxes of biscuits and chocolates to eat to their heart's content. Dhanawathi, Anoma reported, had touched Berty Uncle's shirt sleeve in mute gratitude. This was perhaps the first imported gift she had received in her life. Even the driver, Anoma said, searched – and found – an unfamiliar smile.

Anoma looked radiant as she rattled off the contents of the bags. There was no going back for her. And Quaver was dazzled both by the generosity of the intended bridegroom and the array of imported food and clothing, which were unimaginable luxuries. Although the World Market in Fort had plenty of textiles for sale and the shop shelves were now filled with local goods in anticipation of the 1977 general elections, the days of plenty were still those spoken about in the past tense.

***

As Berty Uncle and Anoma drew closer during the weeks that followed, it seemed as though they had known each other for ages.

Although he was the first man she had ever known romantically, and therefore had no yardstick to measure compatibility, Berty Uncle seemed perfect for Anoma in every way. He had a comforting way of taking charge in any situation and provided the manly figure that had been lacking in her life. With the stability that comes with money, he made bold decisions. She felt safe with him. If he was impatient, she countered with her patience.

At the time, I didn't know anything about loving relationships. On reflection, it didn't sound like a passionate, romantic love, but a friendship that transcended romance. The foundation they built during those weeks was solid. Above all, Anoma was drawn to his kindhearted attentiveness and consideration of her feelings. In her joy, I think she began to wish that she had been more open to life in the past.

Some months ago, before Berty Uncle came on the scene, Anoma had related to me how their silly servant woman had given her intelligent solace when she was particularly downhearted.

Dhanawathi had found a wedding invitation in the mailbox addressed to Anoma and had brought it to her bedroom. Anoma had been seated at the dressing table staring at nothing.

Anoma often wondered how different life would have been had her parents been alive.

She had only a sketchy memory of them. She remembered playing with her father in their garden. He would hide behind a tree and jump out at her or hurl her up in the air, declaring that he was throwing her to the crows, and then catch her at the very last minute. Of her mother, she could only remember her coaxing her to eat, often pursuing her with a balled fistful of rice and curries, trying to make a finicky eater swallow a few mouthfuls.

She was only four when they died in a car crash. She was in the back seat and survived with only a few cuts and scrapes. Why was she spared for this world, she asked me.

Anoma had taken the envelope from Dhanawathi, opened and scanned it briefly. It was a wedding invitation from a girl, barely twenty-three, who had attended cookery classes with her. She had sighed and thrown it in the wastepaper basket.

The reaction had not been lost on the servant woman.

"Anoma babee, who is getting married?" she had inquired.

"Everybody," Anoma had replied.

"Why did you throw that away? Don't you like that person?" The woman had persisted.

"No, I have nothing against her."

"Then why did you throw the invitation card away?"

"I don't want to go to yet another wedding and be asked a hundred times when my wedding is. All the others from the class are bound to be there, and they constantly ask me this question. Besides, I would hate to watch yet another bride and groom walk away, arm in arm."

For a woman who had never been married herself, and for whom a relationship between a man and a woman was as alien as a space voyage, Dhanawathi had offered solace.

"The right man will come one day," she had told her gently. "Then you will be swept away yourself. There is always somebody for everybody."

The words had come from a person whose somebody hadn't turned up. And Dhanawathi's words had come true.

CHAPTER 23

WEDDING PREPARATIONS

B efore returning to Saudi Arabia at the end of May, Berty Uncle set the wedding date for August eighteenth of that year. As Anoma lacked an elderly male relative who could help arrange the wedding, the task fell to Olga Aunty and Nelson Uncle who had by now swept the horoscope matter under the rug and were being swept away by the whirlwind that was an approaching family wedding.

It had been a long time since there had been a nuptial, and our extended family – except for Thatha – threw itself into the chaos. The wedding cake was the bridegroom's responsibility, and the sisters, ably spearheaded by Olga Aunty, made a collective plan to make the traditional dark fruit cake with its layer of sweet almond paste. The cake had to be baked in a commercial bakery, since home-based cake trays and ovens were far too small for the quantity needed. Since the Malsara Bakery accepted baking orders from outside, they decided to cut the fruit and mix the cake at our place.

But things weren't as easy as they sounded. Cookery demonstrations with substitutions for traditional ingredients were still the rage. Recipes for "roti minus coconut," "egg-less cake" and "treacle from coconut water" warranted front-page coverage in the *Sunday Observer*. Colombo Seven housewives, the elite of Ceylon who had once regarded certain food items like sweet potato, leeks, and soy meat with disdain, now gushed they were excellent substitutes that were "so economical as well." But Olga Aunty declared dramatically, echoing the prime minister's famous pre-election promise, that she would get the cake ingredients "from the moon."

For weeks, they all had to scramble and forage to obtain everything in the necessary quantities. Olga Aunty first sent her office peon on a scouting mission to the very bowels of the Pettah wholesale district that harbored – or used to harbor – the dried fruit in burlap sacks. The peon, who had promptly pocketed the proffered bribe of two rupees, had been instructed not to return until he could verify the availability of each item. Once the peon's report came in, Nelson Uncle and Olga Aunty made the trek to St. John's Road to discover for themselves the "sky-high" prices that the peon had indicated with his hands on his cheeks.

The wholesale market is located on a side road away from Pettah's Main Street, past Ram Brothers, Nagindas, and Carvalios, the shops I knew so well thanks to Amma's shopping expeditions. Set amidst squawking chickens awaiting slaughter in pens, mountains of vegetables and traders transporting goods in wooden carts, the narrow street was also smelly. Everyone seemed to be in a mighty hurry but no one went anywhere fast.

Latheefia Stores, dealers in cake ingredients and *biryani*, only carried sultanas from her lengthy list, and they seemed extra-withered. Olga Aunty purchased them all the same, paying a pricey fourteen rupees per pound. At St. Anthony Stores next door, two men seated with bill books at a table that blocked the entrance wobbled their heads in a united "no" when Nelson Uncle queried if they had any ginger preserve. The answer was nay to the other preserves too. What was the point of sitting there with empty shelves behind them, Olga Aunty had whispered to Nelson Uncle. But they were rich in the essence department; big bottles of Star vanilla were procured from the back of the store.

Colombo Stores had a row of dismal looking bottles in a glass case and little else, while Joseph Stores did better, supplying them with the other dry ingredients. But there was one item Olga Aunty could not find: strawberry jam. The Tamil shopkeeper tried to palm-off strawberry-flavored silver melon jam, but Olga Aunty was not to be tricked. She would have the natural product if she had to dispatch her husband to England. As matters turned out, after a fruitless search, bridegroom Berty Uncle was instructed to send four bottles of the stuff through a friend coming on holiday. In June 1976, Ceylon lacked strawberry jam.

The next problem was sugar. The sugar crisis was not only felt in local households; the shortage was supposed to be worldwide, due to decreased harvests and increased demand. After the new sugar-rationing scheme took effect in 1974, sugar, jams, cordials, jaggery, and many other sugary foods kept disappearing and reappearing on shop shelves according to the whims of the traders that were invariably tied to government-controlled price hikes. The latest sweetening method was to lick a piece of jaggery for sweetness and then sip the tea, as the three-quarter pound monthly sugar ration per person barely lasted a month in most households. Wily traders, finding that jaggery was a sought-after and fast-disappearing commodity, had found a way to produce more using *lavulu* fruit as the base rather than the traditional treacle.

When rationing came into effect, off-ration sugar rose to a hefty seven-fifty rupees. Hearing about the impending wedding, Mrs. Vithanage, whose three-person household did not use up the monthly sugar allocation, was happy to sell her share to Amma at the rationed rate of seventy-two cents a pound. Quaver offered to give some of hers, but Olga Aunty wouldn't hear of the suggestion on the grounds of tradition. Brown sugar, which was almost half the price and often watered by the traders to weigh more, was shunned for fear of imparting its peculiar taste.

With Olga Aunty's will, there was always a way. Although it was no easy feat to circumvent those obstacles, in time, the goals were accomplished. On a weekday evening, Nelson Uncle delivered the ingredients to our place.

When she saw the bulging packages, Amma's face was a study in dismay. She could safeguard the precious ingredients from thieves, servants, ants, cockroaches and even a swarm of killer bees from Sinharaja Forest, but her sweet-toothed son was quite another matter. As if reading her mind, Asoka Aiya sauntered into the kitchen as soon as Nelson Uncle departed and began rummaging through the bags.

"Nothing like strawberry jam," he declared, taking out a bottle. "Puts woodapple, guava, passion fruit, papaw and mango in the shade!"

He made a circular motion as if to open the container and Amma immediately snatched the bottle, which slipped and crashed to pieces, spreading its precious contents on the floor. Tikiri bounded in from nowhere and began lapping up the jam, briskly wagging her tail at the unexpected pleasure until I scooped her up before she swallowed any glass bits.

***

The following Friday afternoon, my aunts gathered at home to cut the dried fruit. There were mountains of preserves

240

and dried fruit to get through; pumpkin, candied peel, cherries, chow-chow and ginger, sultanas, currents as well as cashew nuts. Asoka Aiya was banished from the kitchen and he disappeared outside with his cricket bat, wailing his disapproval.

We cut, chopped, and diced into the night. Just a few years before, austerity measures had compelled wedding houses to serve only a piece of cake and a fruit drink, but now, with restrictions lifted, short-eats were back on the table. Yet, nothing was as sought after or as criticized as the wedding cake; perfection was essential in taste and appearance, and quantity was demanded:

Wedding Cake Recipe
Ingredients–
Two kilograms each of semolina, butter, raisins, sultanas and cashew nuts,

Four kilograms of sugar,

Seven-hundred-and-fifty grams of currents and candied peel,

One kilogram each of preserved cherries, ginger, and pumpkin, also chow-chow,

Four bottles of strawberry jam,

One bottle of golden syrup or bee's honey,

A hundred eggs (only fifty whites),

Two bottles each of vanilla, rose, and almond. Brandy optional.

A hundred grams each of cloves, nutmeg, and cinnamon.

For the marzipan icing– Two kilograms of cashew nuts and ten pounds of icing sugar.

For the wrapping– One dozen sheets of oil paper and nine packets of wrapping paper.

The fruit preserves were combined in a new plastic bucket and drenched with essences of vanilla, almond, rose and a cup of brandy, and mixed with bicarbonate of soda. Fermentation took two days.

***

On Sunday, Olga Aunty and Nelson Uncle returned to continue with the cake-making. In batches with a large frying pan, Amma roasted semolina with butter and added it to the mixed fruit. The eggs were broken one by one into a teacup and added to the mix. Nelson Uncle had picked up four enormous baking trays from the bakery, which had to be lined with oil paper before we could pack in the mixture.

The trays were placed on the front and back seats of Nelson Uncle's car to take to the bakery. Being the smallest, I was the only one able to squeeze myself into the back seat to hold the trays so they would not topple. In any case, I don't think Amma would have sanctioned Asoka Aiya's presence anywhere near that heaven-smelling cake batter.

Well into an indolent afternoon, the Malsara Bakery had finished baking – and selling – the morning quota of bread. When we arrived, the premises were as bare of customers as they were of goodies to sell. The young woman at the counter yawned and waved us inside.

Nelson Uncle and I trooped down a passage, opened a rather dirty door and entered the inner sanctum. We both ducked immediately as a multitude of flies whirred toward us like a swarm of locusts in an African field and settled happily on our cake mixture. There was no way to ward them off—the whole place teemed with insects. Those not flying about, crawled over particles of food on the long trestle table that was used to knead the dough. Flies settled on the stacks of bread pans, flour sacks, and even on the long wooden rods used to prod the bread into position inside the oven.

Five shirtless bakers were preparing the trays for the night's bread-making. The handkerchiefs they wore around their heads were drenched with sweat. Even more than the presence of flies, Olga Aunty would have been horrified had she known that one baker's underwear was draped on a semicircular oven door; he had found a quick way to dry clothes.

Nelson Uncle scanned the soot-covered brick ovens and the five shirtless bakers. One muscular young man came our way and explained the process: firewood was burnt under the floor of the oven and the cinders removed. The residual trapped heat was enough to bake the bread and butter cakes. Our cake was going to be baked after the night's bread was done as it required even less heat; the baking time for rich cake was two-and-a-half hours. We would get the cake the next day.

Nelson Uncle and I exchanged glances. Little else could be done apart from abandoning the wedding cake to the mercy of the bakers – and the flies. It was too late to cart the cargo elsewhere. The five shirtless bakers observed us curiously, impervious to the flies that were as much part and parcel of the establishment as they were.

***

After the cake was delivered the next day, I examined its surface carefully just in case any Malsara flies had got baked alongside. There were none. Two days later, when Asoka Aiya was at cricket, Amma broke up the crusty slabs and added the golden syrup and strawberry jam. She had purchased an extra bottle of syrup to make up for the lost jam. Fortunately, Olga Aunty was not around, and Asoka Aiya's trespass went unreported to authorities.

The family assembled once again to add the marzipan paste and cut the cake into individual pieces. We used a steel cutter, provided by the bakery along with the trays. Lastly, we wrapped the cake – first in oilpaper, then in silver patterned paper and lastly in an extra-noisy variety of crinkly cellophane. Again, Asoka Aiya was banished until Olga Aunty and Nelson Uncle were homeward bound in their Austin with the embellished wedding cake stowed in the backseat.

Their job was done, but mine awaited me. As the bridesmaid, it was my duty to control the number of pieces each person took. There would be enough to go around if the guests didn't try to grab half a dozen pieces. I had seen it happen at so many weddings. Even Amma, my sweet and polite Amma, returned from them with an extra piece inside her little pearl-encrusted handbag with its camphor-smelling satiny insides.

There's something in wedding cake that brings out the baser elements of the Ceylonese. Perfectly cultured people turn into schemers who would trick, pinch, cajole or beg to obtain an extra piece or two for that sister, maiden aunt, daughter, servant, someone – anyone – who didn't make it to the wedding. Perhaps they weren't invited.

***

One Saturday morning, Amma set off to the shopping district of Pettah with a long list and returned toward evening, tired but triumphant, with the following purchases: from Kundanmals, material and voile lining for a sari blouse to match the grand Kanjeepuram sari that Berty Uncle had brought her from Saudi Arabia; from Hydramani, rich satin for a matching underskirt; from Visakhamals, a bun-shaped hairpiece and hair net and also a countless number of clips, pins, fasteners, hooks and eyes, elastic tape and safety pins in various sizes; and last but not least, from Pearlridge, open-toed silver shoes "with a decent wedge heel that would not topple me."

I generally liked to steer clear of these headache-inducing expeditions. During the past years, textiles had not been freely available for wholesale purchase and merchants, sporting long faces beside empty shelves, had scaled back operations. But now that general elections were nearing, retail commerce was being allowed marginally by the government, and shelves were gradually filling up with locally manufactured fabric and some imports, albeit at a higher cost than what was doled out by the cooperatives. I couldn't have been ten years old during the pre-import control days, but I vividly remember Amma behaving like a perfect nuisance while shopping.

She sailed in and out of tedious Sari Emporiums and boring Salu Salas on Main Street for hours on end, pointing to endless bales of fabric dormant on topmost shelves. She made salesmen tip them down with their yardsticks or climb up stepladders to retrieve them from their quiescent states, only to disdainfully discard them after examining them not cursorily, but in a dozen different ways including holding up to the sunlight, smelling, puckering, wrapping around her waist, then my waist, and admiring it by tilting her head from side to side.

She also bargained long and hard with the shopkeepers and pavement hawkers before she made purchases. It was no small matter to stand nonchalantly beside a pavement stall with the noonday sun beating on your shoulders and rivulets of sweat coursing down your legs, ignoring the tooting cars and the motley crowd of people staring while your mother saved a few rupees.

During these trips, hitherto hidden characteristics surfaced, imparting strengths belying appearance. Gone was the gentle, unassuming, non-goose-booing lady. In her place stood a black umbrella-waving virago with argumentative powers that could compete with the nation's best advocates. According to her, the salesmen were instructed to snip at least two inches less of the fabric, the shopkeepers exhibited high-quality goods but slipped inferior stuff into the brown paper bag when her back was turned, shortchanged or overcharged her as much as they dared to, and adjusted the prices after sizing up the customer.

It was surprising that there hadn't been a spate of suicides in Pettah in her wake.

Thankfully, as Anoma's bridesmaid, my outfit was the responsibility of the bride's side. I was wearing a sari for the first time in my sixteen-year-old life.

***

As the groomsman, Asoka Aiya got his first tailored suit and was under careful instruction regarding the particulars of his outfit. The suit collar had to be shaped just so, and the trousers had to be flared to the inch. Thatha and he took off to Maulanas in Maradana with the thick Gaberdine suit lengths that Berty Uncle had gifted them. Amma had advised Thatha to get his suit tailored there too. However, at the last minute, after giving their measurements, Thatha had had a disagreement with the Moor tailor about the tailoring cost and had returned in a huff, despite being given a mollifying drink of Orange Barley which was a customary offering to patrons more established and promising. Thatha placed Asoka Aiya's tailoring order at his insistence but decided to entrust his own to the local sewing establishment in the Battaramulla junction where he was an acknowledged customer.

As soon as Amma heard about the argument and the decision to fall back on the local tailor, she launched forth. One could never rely on the tailor-in-the-junction for any number of reasons: he robbed half the cloth and declared the material insufficient, he never finished on time and closed shop early to either avoid irate customers or recover from drinking bouts, and there were always alterations despite the fitting.

But Thatha could not be persuaded to return to Maulanas or any of the other reputed tailoring establishments in Colombo. As usual, money was the deciding factor, and Thatha had better plans for his rupees rather than pay a tailor who, he alleged, was charging him to inhale the perfume-sprayed air inside his snooty shop. He maintained that the local man, despite his less-than-saintly ways in his less-than-sophisticated environs, always managed to turn out things to his satisfaction.

But when Thatha stopped by the little tailoring shop with his Gaberdine cloth, the establishment looked newly arranged. When he parted the multi-hued Batik sarongs that were strung on two lines across the breadth of the shop, he was surprised to see new faces at the Singer machines. A young woman nursing a baby sat on the ground against a glass case containing buttons, beads, and other paraphernalia of the trade; she did not bother to conceal her ample lacteal endowments and carried on feeding.

The tailor shop had had a change of ownership after Thatha's last visit, and the new owner was a newcomer to town. He was also spanking new to his trade, but Thatha did not glean that important snippet of information until too late. He greeted Thatha pleasantly enough and seemed eager for his business.

Given the known-devil-unknown-angel scenario, any other sensible person would have promptly retraced steps through the sarong canopy and returned home with the fabric tucked firmly under arm. But Thatha had had enough dealings with tailors for the week and wanted to finish with his tiresome errand. He took heart from the works-in-progress that were dangling from hangers and the pile of materials awaiting scissors on a table. He succumbed to the measurement-taking under the watchful eye of the suckling infant and hoped for the best. Never mind that the tailor had not even seen a Gaberdine before, judging by the way he kept fingering the woolen material, his twenty-something-year-old face a mixture of curiosity and awe.

***

To put things diplomatically, the finished product lacked sartorial elegance. To itemize, Thatha's suit was deficient in shape, style, poise, and finesse. But what was missed in quality was made up in quantity. The trousers were baggy, flapping affairs fashioned after the street-sweeping elephant pants in vogue among teenagers. The golf-tee, or the "goal-P" as the tailor called it, was about five inches below its intended resting place under the crotch. The sleeves were so long that they covered his hands and had to be turned up to release the fingers.

Thatha swayed about like a restless, caparisoned elephant before the start of a *perahera*. Being more bones and eye socket than flesh and bulk, his skeleton could not support this mass of textile that the Gaberdine and the fashioning warranted, and he sagged under its weight.

"There should be a law to prevent people from becoming tailors if all they know is how to thread a needle," he groused. "How dare he oust my tailor and set himself up, the upstart. What he knows about sewing can be ... can be written on a safety pin!"

"Why didn't you tell him to shape the legs at the fit-on?" Amma cried in dismay, stretching the trouser leg to its elephant-ear width to inspect the damage. "Didn't he understand that when the cloth is heavy, the cut must be slim? Didn't he notice that the sleeves were too long?"

Thatha was noncommittal and beyond practicalities. He continued to bemoan the waning state of the tailoring profession in general, the complete lack of tailoring schools in Ceylon and the mushrooming of fly-by-night clothiers. Listening to him, the establishment's gradual decline was comparable to the rise and fall of the Roman Empire.

He harkened to the past when tailors visited homes; to his father's family tailor whose unannounced arrival was welcomed like rain on parched land, and who would be installed at the sewing machine that was hastily dusted and dragged to the middle of the sitting room and who would hold court spinning tales and sewing until dusk fell and his eyes couldn't see the stitching anymore.

As Amma guessed, Thatha had presented himself for the fitting in a state of drunken stupor. The golf-tee, once cut, might well be cast in stone. He had shouted at the tailor to narrow the trouser legs and shorten the sleeves, but the tailor was not adept at understanding slurred speech—and he was remarkably deficient in sewing skills and vastly inexperienced in adjustments.

***

The preparations in the Rajakaruna household were not without hiccups either. Here, the greatest bone of contention was the invitee list, which kept growing at an alarming rate and had to be contained for the sake of costs. There was much bickering between Nelson Uncle and Olga Aunty about whom to invite and whom to omit. The immediate relatives and their relatives had to be invited, not to mention the cousins twice removed, the poor relatives and the village relatives. Nelson Uncle's family teemed with kin like a termite mound, most of whom had invited them for their weddings in the past. Those who had not were fleetingly considered and then denounced.

Scribbles filled the foolscap. The total extended family on Olga Aunty's side racked up a solid thirteen pax (the hotelier's term for head was "pax," according to the food and beverages manager of the Inter-Continental Hotel, the wedding venue). Then there were Nelson Uncle and Olga Aunty's office colleagues, friends, neighbors both current and past, the area Member of Parliament and government agent, acquaintances who had granted favors and who couldn't be left out and so on. All these people, except for the MP and GA, had had a hand in searching for Berty's life-mate so for gratitude's sake, could hardly be left out. Finally, it seemed as if only the street lamplighter and the kerosene-oil-cart man were not on the list.

The list was dutifully submitted for Berty Uncle's inspection. When it was returned, scratches filled the foolscap.

He had initially said "no" to a *tamasha*, but had gradually succumbed to the idea of a big wedding. As his interest grew, so did his own list of invitees. Berty Uncle was never short of friends and had attended numerous weddings solo, but they were now familied and had to be counted three pax – or four – to a friend. His ex-colleagues could not be displeased, especially as he might be returning to Ceylon soon and needed their help to secure a job. Then there were his university friends, the new friends in Saudi Arabia, some of whom were now resettled in Ceylon, and the usual odd assortment of acquaintances that life brings.

By the time Nelson Uncle tallied up his numbers and added them to Berty Uncle's, there were well more than the hundred-and-fifty allocated to the groom's side.

It was time to talk to Quaver.

***

The music teacher was still trying to adjust to the cyclone, in the form of Berty Uncle, which had hit her household. She had given scant thought to the wedding. While our family sewed clothes and handled hotel arrangements, Anoma told me that Quaver was still trying to fathom the wisdom of her readiness to plunge headlong into marriage. She would launch into almost-daily tirades. She told Anoma that despite his charm, impatience, and swift decisiveness, Berty Uncle provided all the ingredients for a catastrophe. In her opinion, quick marriages were a recipe for disaster.

Nelson Uncle and Olga Aunty trod warily when they brought up the subject of the invitee list.

"Miss Norah," Nelson Uncle had begun gently. "We have been compiling the wedding list and there are so many people almost begging to be invited. I know you will think we are selfish people to ask this, but do you think you could manage with a hundred-and twenty-five invitees instead of a hundred-and-fifty?"

"Hundred-and-twenty-five?" Quaver's big eyes had opened wider and her right hand had gone over her throat.

"Hundred-and-fifty," she had told herself mechanically.

Nelson Uncle had expected an argument and prepared his case well. He sighed and launched his mission to talk her into inviting fewer guests from her side.

But his worries were short-lived. Quaver seemed startled to realize that she had to produce, at short notice, at least a hundred-and-twenty-five invitees for Anoma's wedding. As far as I knew, short of hiring them, she couldn't produce that many people.

By way of relatives, she told Nelson Uncle, all she had was her mother's brother. That's why she invited her teenage pupils, who did not need a chaperone, to her birthday parties.

I know that the parents were excluded, leaving them to resort to speculation and snide remarks to get their share of the entertainment. (*Why won't she invite us; did she imagine herself to be young; fancy having a birthday party for herself when there was a young, unmarried girl in the house.*) The Mrs. Vithanages in the neighborhood whispered and conjectured about it.

In addition, Quaver had no friends, and Anoma had but a few. Between the two, counting their domestics, they could muster a party of perhaps fifteen people. She could rack it up to about thirty if she invited her pupils, but what was the point of making the wedding look like an orphanage outing?

"A hundred and twenty-five?" Quaver had repeated to Nelson Uncle. "Please invite all your friends and relatives. There will be about fifteen guests from my side."

CHAPTER 24

THE BOY

September 1976

C olombo was hosting the Non-Aligned Conference and the world was getting to know our little teardrop-shaped island, its history, and culture. The whole city was agog with the appearances of foreign presidents and prime ministers.

Our prime minister had attended the inaugural conference in Belgrade, Yugoslavia in 1961, consisting of developing countries that were not aligned to a superpower. The world's first woman prime minister had stepped up to her role and graced the international stage.

Now it was our turn to host the event. It was a proud moment for our country.

But not everybody was impressed. The spruced roads had traffic barricaded until a motorcade led by stern-looking policemen on motorbikes hurried on their important way. Some roads were closed for hours on end, and buses were often late. Nelson Uncle was particularly vocal about arriving late to work.

There was the question of costs too. We read about the gleaming Peugeot 504 cars that had been imported to Colombo to provide transport for the delegates.

The newspapers were full of pictures of India's Indira Gandhi with her single, dignified lock of white hair; Cypress's Archbishop Macarios with his long, flowing beard;

Yugoslavia's Marshall Tito, tall and heavily built; and Libya's young Muammar Gaddafi.

In school, they had entered our day-to-day discussions, with Gaddafi featuring more than the others on account of his rugged good looks.

Aruni declared that Gaddafi had waved at her during the opening-day procession that went past their house in the heart of Colombo. Aruni, who could, of late, hardly get through a week without falling in love with a new alpha guy she had set her eyes upon, had fallen madly in love with Gaddafi and made a public declaration to that effect toward the tail-end of a class. The science teacher had stepped out after giving us something to copy from the blackboard. We copied it fast and were making good use of the unsupervised time.

"Fat chance you'll have, the head of a country, married and all," scoffed one girl after the laughter had died down. "I read that he has two children as well."

"Oh, I'm sure he can arrange something if he likes you. After all, being a Muslim, he can have several wives. But what about the age gap? I mean, he must be at least thirty-five years old, no?"

"The biggest problem would be getting his attention. Does he even know of your existence?"

This last question drove the point home, despite the wave, imagined or not. Aruni played with the rubber band that held one of her pigtails. Her pointed face lapsed into moody thought. The bell rang for the lunch interval.

After lunch, I suggested that we opt out of the usual energetic game of rounders and settle into our other favorite pastime. The three of us linked hands and walked toward the ample shade of our favorite *kottamba* tree in a far corner of the school grounds, out of earshot of anyone.

When we were much younger, the protruding roots of the tree were used for a game that we had named "Roots." It had a simple premise. Everyone ran around the tree, and if they were treading on or touching a root, the appointed "catcher" could not get them. The game could get rough and noisy, and we stopped for the occasional cut or bruise, but we had survived childhood on those roots without broken nose or limb.

Now that we were teenagers, we used the roots to perch on during our private discussions. If this tree could talk, it could divulge most of our conversations to the outer world. Usually, it placidly absorbed our deliberations, occasionally waving its leafy arms in agreement to the dictates of the breezes.

"How is Saranga, the dancing master?" Minaka broke the silence, smoothing out the box pleats of her uniform and gingerly seating herself. "Does he still have that interesting lock of long hair that moves up and down to the drumbeat? Or have you stopped following his classes?"

Aruni, still downcast, shook her head and absent-mindedly plucked a few blades of grass from the well-kept grounds. Surely, she couldn't be serious about falling in love with Gadaffi?

I butted in with my story, which I had been burning to reveal all morning.

"Speaking of following, a boy followed me home from school. At least, that's what I suspect, as I don't wear glasses during my walk home in the hot sun. I couldn't see properly if he *was* really following me."

Aruni stopped damaging the grass and looked up. "So then, what makes you think he was following you?"

"*Hmmm*, it's a long story. I hope I can relate everything before the bell rings. You know the spot where the school bus stops in our junction? There's a shop called Upatissa Stores just there. You both get down well before that, so you don't know exactly where the shop is, but I've seen this same boy about three times, waiting on his bicycle on the side of the shop where the coconuts are. He always wears a short-sleeved poplin shirt with a printed design; he changes the shirt but not the trousers."

"It's wonderful how you manage to notice what he wears, with your bad eyesight and all that," Minaka said with a little giggle.

I had noticed his clothes and his tall frame while inside the bus and prior to removing my glasses, which I always did *before* getting off the bus each day due to reasons of, well, vanity.

"Anyway, it doesn't matter what he wears or doesn't wear. What happened?" Aruni demanded.

I had their full-fledged attention.

"Yesterday, before getting off the bus, I noticed him again. This time he was with a friend and not on his bicycle. They both looked at me as I got off, and I pretended not to notice. But I did see the friend nudging him and grinning. The friend looked so idiotic, with pimples all over his face."

"Were you hoping that he'd trip and fall in the coconuts?"

"*Hmm*. But he obviously didn't, as he was accompanying the boy on his mission for part of the way.

"I quickly crossed the road and started walking towards a wooded shortcut I preferred to take because it was shadier.

Amma didn't like me taking it. Sometimes it could be lonely, but at that time, there were other school children and teachers taking it.

I paused for breath and caught Aruni's impatient look. "So?"

"They both followed me at the beginning. I could hear their footsteps and low conversation, but I didn't look back, as I was feeling a little uncomfortable.

"My goodness," Minaka interjected.

"The shortcut leads through a huge field with large cows. I was hoping they wouldn't be there. I sometimes have to run from the cows, so it would have been a terribly comic sight, trying to avoid cows and boys both at the same time."

My two friends burst out laughing.

"For my bad luck, at that time, there weren't any people about, and I was thinking I didn't know what I would do if they stopped me and tried to talk. The public bathing well was deserted, too, when on most days there are a few people bathing."

"Were there any cows? Did he try to talk?" Aruni was impatient again.

"No, that's the funny thing. I began to relax a little bit after I crossed the field—the only cow there was tied to a tree at the far end. Then I saw him overtake me from the other side of the road and go ahead of me. He didn't even look at me and he was alone.

"I thought that was the end of it, but then, he slackened his pace once again and fell behind me."

"This is like the Katukurunda Motor Races, oh please ... go on," said Minaka, with a smile.

A Maiden's Prayer

"It wasn't so funny then. I was very uncomfortable – you know I have never spoken to a boy alone before?"

"I think he's interested in me. When I reached home, I didn't ring the bell at once. I sat down on the doorstep to remove the grass seeds from my socks: I had to do that to prevent Amma from coming across tell-tale signs that I was using the short-cut when she's washing my clothes. – When I looked up, who do I see? The boy."

"This time, he looked directly at me and I think he smiled. I really can't be sure; he was just a blur. He was going back, mission accomplished, which makes me think that he had no business in this neighborhood at all and all he wanted was to find out where I lived."

Aruni asked if I smiled back and whether he was handsome, despite my obvious disappointment of his fashion choice.

"Let me put it this way: he would be very presentable in the drawing room," I announced with a flourish of my hands.

I paused for the laughter and warmed up to my tale. "He is tall, fair and lean with straight, short-cut hair combed to a side. And not a curly hair or a sideburn in sight."

Either of the above would have disqualified him permanently from our common consideration. We were particularly "allergic" to those long ridiculous sideburns that broadened towards the base, taking up half the cheek like a recalcitrant fungus. My brother spent half his youthful life in front of the mirror, massaging and coaxing them to grow "like those of Engelbert Humperdinck."

"As for the other question, banish the thought. I didn't smile at all and treated him to one of my stony stares."

259

Truthfully, despite the display of bravado the next day, I was too scared to smile at boys, just in case they got the wrong idea. I wasn't really interested in getting friendly with this boy – or any boy – just yet. I was only sixteen. And Amma, for all her kindness, would skin me alive.

But all the same, it was exciting to be singled out. When I got home, I sat on the bed and hugged my knees in delight. My spirits were so elevated that while changing from my uniform into a cotton frock, I gave way to impulse and twirled about like a whirling dervish in front of the mirror, clad only in bra and panty. Yes, it was good to attract attention. It was significantly more real than falling in love with the head of a country who didn't know you existed.

***

Two weeks later, the boy followed me home again. This time, he spoke to me.

As I hurried home after school with head down to avoid the scorching rays of the mid-afternoon sun, I approached the field that I was not supposed to cross. There were other children about, bent on the same path of getting home sooner than later. I heard a bicycle approach as the rider slowed down, grinding his brakes. As I furtively glanced back, the boy was suddenly there. He smiled and halted abreast of me.

There was nothing to it, except say "hullo." My heart beat faster than usual in fear and embarrassment, as everybody seemed to be staring at us. I heard myself say, "So?" to mean, "What do you want, and who are you?"

He smiled and seemed uncertain of what to say. "My name is Sanjeeva. You're Tamara, aren't you? Is it all right if I talk to you?" he asked.

"*Err ... huh!*" Was that non-committal enough?

"Is it possible to meet you somewhere? I have something to ask you."

"I'm sorry," I said. "I cannot meet you, as I don't go anywhere by myself." This was partly true. Although I was not chaperoned everywhere like in the earlier days, I did not have the freedom to come and go as I pleased.

"Oh, don't say that. I have seen you walking with your neighbors. I'm sure you can manage something."

He had apparently done his homework well.

"I'm sorry," I said, and walked on hurriedly. I was aware that several school children had been watching the proceedings with great interest. At any moment I could be spotted by one of Amma's teacher friends who would be only too keen to report the news that I had been chatting with a boy. Thank goodness Quaver was tied to her piano at this hour.

Thankfully, he did not follow me, and I heard him reverse the bicycle, turn around, and leave on the same path.

The whole of next week, I didn't take the short cut and instead walked the longer route, hoping to throw him off the scent. And when I didn't see him for a few weeks after that, I thought I had succeeded.

***

That was until Sanjeeva started sending me letters, delivered by Anura with a knock on my bedroom window late in the evenings. They both attended the same school. I didn't reply to them at first. But after the fifth note came, and Anura had repeatedly inquired if I had a reply to be delivered, I knew I had to say something. I wrote saying that I was not interested in meeting him at a cinema hall.

261

How are you supposed to know that you are really in love? What is the defining moment, and how does it happen? Apart from thinking that Sanjeeva looked nice, I felt nothing toward him except anxiety and discomfort in his presence.

When I told Anoma about Sanjeeva, she asked me if I needed a boyfriend just yet. She didn't think I should rush into this just because I was asked. There is time for me, she said, and this did not seem to be the time.

There was sense in her quiet counsel, and I'm glad today that I didn't rush into things.

But all the same, I remember thinking at the time that someday, I would like to be swept away by someone in the manner that Anoma responded to Berty Uncle – instantly and whole-heartedly, without looking back.

Someday I hoped to find out the meaning of caring for somebody. Until then, I was content to follow the love of Berty Uncle and Anoma.

CHAPTER 25

THE WEDDING

August 1976

Berty Uncle arrived in Sri Lanka with days to spare before the wedding because he couldn't get longer time off on account of his frequent visits home that went beyond the allotted times.

The scramble lasted up to moments before the wedding. But he did make time for his bachelor party; his married friends had risen to the occasion to give a robust send-off to his bachelorhood.

Amid the toasting and the revelry in the smoke-filled bar, with many long remniscences, he lost track of time. Although he had a nagging doubt at the back of his mind that there was something more to accomplish before he could let alcohol govern him, he couldn't recollect the errand.

When Berty Uncle finally arrived at Nelson Uncle's house with his best man, Sarath, who was going to spend the night there, it was past midnight. They were waiting up for him. The neighborhood was enveloped in darkness, except around Nelson Uncle's house, which was illuminated by every existing light bulb, within and without. Nelson Uncle paced the front lawn. Asoka Aiya, the groomsman, was there too, and was my witness to the events that unfolded. The house seemed filled with people.

Berty Uncle barely alighted from the car before Olga Aunty, clad in a sari, came bounding out of the house.

"Why didn't you come at six o'clock, as I asked you?" she demanded.

"For what?"

"For lime-cutting."

"Didn't I ask you to forget about that nonsense?"

"Did you collect the suit?" Nelson Uncle butted in.

Berty Uncle froze. That was it. He had forgotten to collect his wedding suit from the Inter-Continental Hotel laundry, where he had taken it for pressing. He was aghast.

"Oh! That's what I forgot!"

"How are you going to take the photograph without the suit? You have to be at Donald's before seven in the morning."

Head spinning, Berty Uncle turned to his friend, the only solace. After all, what are best men for, except to solve problems? Isn't that their role?

"Sarath, what can we do? Do you know what time they open the laundry at Inter-Con? I need to get the suit for the photograph."

"You can't wait till morning. We must go back now and collect it. I'm sure the laundry is closed, but let's make some inquiries."

Sarath went to the phone, looked up the directory and called the hotel. The night manager was sympathetic, but compassion didn't solve problems. He did not want to open the laundry without permission from the laundry manager. Further inquiries revealed that, on occasion, Sarath had met the laundry manager in clubs along with his drinking buddies. On the strength of the acquaintance, Sarath did not hesitate to call him, in spite of the wee hours, to get his consent to release the suit.

A Maiden's Prayer

As they prepared to walk back to the car, Olga Aunty barred their way and demanded that Berty Uncle attend to the lime-cutting before leaving. "The man has been waiting for you since three o'clock, when he started getting everything ready. He was so restless and kept asking me when you'd get here," she said, without taking pains to hide her agitation.

Before he left the house in the morning, Olga Aunty had requested him to return in time for this ritual. He had asked her not to indulge in village traditions but knew that his sister-in-law wouldn't take no for an answer. He had meant to sit through the exercise only to humor her.

Olga Aunty led him away like a prisoner to the docks. She presented him to a middle-aged man who was sitting cross-legged on the ground in a far corner of the sitting room. He had the trademark hairstyle of a village occupation — longish hair tied in a little knot at the back. He cast an irritated look at the errant bridegroom.

The *kattadiya*, or the shaman, motioned Berty Uncle to sit on a mat placed in front of an elaborate little platform holding the paraphernalia of his assignment. The little shelf – the afternoon's labor – was made from bamboo stems, lined with banana leaves, and decorated with woven coconut leaves. His task today was comparatively simple. The man who traveled to remote villages to dance into the night exorcising evil spirits from afflicted mortals, who cast complicated voodoo spells and tied life-protecting talismans around portly bellies, had only to ensure Berty would enter wedlock minus the malevolent effects of evil eye.

Berty, the least of his demoniacal clients, sat with his eyes shut tight. His head spinning from the dual effects of alcohol and consternation, Asoka Aiya said Berty Uncle must not even have noticed the shelf or its trappings. He must have thought of Anoma, who was blissfully unaware of his predicament. This was a prickly bush from which he had to disentangle himself without thorns. After all the remote-controlled, elaborate planning of the past months, Berty Uncle could hardly sit for his wedding photograph wearing any suit he happened to have. His outfit must match the materials he had sent to the groomsman and the best man.

Berty Uncle opened his eyes and stared at a long strand of coconut flowers that curled toward him out of an earthenware pot. He shifted and fidgeted, then looked at his watch. It was 1 a.m. The man had to catch some sleep before his wedding, too, Asoka Aiya thought.

The *kattadiya* chanted softly, all the while fingering the pile of limes that received pride of place among the assortment of fruits and flowers. Nobody knew whether the lime or the reciting did the trick; but jointly, they were supposedly endowed with the power to ward off harm.

From tomorrow, Berty Uncle was going to be responsible for another person's happiness. He had to be more careful with his life. Asoka Aiya looked up sleepily to find the *kattadiya* had set one of the limes in between the sharp blades of an areca nut cutter and was circling the fruit around Berty Uncle's head.

The lime was now in motion, alongside his body and down to his toes. Crunch! It was halved in a quick motion, releasing its tangy aroma, and plunked into a basin of water.

Seven halved limes were plopped into the water before the *kattadiya* was satisfied that Berty Uncle would elude the spirit world. "*As waha, kata waha, apala dosa duru vuna* (evil eyes, evil words, malefic results, they have been vanquished)," he declared in a rumbling crescendo, to the satisfaction of Olga Aunty. He instructed her to discard his organic shelf, together with the fruits and flowers, at a three-way junction.

Berty Uncle grabbed his friend by the arm and rushed to the car, even before the *kattadiya* had time to examine the money that he gave him. Asoka Aiya found out that Berty Uncle had paid him twenty-five rupees; double the payment due because of his inordinately long wait.

***

The bridegroom had forty winks before it was time to get up. His mission to the hotel laundry in the dead of night had been successful, and the suit was in his possession. The sleep-deprived best man, Sarath, and the groomsman, Asoka Aiya, were dispatched with the bride's and bridesmaids' bouquets to Anoma's residence by 5:45 a.m.

***

The morning photography session at Donald's Studio went without a hitch, except that the flower girl and the page boy, both five years old and too young to understand their duties or responsibilities, were constantly crying for their mothers. As a result, the photographer spent what seemed like hours trying to soothe and distract them with a squeaking ball and a rag doll. I felt just like that doll after smiling at the dark spot above the black cloth-draped camera for the sixteenth time.

***

By 8:30 a.m., the bridal party was whisked away to a hotel room on the eighth floor until it was time for the wedding, which was slated to start at the auspicious time of 10:14 a.m. Berty Uncle and the members of his entourage got back into

267

the car and drove off to Galle Face to while away the time. He was not supposed to be with the bride at this time.

On the way, however, Berty Uncle was struck with what seemed a good idea. There was plenty of time to fritter, so he thought it was a good opportunity to accomplish something he had been toying with for the past few days. Anoma had noticed Berty Uncle's graying hairs and suggested he dye his hair before the wedding. Berty Uncle pretended to be offended. He was marrying her without asking her to change anything about herself. Why could she not do the same? Anoma had let it rest.

But here he was, passing the well-appointed Salon Seaside with plenty of time to spare and already becoming restless. He spoke his plan out aloud. Both Sarath and Asoka Aiya saw nothing wrong with it. After all, Salon Seaside was situated near enough to Inter-Continental Hotel, and even if there were a traffic jam, which was unlikely after the morning rush hour, they could walk to the hotel from the hair salon.

The trio walked into the salon. Berty Uncle explained his mission and soon, a young man arrived with gloved hands, covered him with a black gown, emptied a tub of foul-smelling cream all over his head and massaged it gently into his hair. Berty Uncle settled back and picked up a magazine.

The young man disappeared. Time passed. Berty Uncle became restless. The auspicious time for the *poruwa* ceremony, which was the traditional ritualistic part of the wedding, was approaching. Since it was still early in the morning, there were no other customers about. Sarath went further in and tapped on the door. The young man emerged and raised an inquiring eyebrow.

"Could you please finish the hair dying?" Berty Uncle asked from his chair.

"Oh, it has to work on the hair for an hour."

"One hour?" Berty Uncle jumped up from the barber chair. "But I'm going to a wedding!" He groaned.

"Well, what's the hurry? You can go a little late," suggested the young man. "After all, you're not the bridegroom."

"I am the bridegroom."

"Oh!" he said and hurried up to Berty Uncle. "Why didn't you tell me before? The dye has to be on for at least an hour to take effect." He snatched another pair of gloves and began rubbing Berty Uncle's head with blender-like movements.

***

A quarter of an hour later, the bridegroom and his party hurriedly made their way to the hotel. Berty Uncle joked that he still felt as though an electric beater was massaging his head. Only minutes remained for the ceremony to start. They parked in the first available parking space, which was towards the back of the premises near the hotel kitchens and hastened from the car. Their rather undignified entry did not lead the security guards to think that the bridegroom was among them.

The Inter-Continental, like many of the other Colombo hotels, was hosting several meetings connected to the Non-Aligned Summit that was taking place from August 16 to 19. Today was a busy day for them, with the likes of Yugoslavia's Marshall Tito and China's Chou En Li part of the delegation.

Three security guards rushed at Berty Uncle and his party and barred their path to the wedding hall.

"Where are you going?" they demanded.

"To the wedding," Berty Uncle replied.

"Show us your invitation," they said.

For the second time that morning, Berty was forced to declare that he was, indeed, the bridegroom.

***

Thankfully, the rest of the wedding was more predictable.

Anoma wore the traditional white sari, embroidered with sprigs of roses. Silver sequins sparkled when she moved. In a practice adopted during British rule, she wore a net veil that was pinned to her hair, styled in an elaborate coiffure. The veil and the hairstyle together gave her added height.

The man who applied the makeup had gone to town with pink blush. It may have been caused by the early hours he had begun working and helping to dress the bride, apply makeup, and pin the veil. Thankfully, he had spared her eyes, which were softly accentuated with black liner. Lipstick was also used in comely moderation.

Despite the prominent pink cheeks, Anoma's radiance was what you noticed about her first. Her eyes shone. It was a happy bride who was helped on to the *poruwa* – a decorated structure symbolizing a home – by the one available uncle. This part of the ceremony, administered by a village elder that Olga Aunty had procured, was nearly one-hour long and seemed one endless chant. Berty Uncle fidgeted but obliged the man's bidding. The couple's fingers were tied by a sanctified thread, and water was poured over the nuptial knot. Later, they worshipped their elders by presenting them with sheaves of betel and reached down to touch the elder's feet.

Next, Berty Uncle endured a bevy of pre-adolescent girls dressed in white cloth singing a string of verses called the *Jaya Mangala Gatha* from the Buddhist scriptures. We learned in school that each stanza was taken from the Buddha's life story of how he overcame obstacles and challenges with his virtues.

We bridesmaids looked smart in orange. After standing still during the formal ceremony, we became active, fulfilling our most important role of serving the cake. As instructed, we were on full alert, but stocks depleted fast because stockpiling cake at weddings is an evergreen Ceylonese sport.

From the guests' point of view, it helped if you knew the bridesmaids, but if not, a compliment or two on their embroidered saris did the trick to break the ice and allow them to help themselves liberally from the tray. More than half the guests put their cakes away: the ladies clicked open the silver or gold clasps in their handbags and nestled them on the satin-lined vanity bag in between the Chanel 5-scented handkerchief and the wedding invitation. The males slipped it inside the square pocket of their coats. Those who lived for the moment uncurled the extra-crinkly wrapper, making a din that drowned out the band playing *The Blue Danube*. The silver paper and the wax paper were removed also, and then they popped the moist fruit cake in their mouths.

Electric fans whirred above, but the guests huffed and puffed in the tropical heat. The males kept tugging at their collars and loosening their ties, while the females, looking weighed down by their heavy saris and gold jewelry intermittently fanned themselves with the wedding invitations.

Quaver looked every bit as sad and every bit as proud as she ought to be. She also looked different in a hakoba-embroidered sari; this was the first time the rest of the world had seen her in any outfit other than her long, white twill, walk-the-dogs dress and her trademark tight-around-thighs, boat-necked shifts.

Dhanawathi and the taciturn driver were expected to blend in with the furniture, as all servants should. But it was nearly

271

impossible to keep to their traditional roles that day; their *baby-nona* was getting married. From the beginning, the servant's exuberance was such that she started ushering and welcoming the guests until, I observed, Quaver spotted her unusually bold hospitality and squashed it with a stern look.

Dhanawathi was also decked out in a sari that day, a yellow butter nylon that Quaver had purchased for her. She had tied her hair in a knot at the nape of her neck; her one adornment was a small white flower pressed into the knot. The taciturn driver wore a national suit— a long white tunic shirt and cloth and a pair of brown slippers. The slippers were noteworthy because the driver never shod his feet.

Most brides cry when it is time to leave. Anoma clung to Quaver amidst cascading tears, while bridegroom Berty Uncle looked on sheepishly. It was not as though she was unhappy to leave with him, but this was the inevitable, heart-wrenching moment of parting familiar to every Ceylonese bride. She was leaving her nurturing environment and about to cross the point of no return.

Despite the emotions on display, Berty Uncle looked charming and happy. Thatha observed, too loudly, that "most husbands were cheerful at this stage in the game."

When she simply could not delay her departure any longer, Anoma bestowed one last tremulous smile on Quaver and the bridal couple rushed out of the wedding hall. Pelting them with grains of rice and confetti, the guests followed them to the waiting car. The younger folk had assembled some empty tins and coconut husks and affixed them to the back of the Mercedes-Benz. The assortment rattled along the ground as the chauffeured wedding car pulled out.

CHAPTER 26

MARRIED LIFE AND NATURAL DEVELOPMENTS

Time has a way of rushing when it should slow down and crawling when it should hurry. For Berty Uncle and Anoma, the days after the wedding flew by in a flurry of wedding visits, a trip to the cooler climes of Kandy in the upcountry and stays in picturesque rest houses overlooking misty paddy fields. Anoma did not tell me about the less hurried, sweet and intimate moments, but seeing them together, it was evident that they were drawing closer.

Just as certainly, the inevitable day of Berty Uncle's departure was drawing near.

Berty Uncle had found his anchor. The incessant clamor within him had ceased, giving way to an inner peace that quietly settles deep down inside when two people love each other. He did not actually say that to Thatha; it's my imagination.

Anoma told me that they were constantly making plans.

"Do you really have to go?" she would ask Berty Uncle for the umpteenth time, seated on the little cane chair that was in their temporary bedroom at Quaver's house, and not part of the sitting room quintet that Berty Uncle had learned to skirt around the past two weeks. It was too early for the racket at the piano, so they could speak without disturbance. Or so they thought.

"I can stay here, but my job is a good one with a lot of prospects." Berty Uncle offered the same reply. "How many people get a salary like mine with this many weeks of holidays, plus an air ticket to visit home?

The other thing is, don't you want to see the world? We can travel to other countries without coming to Ceylon on holiday all the time."

"See the world ...?" Anoma had not yet realized that her marriage had opened the door to overseas travel.

"England, I would like to see England," she enthused. "When I was small, I thought to go abroad meant going to England because nobody went anywhere else."

"England, Ireland, Scotland, Wales; you name it and we can go," replied Berty Uncle, counting them off on his fingers. "It's ..."

"Anoma! Berty! Why don't you come to Ceylon when you get your holidays? You can't forget your relatives like that." Quaver had been eavesdropping on their conversation from her bedroom and could not restrain herself. A few quick steps and she stood just outside the door curtain where Berty Uncle and Anoma could see her Bata-slippered feet. Before Berty Uncle could think of a suitably polite but firm retort, Dhanawathi shuffled into the hallway and told Quaver that the potatoes were growing eyes, and "it was time we cooked them."

In a little while, piano lessons would be in full swing and with that, the hated, endlessly repetitive scales that seemed to echo through the little house long after the students departed.

Everyone (except Anoma) – and everything – in that miniature household tested Berty Uncle's patience. It would be wonderful to start married life in a foreign land where no one would listen in on your bedroom conversations.

While Berty Uncle found it impossible to live there, even for a few weeks, Quaver had repeatedly asked Anoma why they couldn't settle down in her house. She bemoaned the fact that life would feel futile if she were to live alone. Besides, the house would belong to Anoma one day.

The same situation prevailed at Nelson Uncle's house. The hospitality factor was large, but the privacy factor was small, even though that house was considerably larger than Quaver's, Berty Uncle told my parents. If they were to settle in Ceylon, they had to have their own place.

Berty Uncle began to speak longingly of his Panadura estate. Was it time to ask Elisa Aunty to move out?

But then there was the question of getting a job during these bleak times. While pursuing a path of nationalization, Sirimavo Bandaranaike's coalition government had all but killed the private sector. The economy was shrinking, and large companies were closing. Engineering jobs in the construction industry were hard to come by. The few available jobs were in government corporations, but you had to know a politician to get one. Everybody was trying to cozy up to them, but only those with the strongest ties could hope to fill the limited vacancies.

For Berty Uncle, the only hope was re-joining the private company he had left, but he would have to wait until someone retired or they embarked on new projects.

Anoma was content either way. She was happy to begin her new life surrounded by familiar people in the place she had grown up. She had no inclination to abandon the one person who had been the only constant in her adult life to the woeful company of Dhanawathi and the reticent driver. But the prospect of living in a new country and sampling luxuries that she could only imagine – and visiting exotic places that she had heard about – was delightful.

So Berty Uncle decided to return to his job as planned. But before they could gallivant in Europe, he had to bring her to Saudi Arabia.

***

Spouses of Asian workers were not exactly welcomed with open arms in the Kingdom, and the lucky ones who had families with them were at the very top rungs of the ladder. Americans and Europeans were privileged with a completely different set of rules.

Berty Uncle wasted no time in approaching the personnel department through his manager to apply for a visa for his wife. He filled out the paperwork and handed over the required documents. Then he waited. He grumbled to Anoma about how slowly things were moving. The Saudi Arabian clerk who handled immigration matters greeted him with a robust "*As salam alaikum!*" and kept assuring him that his papers would be filed soon, but no sooner had Berty Uncle walked away from his table than the clerk conveniently forgot all about it.

"It's in their national make-up to delay things," Berty Uncle groused to Anoma on the phone. "Every day he says it will be done, but when I check the next time, they are still lying on his desk with a hundred other documents on top.

"All they want to do is sit in a circle drinking qahwa, talking at the tops of their voices in their guttural tongue."

"That must be why they need so many expats to run the show," Anoma volunteered.

"Exactly."

A whole month went by. Berty Uncle called Anoma daily, and sometimes twice in a day. His attachment surprised him. In his mind's eye, he saw her doing what she did best: bent over the keyboard, her long, loose hair caught in the dappled sunlight streaming through the window while the little house rang with a dulcet melody. He played back their conversations over and over again. In the office, his "in" basket was piled high and the "out" basket was near empty, he told Anoma. All sorts of little worries kept cropping up too, and he was fast becoming like the married friends he had scoffed at in the not-too-distant past. He had to bring her there.

He enlisted the help of an Egyptian clerk who pushed the visa application through to the labor office and was awaiting its confirmation impatiently when there was a new development. Anoma told him, hesitantly, that she had been nauseated several mornings in a row.

It could mean only one thing, but Berty Uncle was cautious. He told her to go with Quaver to see a doctor. He thought it was *saankawa*, a psychological effect of missing somebody that manifests itself physically.

A test confirmed that Anoma was pregnant.

***

The news was hailed with great joy around the family circle. "Now you must be very careful," Olga Aunty told the blushing young woman. "I hope it's a boy."

She and Nelson Uncle had driven around the same evening that Quaver had phoned with the news. We dropped by too, which meant just crossing the road. We all milled about the cane chairs, too excited to sit down and unbothered about dislodging the decor.

277

"I'm sure it will be a lovely baby girl," Thatha declared loudly, just to invite trouble. He was rewarded with a scowl from all the females present except the mother-to-be who hadn't figured out what to make of this sudden development.

"*Shhh* ... Keep your voice down. We don't want the neighbors to know yet. Don't you know that these things are kept quiet at the beginning?" It was considered inviting evil eye and bad luck to tell outsiders before the first three months could settle a pregnancy. Olga Aunty made everyone promise not to reveal the news; she even went to the kitchen to warn Dhanawathi.

When the dust settled and Anoma managed to control her blushing, the more practical side of the situation began to emerge. The baby was throwing life into disarray the way impending babies usually do.

It was unthinkable for Quaver and Olga Aunty that Anoma should go to a foreign country in her condition, and they surmised that Berty Uncle must return to Sri Lanka. They remembered the horror stories that Berty Uncle had related about quack doctors from neighboring Arab countries that "treated you for a headache if you went in for stomach pain." Berty had related these stories during his vacation Scheherazade nights. These anecdotes had lodged in their consciousness, and stripped of mirth, they stirred misgivings.

They didn't want her to go through a pregnancy and delivery without the family around.

Berty Uncle was the first to concede that Anoma would find it difficult to have a baby in a foreign land. Although hospital facilities in Saudi Arabia were second to none since Americans had set up the medical system in a no-money-spared scenario, there would be few other females, if any, to support her. What he knew about childbirth could fit onto that proverbial pinhead.

***

As Berty Uncle began contacting his friends in high places, Nelson Uncle and Olga Aunty were already working to retrieve his property. With a child on the way, they had fresh ammunition to move Elisa Aunty out of the family home. Despite cajoling, however, Elisa Aunty did not give a firm word about leaving. The baby was expected in July.

***

After the initial bouts of nausea abated and the first trimester passed, Anoma began to enjoy her pregnancy. It was impossible to do otherwise, she told me.

The food – and the love – came from all points of the compass. Early every Sunday morning, Dhanawathi was sent with the taciturn driver to the *jathika pola,* Colombo's weekly fair, for food and other necessities. Usually, Quaver went on this weekly market spree, but she was loath to leave Anoma by herself, so Dhanawathi was dispatched with a directive to bring the choicest slabs of seer fish, the freshest bundles of *gotukola* and the ripest *korathukolam* mangoes. Later, Quaver would supervise the cooking even while her pupils were at the piano, without allowing Dhanawathi to be left to her own devices in the kitchen.

Amma plucked ripened passion fruit from the profuse vine in our back garden. She made fresh mint sambol, an Anoma favorite, from glossy leaves gathered from the little vegetable plot that yielded produce without much prodding. She made her special, tempered dhal curry with its caramelized onion, causing a heavenly flavor that became an instant favorite of those who partook of it. I delivered the food to Anoma.

Maya, Mrs. Vithanage's wisp-of-a-servant-girl, often knocked on Quaver's door bearing a plate of breadfruit, a starchy fruit that grew in her back garden. Whether fried into chips, cooked in a creamy coconut milk curry, or just boiled, it was equally delicious.

Olga Aunty arrived with her special brand of nourishment, the results of Soma's cooking prowess. These ranged from *polos,* sweet sago pudding, and green jackfruit curry immersed in oodles of coconut milk, to large bunches of king coconuts from Berty Uncle's estate.

Even those from the poorer parts of the neighborhood, with whom Quaver only held a nodding acquaintance during her evening rambles with the dogs, exhibited their generosity with a fruit, a few leaves, or a sweet offered with a humble, betel-stained smile. Every woman was expected to bear children, yet every pregnancy was special and nurtured by all.

With her growing belly lightly supported by long cotton dresses in pastel pinks, blues, and yellows, Anoma returned to the piano, propped on the soft cushion Quaver had placed on the bench for her. *A Maiden's Prayer,* which had been neglected for a long while anyway, was supplanted, sometimes by the bubbly tempo of Beethoven's *Ode to Joy,* and sometimes by the slow and emotional *Angel's Serenade.*

***

Toward the end of February, when Berty Uncle gave up his job and returned home forever, Anoma's joy was complete. Berty Uncle unpacked bags full of baby paraphernalia that he had brought, faithfully adhering to the list that Anoma had sent him. Everything matched with everything, down to the large, pink and blue safety pins that would secure the cloth nappies. Anoma showed them to me proudly, basking in a maternal glow.

CHAPTER 27

ELECTION FEVER

June 1977

W hen he reached voting age, Asoka Aiya developed an interest in the political situation. He wasn't an exception by any means. It was a sign of the times. From the young student to the pensioner, everyone had been affected to some degree by the country's situation, and they were all gripped by the impending general elections.

Asoka Aiya opposed the ruling government with a vehemence that spread around our home and went over the fences into neighbors' homes, where it joined a patchwork of communities made up of those with similar thoughts.

But nowhere did his emotion find more fertile ground than in the house opposite us. This was the one subject that Asoka Aiya and Quaver saw eye to eye, and an alliance had been forged from their mutual dislike.

One Sunday, our family, like many others in the vicinity, was shaking off the past week's toils by taking in a leisurely breakfast. The coconut *roti* and *onion sambol* that Amma had made were spicy but amicable companions for the lazy morning, but the morning's tranquility was broken when a voice from a loudspeaker was heard intoning in increasing decibels.

Presently, a van decorated gaudily with green streamers and with a loudspeaker attached to its hood could be seen through the long windows, making strident rounds of the neighborhood and announcing that a United National Party election meeting was to be held that evening in the Battaramulla Junction. The guest of honor was Junius Richard Jayewardene, or J.R., as he was better known, the United National Party leader who was touted to win and form the next government. The newspapers introduced him as "a shrewd politician, cunning in the extreme, erudite, a good judge of people and a strategist superior."

Quaver rushed out of her house in one of her boat-necked shifts and stopped at the rusty iron gate that led to our house, and Asoka Aiya, Thatha, and I got up from the breakfast table, compelled outside by the commotion.

Maya, Mrs. Vithanage's wisp-of-a-servant girl, who needed little to be distracted from her chores, also emerged, followed by the purple house-coated form of Mrs. Vithanage herself, just as the van left the immediate neighborhood with two stray dogs running after it, barking in unison. Residents could finally resume thinking and hearing each other speak.

Election fever was at its height.

"Are you going to the meeting today?" Mrs. Vithanage asked Quaver and Thatha.

"J.R. is coming too," she added, her voice a hushed tone of respect. "Just imagine ... J.R. coming to Battaramulla?"

A son of a Supreme Court judge, J.R. hailed from a privileged and respected family in Colombo. He had followed in his father's footsteps but had also developed a career in politics since the 1940s. After three decades of waiting in the wings and watching a succession of prime ministers rule the country, everybody said that he was ready and able to govern the country.

"Everybody is the same," Thatha dampened Mrs. Vithanage's enthusiasm. "You wait and see what will happen if they win. They are all crooks!"

"They are all crooks, but if this government wins again, there'll be more shortages and rations," Asoka Aiya piped in. "At least, with the UNP, there'll be food on the shop shelves, and I won't have to stand in a bread queue at five in the morning."

It almost sounded like Asoka Aiya had political aspirations. It wasn't only his early morning excursions to the bread lines and the shortage of shirt lengths that colored my brother's dislike of the present administration. Asoka Aiya, going on nineteen, had passed his G.C.E. Advanced Levels with more than average results, despite the fears of our parents, and was looking for a job. Months had passed but none of his applications, close to forty at last count, had so far found favor with an employer or resulted in being called to an interview. There were many Asoka Aiyas fresh from school — about 700,000 people were unemployed — and few opportunities for them to start life.

Before Thatha could answer, another vehicle, this time adorned with flags of the ruling party's blue, could be heard, and seen coming down the road. Thinking that the group had congregated in their honor, the driver of the Morris Minor slowed down, and the man on the passenger seat launched a piercing announcement of a Sri Lanka Freedom Party election rally that was going to be held on Tuesday evening.

Mr. Vithanage, who had also ambled over by then, nodded his head vigorously up and down to indicate that his presence could be counted on. I knew that he would never go. He had a permanent hard-up pensioner's gaunt frame and a hollow look in his eye.

"I like the way they ease shortages when elections are around the corner," Quaver said. "We can now buy most foodstuff without a problem."

"Their policies are not that bad. They wanted to increase local production, but the way they did it was wrong." Just to be different, Thatha continued to support the government. "They are trying to make the country self-sufficient, but it was done in such a drastic manner that everything went wrong."

To the prime minister's credit, there was an international food crisis, and part of the tribulations that were felt by our people was brought on by forces beyond her control. Grocery staples such as sugar, flour, and rice were in short supply in the world market and had seen steep price hikes. She had taken the politically sensitive, drastic step of cutting down on imports that could be grown or substituted in Ceylon.

"It didn't help that they were having a good time, with foreign trips and imported food for themselves," Quaver muttered.

"On my way from work recently, I stopped at a government party meeting in Borella and listened to them," Thatha said. "They also had their arguments; 'how long can we depend on food imports? After all, we had always been a country that produced its own food before the British came. Why can't we do it now? As long as the imports are there, nobody will care to grow anything.'"

"Everything sounds good on paper, Thatha," Asoka Aiya replied. "It's when you go to implement the policies that it's difficult. It's the people who suffer."

"Yes, I prefer the UNP's policies, too," agreed Quaver. "People can make money and have a decent life."

"The UNP is known as the party for rich people. That's why the ardent leftist ideology is so strong now. The LSSP says they are working for the poor and that's why they are behind the government," Thatha rejoined.

"Everybody is so bitter at these election meetings," Asoka Aiya said. "If you go to a UNP meeting, you'll understand how much they want a change. They call it the seven-year curse."

"I think I'd like to go and see for myself what you've been describing to me all this time." Quaver paused as if hoping Asoka Aiya or Thatha would invite her to come along. But Asoka Aiya was going with his cricket friends and, not to be left out, I was going with Thatha.

***

The road to the election meeting was a sea of green decorations. Some were elaborate affairs in the shape of elephants – the UNP symbol – woven out of coconut leaves, while others were simple flower heads made of green polythene. Supporters handed out paper hats so that attendees could fill in any empty spots that were not of the party color.

In the middle of a small park, a stage had been erected. Rows of chairs covered in white cloths were awaiting dignitaries. More green was evident here, beginning with the backdrop that looked suspiciously like a butter nylon sari that snaked across the length of the stage and was pinned to wooden planks on either side. A dozen potted palms had been placed for good measure.

Until the distinguished guests arrived, party workers had devised entertainment to sustain the support and persuade anyone who may have been on the fence, to stay on. A man walked across the stage bearing a long stick, on top of which was an upturned, empty sardine tin. The crowd roared with laughter. They caught the joke at once. The government had recently imported a consignment of sardines and allowed every household one small tin so that each person had a scraping to wipe their bread. The mockery of the fishy election ploy was followed by another man bearing a long piece of paper, on which was written a litany of tribulations that had beset our country during the extended government of seven years. He proceeded to sing this in verse, pausing long and hard between each phrase to give onlookers time to absorb each incident and react accordingly. "The upcountry tea pluckers ate grass," he sang, "beggars ate dog flesh and banana skins, infants were malnourished, the middle class drank sugarless tea and ate tapioca for lunch while Sirimavo and her government globetrotted, divided the cabinet positions among relatives and celebrated the 80-lakh Non-Aligned 'wedding.'"

The ditty had the desired effect. When J.R. arrived at last and greeted the crowd with his palms together in front, he was, in turn, greeted with a thunderous roar of approval.

The quintessential politician, looking the more pristine in his spotless white national suit, played to the crowd. He told them exactly what they wanted to hear. He criticized the present government. He spoke of the just and free society that he would create, the basis of his platform.

He promised to reduce prices of essential goods, banish the queues, let people purchase commodities from anywhere they wished, create jobs for youth and resume imports. The crowds saw Bombay onions, Maisoor dhal, Maldive fish and bales of colorful chintz cloth. Some even saw Kraft cheese.

That balmy evening, J.R.'s promises were like a refreshing breeze. He wooed the crowds with staid dependability that emanated from his tall, statuesque frame. Everything he said seemed attainable. To them, he didn't appear like a con man dispensing impossible assurances. Above all, there was no rice from the moon.

That day, it was impossible to know that Sri Lanka was going to exchange a blackened pot for an equally darkened kettle.

CHAPTER 28

SODDEN FRANGIPANI

July 1977

On July 3, 1977, Thatha celebrated his fiftieth birthday with a stay at the General Hospital. Olga Aunty, Nelson Uncle, and everyone else was due to come home for lunch that Sunday, but they all crowded around the hospital bed instead.

Amma spoke to the doctor, a serious-looking young man who looked only a few years older than Asoka Aiya, who had a "chat" with Thatha on his Player's Navy Cut habits that could have had a more-than-minor role to play in his chest pains.

Those three days in Thatha's life should have robbed him of the desire for that amber liquid. Even if the collective "we told you so" looks bestowed upon him by his relatives were useless, the patient on the next bed, another hard drinker who slipped away from this existence with cirrhosis of the liver, should have jolted him. But it did not. For an alcoholic, memories are fleeting. Once out of the depressing hospital ward, after a few days of hope Amma palpably nurtured, he calmly went back to his ingrained habits. Before long he was "squeezing out" the last sixteen drops he insisted there remained in an empty arrack bottle.

***

On election day, July 21, Asoka Aiya and I stayed up all night, coloring the electoral map of Sri Lanka when the Sri Lanka Broadcasting Corporation announced each winner. My green felt pen ran dry.

J.R. came into power with a resounding majority and promised to create a benevolent society at a difficult time.

***

Over the next days, the papers were full of the new leader. When he addressed his fellow countrymen from the *Dalada Maligawa*, the Temple of the Sacred Tooth in Kandy, the largest ever crowd surged to the hill capital. People had even slept on the wayside from the previous night to glimpse him. During this historic occasion, the hill country echoed with cries of *sadhu sadhu*, the newspapers reported that he was venerated almost like a god.

That rainy Monday afternoon, I had returned from school and we were listening to a repeat broadcast of J.R.'s speech when there was a sharp tap on the door. It was Dhanawathi, wet and wide-eyed with the news that Anoma's time had come. Berty Uncle was at work; despite his fears, he had secured employment in a short time. Amma hurriedly wrapped a sari around her waist, snatched an umbrella and was off to the front house in a matter of minutes.

I followed her in the pelting rain. Dhanawathi clucked and hovered in the background. Because of the bad weather, the telephone lines were down, and Berty Uncle could not be informed. They were planning to call him from the hospital. Quaver and Amma piled into the Morris Minor and huddled near Anoma, birth pangs, extra pillows, packed bag, umbrella and all, while the taciturn driver, aware of the responsibility ahead, sat at the wheel, foot on the clutch and hand on the gear.

Off went Anoma.

What I learned next is from what Amma told Thatha later that evening.

***

At first, everything appeared to be progressing normally. Quaver and Amma had been with Anoma throughout her intensifying pains, murmuring words of encouragement, mopping her brow, and holding her hand. From time to time, Amma said Anoma had a spanner-like grip on her hand. The doctor arrived just in time to deliver the baby boy, who announced his entrance with a gusty cry that penetrated the rain. The umbilical cord was cut, the toes and fingers were counted, the blood was wiped off, and the baby was placed on a scale, where the arrow had leapt to the six-pound mark. There were no worries on that score.

Then, Anoma told Amma that she had fresh discomfort and was nauseous. She began to throw up, and a few moments later, she slumped. She started bleeding profusely and turning blue.

The medical team had turned their full attention to Anoma, and fresh doctors were summoned. The baby was whisked away to the nursery. Another nurse quickly shepherded Amma and Quaver away from the bedside and out the door.

***

Amma and Quaver sat on a wooden bench along the corridor and waited. They didn't make conversation, but their pounding hearts communicated with each other. Outside, the rain beat incessantly on the tiled roof of the private maternity

291

hospital. The air was chilly because some of the wind and mist permeated the high windows and wafted through the corridor. They were loath to go into the reception room even though the chairs were comfortable, and the room was sheltered from the elements.

They didn't want to leave the vicinity of Anoma's room in case they missed anything or were wanted inside. Even though they couldn't do anything to help her medically, Amma and Quaver felt that their loyal presence would help reassure Anoma in some subconscious way.

Half an hour passed. As Amma and Quaver sat waiting, a beaming family passed through the corridor, stopping to show off their newborn baby girl swaddled in pink.

Berty Uncle had still not arrived.

The bustle within intensified, with nurses hurriedly going to and fro and muffled sounds emanating from the room. They brought in an oxygen tank, as two hospital orderlies dressed in shirts and ankle-length white cloths hurried past them. One carried a pile of blankets and the other, a basin. Amma asked them how Anoma was faring, but she shook her head vigorously from side to side, went in, and quickly shut the door.

For an hour, they struggled to save Anoma, but they couldn't stop the bleeding from her semi-conscious body. She slipped away. Berty Uncle was delayed by a frangipani tree that had blocked his path, forcing him to drive a circuitous route to get to Anoma's side. When he arrived at last, Amma and Quaver, both sobbing uncontrollably, had to break the awful news: Anoma was dead.

The enormity of it all didn't register with Berty Uncle until he asked to see her. By that time, the blood had been cleaned up and the room smelled of antiseptic. Anoma looked peaceful, with nary a trace of the struggle she had endured just minutes before. Berty Uncle cradled her in his arms and wept before collapsing at her bedside. His son was in the nursery and he didn't see him on the day he was born.

***

Anoma's medical records showed that she suffered an extremely rare obstetric condition called amniotic fluid embolism. Respiratory failure had followed. It's caused when amniotic fluid, fetal cells, hair, or other debris enter the mother's bloodstream and trigger an allergic reaction. The emergency is so rare that most doctors never encounter it in their careers. Sometimes, the baby doesn't survive the ordeal either. This one did.

***

Afterward, Berty Uncle could only talk about the tree, as though he could have saved his wife if the tree had not delayed him. I think he masked his pain by talking about how a huge frangipani was toppled by the wind and blocked his exit to the street, just as he pulled out of the office car park. This effectively blocked his exit to the street as though unseen forces were at work.

Weeks later, he told us that, in his mind's eye, he could still see the stately bark and its widespread branches, the glistening green leaves, and the sodden white flowers lying limp about the water-logged parking lot.

***

A week after the death, we performed Anoma's seventh-day almsgiving at Quaver's place to transfer merit, a customary Buddhist tradition. We believe that the departed sometimes does not go on to its next birth immediately and the almsgiving may help to bolster merit, or good karma, to help attain a good birth.

Thatha, who works in a bank, had a financial simile to explain this to us. "Think of it as a bank account," he said. "Your past merits, or credits, are used up this birth and debited just like the money in your account. You are expected to deposit more funds or gather more merit during this birth to carry it forward for use in the next."

The evening before the almsgiving, Thatha and Asoka Aiya moved the furniture from Quaver's tiny drawing room into Anoma's former bedroom to accommodate the flat cushions that we brought from the temple. We covered the seating with white cotton saris and tablecloths and propped them against the walls. They made a stark contrast to the polished red floors. Woven mats were placed on the floor for us to sit on because, as a mark of respect, Buddhists don't sit on chairs when monks are present.

Early next morning, the family's cooks – the aunties and their servants – assembled to prepare and serve a nutritious and hearty mid-day meal to ten monks. The kitchen was small too; hence much of the preparation was done in the backyard that had also been set up for cooking. There was some spillover to the kitchen at our home as well.

This is the collective good deed that would produce merit. Buddhism teaches that this virtue may be transferred to those who may need it, and they can be either living or departed.

After lunch, the monks chanted from the sutras and then the head monk presented a sermon. We happen to be with the same people – family, friends and enemies included– in this life to work through unresolved issues from past lives, he said.

If people continue their alliances for over multiple lives, I hoped Berty Uncle and Anoma would have more time to resolve their issue when they meet in a future life. And hopefully, they wouldn't need us to bring them together.

During the bleak days that followed Anoma's funeral, I was guilt-ridden about our family's role. If destiny had sent that burglar into our house, did we unwittingly function as destiny's assistant, to arrange that fateful meeting between Berty Uncle and Anoma? If not for us, what were the chances of a sheltered young woman like her meeting a man who didn't even live here? If we had no hand in it, would destiny arrange for someone else to perform the chance meeting?

Also, did Berty Uncle accumulate bad karma by disappointing so many women and is this a fitting punishment?

Why didn't Berty Uncle and Anoma listen to the astrologer's advice? If they had waited five years, as he had indicated, they may not have had a baby and this tragedy could have been avoided.

Like a moth that encircles a lamplight, drawing closer and closer until it perishes in its heat, Anoma had been pulled toward Berty Uncle. Innocently, she had been drawn into the vortex of karma, and we were unconscious helpers.

These thoughts disturbed me the most. Additionally, Anoma's unexpected departure was a blow to me as well. I was beginning to rely on her serene wisdom, especially in the absence of an elder sister sounding board. Aruni and Minaka could only step in so far, and besides, being my age, they were faltering similarly on the journey of life. I couldn't see myself appointing Asoka Aiya as my confidante; he was of the wrong gender.

What was in store for me? Maybe I should follow the guidance from the horoscope to prevent calamities like these. I remembered the grumbling and the impudence I had exhibited during those first days of puberty. Maybe I should have endured the traditions without complaining; after all, I only had to sit inside a room for a few days surrounded by books and a female relative.

The priest also spoke at length about the impermanence of life and the inevitable suffering that follows birth. Rather than spending our time seeking enjoyment, which is short-lived and will only lead to more disenchantment and suffering, he said we should be mindful of using our lives to eliminate common vices such as greed, hate, and ignorance, as this will help bring peace to life.

***

Peace was the last thing our family could claim at that time. There were so many things to settle before we could allow time for private reflection and follow up on the priest's counsel.

Although Berty Uncle had eagerly awaited his child's birth, now that the baby was here, he didn't take to fatherhood as readily. Chanake saw even less of his father than of the other male figures around him, and that was not just because Berty Uncle was busy taking care of affairs after the funeral. It was because he was watching him from a distance. He was unable to reconcile himself to losing Anoma because of Chanake's birth and saw him as an intruder.

I think a mix of emotions crowded his brain. If he thought clearly, he would've realized that the baby was the only thing left to him of Anoma. She gave him a priceless gift before departing, but he didn't recognize it at the outset.

I heard Amma and Olga Aunty discuss how Chanake would most certainly develop some physical features of Anoma as he grows up that would constantly remind Berty Uncle of her. Just now, he looked like any baby, with a scanty head of soft black curling hair, toothless gums, and jerky limbs during the rare hours that he was awake.

To make matters worse, another storm brewed, heading straight toward poor Berty Uncle.

Berty Uncle and Anoma lived at Quaver's home while they were expecting their child, with the understanding that he would leave with the family once the Panadura house was vacant and renovated.

But after Anoma's passing, Berty Uncle told us he didn't want to take the baby to Quaver's home. He couldn't go back to sleeping in that bedroom with the memories of her fresh in his mind. Neither did he want to be part of the music teacher's structured household, nor want the longer work commute from her place.

The music teacher had stopped giving lessons, spoke little, ate even less and was given to brooding for hours. Given the changes, the family deemed that Quaver wasn't in a frame of mind to look after herself, let alone a few-days-old baby. So, when Olga Aunty had volunteered to look after the baby, Berty Uncle had jumped at the offer. Although she didn't have the experience of infant care, Soma could help, and the extended family supported his reasoning. There were also three loving sisters who were more than happy to share their knowledge. Also, the August school vacation was approaching, and Olga Aunty would be home for a whole month.

Pushing past the initial agonizing days of hopeless grief, Quaver begged Berty Uncle to fetch the baby home. By that time, Olga Aunty was in charge, once again, with Soma at the epicenter of all things baby. Berty Uncle didn't have the heart to move Chanake and unsettle everything once again. His response was to issue an open invitation to visit them as often as she liked.

That's how almost every single day, Quaver would visit Olga Aunty's place in Borella. She spent time in the nursery whence she issued brisk instructions to an overloaded and bristling Soma and found fault with both for their handling of the baby.

Olga Aunty called it meddling.

It didn't take long for the two women to openly develop a major tug-of-war to take possession of the baby and push the other away. They argued about the milk (Olga Aunty wanted to use Nespray for convenience, while Quaver recommended fresh milk be delivered every day, despite milk delivery becoming increasingly rare), the best method to put baby to sleep (Soma demonstrated that rocking fast, a type of bouncy movement up and down, did the trick, while Quaver believed in a warm bath, massage and singing a soothing lullaby), and the better food (Olga Aunty wanted to supplement the milk with store-bought powdered cereal and vegetables in baby food jars, while Quaver upheld that home-made blended greens and fruit were healthier).

The battle showed no signs of abating. All I could sense was Soma's plight, sandwiched by two substitute mothers and drowning in her workspace surrounded by pails of dirty nappies: a blue one marked #1 and a red other marked #2. Fortunately for her, Dhanawathi, was a welcome accompaniment to Quaver's visits. Entrusted with tackling the nappies, she washed and hung them on a clothesline to dry and even steam-ironed the cotton to kill any errant germs.

Back in our neighbourhood, there were no lullabyes to be heard, but sundown still ushered in melody along with the mosquitoes.

In the gathering hue of dusk, Quaver installed herself at the piano and banged out her new version of *A Maiden's Prayer*. She gave the andante piece a quicker tempo than it warranted and what she had meticulously taught us. I don't think the Polish composer intended the maiden to engage in a desperate gallop. Quaver abandoned the graceful charm and blushing romance of the ultimate drawing room refrain as she raced faster than the metronome on top of the instrument.

Then, when she came to the trills, she kept on trilling far longer than the standard length of the note, suspending the music in mid-air.

It was impossible to ignore the lull and continue with whatever we were doing. Everybody waited for her to resume. Cars slowed down outside the music teacher's gate and seemed reluctant to gather speed; youthful cricketers going home after a game piped down their discussion and suspended their imaginary bowling animations; Maya, Mrs. Vithanage's-wisp-of-a-servant-girl, aimed the water hose on the concrete and missed the plants. At home, Amma paused with the soup ladle held aloft the steaming hot liquid and burnt her forearm. At Quaver's place, the taciturn driver left his labors inside the garage and hastened to the window to peep in at the mistress through the grill.

After the prolonged trilling, the music ceased abruptly. Then Quaver emerged in her white twill dress with the dogs. I guess she was in a hurry to walk them, the one custom she didn't relinquish to the servants.

Her grief seemed to ebb and flow with her twilight meanderings that would now stretch into nightfall. Some days I could see Dhanawathi anxiously peering into the darkness, awaiting her mistress by the gate. The dogs, exhausted when they returned, flopped on the garage floor with their tongues hanging out, but Quaver was upright and even more energetic than when she had started out.

My guess is that during those long walks she was plotting her next steps.

***

Two months after Anoma's passing, the whole extended family was gathered at our house, including Quaver. What should have been a time of celebration was one of immense sorrow. Gone were the light-hearted conversations, hilarity, and games of our usual spend-the-days. Even Dhamith sat on a chair and stayed still. There was a simple meal of red rice, fried fish, a few vegetable curries, followed by bananas and papaw for dessert.

As expected, the chief topic of conversation was Baby Chanake.

Berty Uncle's son was now a bundle that spread joy in two ways — with an unexpectedly dimpled smile, and bright eyes affixed solemnly on us. If he missed his mother, he didn't show it. In any case, that day, there were so many people mothering him, taking turns to carry him, coo to him and embrace his chubby frame, that he was sunny and content.

Everyone avoided dwelling on Anoma and concentrated on his welfare.

Olga Aunty was vehement that Chanake would best thrive under her continuing care while Berty Uncle was at work. She was talking about giving up her teaching position and going into early retirement. She had also sent out word to friends and acquaintances that she was looking for a suitable woman to take over the kitchen, relieving Soma to dedicate her time just to the child. Soma, who had brought up a daughter, had proved herself to be a perfect and trustworthy ayah.

We all had an ayah when we were little; they were like a second mother, washing our clothes, making the bed, tidying up the room, feeding, soothing us when we cried and performing a multitude of tasks to make our lives comfortable.

Olga Aunty was the only aunty in our family who didn't have children. That meant that she didn't have any experience handling them, either. Quaver repeatedly pointed out the same argument.

Listening to my aunts, however, it seemed as though Quaver was the inexperienced person, even though she had raised Anoma, who was her sister's child.

This exchange would have gone on for hours if not for another unexpected guest. It was Quaver's old uncle, a frequent visitor nowadays, dropping by to inquire about her welfare. Dhanawathi had directed him to our place.

By then, Quaver was visibly rattled. She had barely greeted her uncle, who had found a chair and sat down, when she stood up and addressed us, hoarsely: "I couldn't bring up my daughter, but I'm not giving up my grandchild. This child," she pointed to him, "is of my own flesh and blood and belongs to me because he is my daughter's child," she announced.

301

Before anyone could utter a word, she pointed her finger at her uncle and beseeched him: "You tell them everything. Please tell them everything that happened and how I came to live in this neighborhood."

Saying those words, Quaver hurried out of the door as fast as her narrow shift dress and high heels allowed. We stared at her vanishing figure in mute disbelief. Then Berty Uncle rushed after her. We saw them sobbing and embracing wordlessly for many minutes before Quaver disentangled herself from him and fled inside her house.

CHAPTER 29

QUAVER'S STORY

At the time of Berty Uncle and Anoma's marriage, our family, along with the rest of the neighborhood, knew nothing of Quaver's story apart from what we had presumed, imagined, or eavesdropped about.

My empathy for the music teacher grew after the gritty details of her youth were divulged by the old uncle, who was perhaps the only living person who could attest to her true story.

I knew that he was good at ballroom dancing, as evidenced by his routine at every birthday party following a tot of arrack.

I had no idea that he was also a brilliant storyteller. To use a hackneyed phrase, the plot thickened considerably. He didn't spare any details, and it seemed as though he was waiting for a chance to expose his family's skeleton that had been concealed in the closet for decades.

We were just after lunch and it was past teatime when he finished his account. Partway through, I slipped away to my room and fetched my notebook to record some of the colorful images he recreated on that unforgettable day.

***

Quaver's story reverts to 1945, to the sleepy hamlet of Thelikada, near Sri Lanka's southern port city of Galle. With its patchwork of green fields and coconut plantations, the tiny village was so far removed from the hustle and bustle of its nearest city that its inhabitants almost required a good pinch to wake up in the morning.

Norah Dias was the younger of two daughters born to a pair of respectable parents of modest means who breathed life into the expression, "poles apart."

Her mother, Rosa, was from the capital city of Colombo. She had once frequented posh restaurants, walked the breezy promenade of Galle Face, and tucked into many-decked sandwiches and jelly ice cream.

As an English teacher, Rosa's first teaching appointment was in Thelikada. When she met the principal of the *maha vidyalaya*, fate had played its role. It was difficult to fathom if she had repented at leisure her decision to marry the principal even before the first school term had lapsed. She had been about twenty-two years of age then. The uncle was reluctant to comment. He would willingly wash in public only so much dirty linen. But what did it matter? They were both long gone.

Rosa was forced to adapt to life in Thelikada, where country folk bathed in public wells and made a pastime of making thick buffalo curd in clay pots, drying lime pickle and rearing chickens and goats in their backyards. In this environment, she found few with whom she could converse in her excellent English and fewer yet who could appreciate her gifted piano-playing.

Norah's father spoke only Sinhala. As principal of the school, he resolutely wore the pure white national attire of his countrymen without adopting the British garb of shirt and pants, and maintained that his surname, Dias, an inheritance from a name-taking ancestor angling for favors from his Portuguese masters, was the only foreign thing he would tolerate in his life. He had sanctioned his younger daughter's first name only after a great battle. The elder daughter was named after a flower that occurs often in Buddhist scriptures as a comparison point because of its purity and beauty in spite of growing in muddy water: Nelum or lotus.

Consumed by occultism, the principal tiptoed around auspicious timings and ancient Sinhalese beliefs. A cawing crow meant impending visits by relatives, a screeching gecko meant an important decision should not be taken and a howling dog at the front door portended bad luck. Glass breaking on the first day of the month meant a series of breakages lasting several days. He never left home on an important undertaking without consulting the *horawa*, or favorable time of day, and figuring which way he should face when he took his first step. One day, finding that none of the doors in the house faced the appropriate direction, he opened a window and sprang on to a flower bed and fell into a pat of gooey cow manure, but picked himself up and proceeded unfazed while the rest of the family looked on, amused.

During school holidays, the principal spent his time visiting the village temples in the area and strengthening his friendships with the Buddhist priests he had known since childhood. He would often sit with them in the sermon halls, learn difficult concepts of the religion and practice the knowledge on his wife, thereby reinforcing it in his own mind.

The religion's basic concepts of *dharma, samsara, karma,* and *ahimsa* had taken on rice-and-curry familiarity in the family. Dharma refers to the teachings of Buddha; samsara to the life cycle of birth-death-rebirth; karma to the effects of good or bad deeds on a person's rebirths; and ahimsa, the doctrine of nonviolence toward living things.

Dhammapada, the encyclopedic teachings of the Buddha, deeply influenced the principal's life. Barely would the evening shadows fall without him reciting a stanza or two in his school principal tone.

"As a deep lake is tranquil and undisturbed, so do wise men become tranquil heaving heard the Teachings," he would intone to his daughters.

"Oneself is one's own protector. Who else could the protector be? With self well-subdued, one obtains the protection which is difficult to obtain."

I wished Norah would have taken this stanza from Dhammapada to heart.

The village school, like all impoverished government schools in sleepy hamlets, was Spartan in resource. Norah was sent here despite the drawbacks, not of her parents' choosing, but because there were none to choose from in that godforsaken place. They were far too young to be sent away to a boarding school in Colombo. Rosa ensured that they were fluent speakers of English language and trained them to play Western music on the piano.

Regardless of being the principal's daughter, the books that Norah received were the regular dog-eared editions that were handed from each graduating class. The principal had his principles, and favoritism was disallowed.

Norah and her sister Nelum traveled to school in a little buggy cart, called a *tirikkele*, drawn by a bull, around whose neck was a chain of bells that announced its arrival. Urged on by the carter, the bull – along with the cart and its occupants – often overtook their classmates kicking stones while walking to school.

Some of her classmates helped their fathers at brickmaking, which was a local industry. Hence their clothing, whatever they had, was patched and stained.

While Norah put on a clean white uniform every school day, most of her classmates wore the one uniform they owned, which was subject to constant scrubbing at the community well. The school boasted of neither tie, badge, nor buckle to give itself recognition and standing. Alas, some of its students arrived sans belt.

But everyone was level on the playing field. During the interval, the girls played *batta*, or hopscotch, pushing around a piece of slate that stirred the red earth under the leafy canopy of the jam tree. The boys played cricket; wielding bats fashioned with the sturdy stem of a coconut branch. Designer willows were not within their reach, but the air rang with exuberant "howzaaats," raucous umpires settled disputes at the pitch and windowpanes shattered all the same.

It was underneath that same jam tree that Norah and her classmates sat for lessons on days that the sun was not scorching and the air cooled after the monsoon rains. While the teacher droned from the textbook and the buffalo mewed from the nearby paddy field, the children engaged in what was deemed a more fruitful pastime; they looked up and scanned the branches for the tiny, yellowing jam fruit; the boughs were constantly plucked bare of its delicious harvest.

Norah hardly ever left the village, her uncle recalled. During her childhood, she had never seen the sea, although the port of Galle, its treasured marine harbor with its famous lighthouse and the ramparts built by the Dutch colonialists, were only a few miles away. Servants referred to the sea as the *hogana pokuna,* or the roaring pond. But as a child, she was

307

never to know that her curiosity to lick the salty air would propel her toward a disaster that would change her life forever.

* * *

Early school life passed gently enough. Unlike Nelum, who had been married off to a doctor as soon as she passed her eighteenth birthday, Norah had shown promise in scholarship. The principal, keenly expectant of a learned offspring, rewarded her by enrollment in higher studies at the revered Sacred Heart Convent in Galle. Feeling that she would be happier in a home atmosphere rather than in the school boarding facility, they installed her with a family that they knew who resided close to the school.

During the first two years, Norah came home during long weekends and school holidays. Her father would either come himself or send a servant to accompany her on her bus journey to Thelikada. Later, as she progressed into advanced level classes that required more serious study, she came home less and less.

Past adolescence, Norah was fast shedding her baby fat and growing into a good-looking young woman. She had an angular face made the more arresting by large eyes. A luscious plait of straight hair swished below her waist when she walked – that and her long legs began to hold the attention of those who beheld her.

When the uncle made these comments about the youthful Nora's appearance, his wrinkled face took on a look of abject sorrow.

Among those who noticed her, was a young cousin in the household in the first flush of adrenalin. But hardly had the cousin started making inroads into her schoolgirl existence, when Norah found herself befriended by a relative who frequented the house. With the maturity and the lasciviousness that comes with middle age, the relative used his cunning and lured Norah on a trip to show her the sea.

***

Nothing untoward happened to Norah during her initial trip to the ancient Galle Fort, which she managed to pull off in the guise of attending a tuition class. Even though she was a boarder, the family was under instruction to monitor her movements.

Norah and the man walked along the breezy waterfront toward the white, conical tower of the lighthouse. She delighted in the vastness of the sea's azure waves and hurled a coconut shell into the horizon with the abandon of an urchin.

When she smiled and licked the salt off her lips, rubbed her palms together to discard the last grains of sand and looked about, her face was a picture of rosy good health. Fate should have rung a warning bell, the uncle said.

Every fifteen seconds, the lighthouse flashed two white lights to warn seafarers about perils, but it didn't do anything to caution Norah about impending doom, the uncle said.

The clocktower and the stilt fishermen in the shallow sea should have kept a watchful eye. They didn't, the uncle said.

No harm came to Norah during subsequent trips when she found herself exploring the historic Dutch ramparts that dotted the fortified city. But trust was established, and along with trust, she was attracted to this man. The relative was self-assured and charming, unlike the youth who bumbled about for her attentions with a voice that still bordered on squeakiness, and a chin that featured a few straggling hairs.

When they drew closer, Norah was a willing partner to his all-encompassing embrace and quietly believed that his emotions were as involved as hers. She didn't question his motives or marital status.

***

A few weeks later, when her mornings were nauseated and the household was noticing a change in her temperament, the relative vanished into the sunset. Norah was dispatched home, a disoriented young woman returning to a pair of bewildered parents.

The principal took refuge in Buddhism. He shut himself for hours in his study room surrounded by the Dhammapada and other instructional books and the remnants of an occasional rice and curry meal. He could barely look at his pregnant daughter.

But her mother didn't express her desperation at the piano. Rosa took matters to hand when her husband didn't emerge from his study despite loud entreaties and bangings on the door. She quickly sent Norah to her sister who was now in the eastern city of Trincomalee with her doctor husband. To the villagers and their relatives, she maintained that Norah was in school.

Fortunately for Norah – or unfortunately, depending on how you look at the circumstances – the sister was childless after six years of marriage. After the baby girl was born, she gladly took over her mothering and the husband took a transfer to another city where they would be unknown.

It took a few years for Rosa to convince her now-introverted husband that they had to do the same: retire from his employment, sell their property in the village and move into the suburbs of Colombo like the rest of the post-war migrating population. Their only strength came from the uncle himself – privy to the story, he assisted them during the upheaval and helped resettle them in the small suburb of Battaramulla. It was no easy task to uproot and transport the village principal with his cultural beliefs, but it was accomplished, the uncle said, with more than a modicum of patience on Rosa's part.

In the suburbs of Colombo, away from prying eyes, they could start life anew. They knew it would be impossible to get Norah married unless they were away from the well-meaning but gossiping villagers who generally appraised each other of every tidbit of news at the community bathing well.

Then destiny dealt another blow. Nelum and her husband met with a fatal car crash.

***

The uncle paused and wiped moist eyes with his handkerchief. The adults looked away. Dhamith went to him. I fetched him a welcome glass of water.

When little Anoma came to live with them, Rosa and Norah raised her, he resumed. By then, both had started giving music lessons to neighborhood children and were making a lucrative income.

Although the principal was no longer employed and drew only a pension, money was not a hitch to the family. They maintained a household with many upper middle-class amenities such as servents and a vehicle with a driver. But marrying off Norah, who showed a marked distrust of all men, posed a problem. The young woman refused several advantageous marriage proposals that came her way.

In the years after her parents died, Norah continued to isolate herself and live in her inherited Battaramulla home

Srianthi Perera

opposite to ours. She was independent and lacked no material comfort.

***

But people like Norah, whose lives did not fit into the mould sanctioned by society as the only proper one, invited speculation. A self-sufficient, unmarried woman in her late forties was a foreign body lodged in a place where it did not belong. They felt a misguided pity for her and took a vicarious pleasure in digging into her life. They imagined the problems she must face and the tribulations that were different from those that challenged themselves.

Whenever I overheard Amma and next-door-Mrs. Vithanage conferring about Quaver, even they mustered a tone of pity, although Quaver was better off financially than either of them, and even owned a car.

Fearful of neighbors finding out and apprehensive of saddening Anoma further, Norah never divulged to Anoma the secret of her birth. She contended that a birth out of wedlock would scar a woman even more than a pregnancy out of marriage.

***

Nobody moved a muscle, except for Olga Aunty, who looked shamefaced. I knew what she was thinking. There was no further argument to make: she was Berty Uncle's sister-in-law, which made Chanake her nephew by marriage, while he was Quaver's grandchild.

Quaver's dilemma was such that she risked revealing her long-guarded secret to the detriment of what society thought of her, to help claim her kinship to Chanake.

CHAPTER 30

OPENING A DOOR TO HOPE

Elisa Aunty didn't move out of the property without a fight. Although there were some acres of land that still belonged to her, she didn't have the wherewithal to build a house. The nephews were still staking out their territory there as well. The only way we could get them to vacate it was with a chunk of cash from Berty Uncle that could go toward renting a home at first and then building something of their own later.

Berty Uncle didn't care about how he spent his bounty from Saudi Arabia. He wouldn't have bothered about the ancestral house either, except that his ailing father had made him promise to keep it in the family. He was doing his best to defer to those wishes.

***

Nearly three months following the tragedy, Berty Uncle took possession of his Panadura home, grudgingly vacated by Elisa Aunty and her brood. Everybody accompanied him on his first visit with the door keys, so that he wouldn't feel alone in the world. That is, everybody except Quaver, who was home with the baby. It was her turn to bond with him.

"Nobody is going to be a winner when you fight for properties. There's always an unhappy ending to these quarrels," Thatha commented when Berty Uncle was out of earshot, inspecting the kerosene kitchen stove that had all but disappeared in progressive layers of soot.

"That's the only bit of sense Oswald has uttered in his adult life," Mary Aunty whispered to Beaula Aunty, who narrowly escaped from crunching an upturned, long-dead cockroach beneath her chappals.

Malkanthi sighed behind them, smelling of a medicinal balm that was welcome just this once, in the confines of that grimy kitchen.

As one, we moved through the dank rooms, clad in ghostly white and gray in observance of the three-month mourning period for Anoma. Berty Uncle made notes in a small black notebook, and I wondered if he were jotting down memories or simply something concerning the repairs to come—most likely the latter. The dark circles beneath his eyes spoke of the wakefulness of lonely nights.

Wordlessly, he noted the peeling paint on the ceiling and cobwebbed light fixtures; the faded cream wallpaper and grimy walls. Brick had become exposed here and there, and the windows that had always proved stubborn to open were now pocked with broken panes and loose jambs.

We took the stairs in single file lest we overburden the steps. The landing was bordered by a wrap-around verandah that looked out into the back garden and a portion of the roof below.

The bright section of new red roof tile shone like a medal of honor pinned to the other dull gray shingles. We scanned the grounds, which were too wild to explore, but we could see the thriving fruit trees in the thicket beyond. Hearing our babel of voices, a pair of mynah birds left their camouflage in a mango tree and fled into the distance.

A Maiden's Prayer

We began exploring the rooms. Berty Uncle brightened when he entered one in particular. This was the bedroom of his boyhood, he told us. Residual bric-a-brac and long-ago family treasures, like the old rocking horse, were scattered about the room and relegated to shadowy corners. Due to its sorry state, it hadn't been inhabited by the last occupants. Berty Uncle set the wooden toy in motion and simultaneously released a steam of dust. He voiced his remembrance of clutching the strong handles and rocking himself for hours.

"I can see Chanake doing the same in here," he said, thoughtfully. I saw Olga Aunty and Amma exchange a tiny smile after a long time.

Olga Aunty told Amma that it would be months before he could make the place habitable for his son and mother-in-law. It was good for Berty Uncle to have this huge project on his hands to take his mind off things, she whispered.

Berty Uncle's cumbersome inheritance was a blessing in disguise. He would be engrossed in the work he did best while being wrapped up in the greatest healer's embrace.

At the end of the tour, Berty Uncle felt he had plenty to do inside the house before tackling the outside. Wearing his civil engineering hat, he had filled many pages of his notebook. But, from time to time, the hat dislodged, and his face reflected the haunted look of a man who had lost his way. That's when the vertical worry lines above his nose became pronounced and his usually alert eyes became vacuous. That's when he was more wilting than alive.

Downstairs, I peeked through the glass-fronted cabinet that had sheltered the now moth-eaten Mudaliyar coat, a ceremonial costume of the British Mudaliyar class of Sri

Lankan history, for more than a century. One of its silver buttons had come loose and fallen away into the darkness.

I sighed. Given time, everything could be repaired. Everything that is, except perhaps Berty Uncle's heart.

Make an author happy today! If you enjoyed this book, please consider posting a review on amazon.com/author/srianthiperera. Even if it is only a few sentences, it would be a huge help.

GLOSSARY

Ambul bananas: A variety of small, chubby, and sour bananas.

Aney, Aiyoo, Chee, I say and *Myeee*: Sri Lankan expressions used frequently to denote a spectrum of emotions such as surprise, dismay, sorrow, and sarcasm.

Baila: A form of lively, danceable music that originated in Sri Lanka with Portuguese influence centuries ago.

Bothaal, pathraiii: Bottles, paper.

Dasha kalaya: Planetary period.   *Marakaya:* Planetary period with negative result.

Dagaba: A dome-shaped shrine that may contain relics of the Buddha, also known as a *stupa, chaitya* or *vehera.*

Dhobi: Washer caste folk who regularly wash clothes for families.

Duwa: Tamara de Silva is also referred to as Duwa, meaning daughter, Akki, meaning elder sister and Baby or Baby-Nona, which is a common servants' term of respect to a child or member of the younger generation in a household. (The Dhobi uses the iteration Babee.)

Enid Blyton: A prolific English children's writer whose work is immensely popular in Sri Lanka. Her series includes The Famous Five, The Secret Seven, Mallory Towers, The Circus Series, The Mistletoe Farm, St. Claire's and Noddy.

Ethin Kohomada: So, how are you?

Forward Peter: A childish term for a bold person.

Bodu Govi: Sinhalese belonging to the Govi caste and Buddhist religion. About half of the Sinhalese population belong to the Govi caste, which is agricultural in origin.

Frangipani: Also known as plumeria and *araliya,* this deciduous shrub is related to the oleander. The flowers grow in clusters and some varieties emit a fragrance.

Habarala **leaves:** Large leaves of the taro tree that can provide shade from the elements.

Handahana: Horoscope

Kottamba **tree:** *Terminalia catappa* is the botanical name of Sri Lanka's own tropical almond tree.

Lascarins: Indigenous soldiers who served during colonial times.

Lavulu: Eggfruit, a yellow-orange fruit which may be scooped out in the manner of an avocado.

Mahattaya, Loku Mahattaya: Sir and Senior Sir.

Malefic horoscopes: A planet placed in a horoscope to bring a malign influence on a person's life.

Mallum: A dish of finely cut green leaves.

Manioc and *Koss ata*: Kasava and seeds of the jackfruit tree.

Milk rice: Rice cooked with coconut milk, usually partaken during personal, cultural and religious celebrations. *Kavum, kokis* and *athiraha* are sweetmeats made with rice flour and honey made for such occasions.

Yes men/No men: A Sri Lankan expression that does not attach any meaning but reinforces the expressed sentiment, either positively or negatively.

Nona: Madam.

Ola leaf: Leaves from the Talipot palm tree are used as the base to write/carve horoscopes.

Perahera: Sri Lankan street procession with caparisoned elephants, traditional dancers, musicians and religious dignitaries. The largest, the Kandy Esala Perahera, is held in July and August in Kandy. It is also known as The Festival of the Tooth because it pays homage to the Sacred Tooth Relic of the Buddha housed in the Dalada Maligawa.

Pirith **chanting**: Buddhist blessing invocation.

Porondam: Twenty factors of compatibility for a marriage such as long-term attraction for each other; status of the subconscious mind; a stable bond; genealogy; caste and family background; and life expectancy.

Poya: The full moon day of each month is known as Poya and is a public holiday to allow time for Buddhist practices.

Putha: Son.

Roti, stringhoppers, hoppers **and** *pittu*: Sri Lankan meal staples made of rice flour combined with shredded coconut/milk.

Somerset Maugham: A popular English novelist in the mid-Twentieth century.

Sutra: Buddhist scripture.

Tamasha: Party.

Veda Mahattaya: Village doctor who practiced Ayurvedic medicine.

RECIPES

Following are some recipes from Blossom de Silva's kitchen. As you know, Blossom is a great cook and has a stash of recipes to display her prowess. These were selected for their availability of ingredients in the Western world; in some cases, substitute ingredients are offered. A couple of them were sneaked in because they are Tamara's favorites. Please note that a visit to an Asian store (preferably Indian) is recommended to gather the items.

Kiribath (coconut milk rice)

2 cups white short-grain rice (not Basmati)
5 cups water
3 cups coconut milk
Salt to taste

Method:
- Rinse rice and combine with water in a large pot, then bring to a boil uncovered.
- Cover and simmer on low heat until water is absorbed and rice is tender (about 20 to 25 minutes).
- Add coconut milk, stirring until well mixed.
- Simmer on low heat until coconut milk is absorbed by rice (about 15 minutes).
- Remove from stove, and cool for about ten minutes before turning into a 2 ½ quart (2.3 liter) glass pan.
- Flatten, cool, and cut two-inch squares.

- Serve with chicken curry and seeni sambol for a spicy meal or with a banana, honey, sugar or jaggery (brown sugar block) for a sweet snack.

*You may also make this dish in a rice cooker. First prepare the rice and water according to the cooker's direction. Open cooker and mix in the coconut milk and salt. Reset the cooker for about five minutes. Flatten onto a 2 ½ quart glass dish and cut into slices.

Chicken Curry

2 pounds chicken cut into pieces; bone-in is more flavorful, cut smaller pieces if boneless
1 tablespoon of Sri Lankan curry powder
1 teaspoon red chili powder
Salt
¼ teaspoon turmeric
1 stick of cinnamon
1 tablespoon tamarind paste
Cooking oil
2 cloves garlic and 1 inch-sized piece of ginger
1 large tomato
1 cup of coconut milk, sour cream, yogurt or regular milk
3 sprigs of curry leaves chopped into inch-size pieces
½ large red onion
½ cup water

Method:
- Marinate chicken with spice powder, turmeric, salt and chili powder. Then rub tamarind. Refrigerate overnight.
- Add garlic and ginger to heated oil and sauté over medium-to-high heat until aroma rises.
- Add the onion, cinnamon stick and the leaves, and continue to sauté about four more minutes.
- Add the marinated chicken.
- Mix and add water and then the chopped tomato.
- Reduce heat and simmer for about half an hour, turning the pieces intermittently.
- Add milk and cook another 5 minutes, or until the gravy thickens.

Seeni Sambol
(vegan, sweet, and spicy onion relish)

5 large red or yellow onions diced (the reds are known as
Bombay Onions in Sri Lanka)
vegetable oil
3 sprigs of curry leaves chopped into inch-size pieces
3 stalks of lemongrass, each cut into thirds
2 teaspoons of tamarind paste diluted in a little water
4 cloves of garlic, a half-inch piece of ginger, stick of
cinnamon
1 teaspoon of black or brown curry powder from Sri Lanka
(Available in South Asian supermarkets, if not, substitute
with one from India).
½ a spoon of coarsely grounded chili
1 teaspoon sugar
Salt to taste.

Method:
- Sauté onions with oil over medium heat, stirring from time
to time.
- Add the lemongrass, curry leaves, cinnamon, salt, and the
spice powders.
- In about half an hour, when the onions darken, add the
tamarind and sugar.
- Keep stirring until the mix is caramelized further and
remove from the heat.

Vegetable/Egg Fried Rice

2 tablespoons each of butter and vegetable oil
2 cups of Basmati rice, washed twice
3 cups of water
1-inch piece of ginger
4 cloves of garlic
6 pepper corns
3 cardamoms
2 sprigs of curry leaves
2 Bouillon soup cubes (or a tablespoon of paste), chicken or vegetable flavor
salt and pepper to taste
2 teaspoons of coriander and cumin seeds powdered together; if you do not have both, one will suffice
2 medium carrots, 1/2 a head cabbage and 1 stem of leeks lightly sautéed together for about 5 minutes in vegetable oil.
Topping:
For egg rice, make omelet out of four eggs and break it into pieces.
Roasted cashews.

Method:
- Heat the butter and oil in a large pan and sauté the uncooked rice along with the garlic, ginger, spice powder, soup cubes, pepper corns, cardamoms and curry leaves.
- Transfer to rice cooker, add water and cook to done.
- Add vegetables to rice, along with pepper and salt to taste.
- Transfer to serving dish and top with cashew nuts and/or omelet.

Sri Lankan Roti/Flatbread

1 cup wheat flour
1 cup grated unsweetened flaked coconut (fresh is best)
Salt to taste
Shortening for the griddle.

Method:
- If coconut is not freshly grated, add about a quarter cup of warm water and allow it to fluff up a bit.
- Add flour and salt and mix with cold water to make a wet dough that can be molded by hand (add flour if it's too wet).
- Separate with a wooden spoon into two-inch thick pieces.
- Heat an oiled griddle. Rub some cooking oil in your palms, take each ball of dough, flatten it to a round shape on a greased saucer and transfer to griddle.
- Cook over medium heat, turning with prongs or steel spatula.
- Repeat until all the dough is cooked.
- The finished roti will have brown patches but take care not to burn them black.
They are delicious with butter and jam.

Tempered Lentils (dal)

½ cup orange lentils
1/2 cup coconut milk
1/4 teaspoon turmeric
1/2 large red onion
3 sprigs of curry leaves
1/4 teaspoon of coarsely chopped red chili, add more if
desired
2 tablespoons vegetable oil.

Method:
- Wash lentils, then add to water and turmeric in a saucepan
and bring to a boil. They will be soft when done.
- Transfer the lentils to a glass dish and add the coconut milk
and salt.
- Return the saucepan to the heat, add the oil, onions and
curry leaves, then sauté. Add the chili and continue
caramelizing until aroma rises, about ten minutes.
- Add the lentils and coconut mixture back into the saucepan
and reheat thoroughly.

Sago Pudding

3/4 cup small-seeded sago
3 cardamoms, bruised (if using powdered, use ¼ teaspoon)
2 cups water
1 cup cow's milk
1 cup coconut milk
3/4 cup white or brown sugar or one cup grated jaggery
10 cashews, sliced almonds or walnuts
A tablespoon of raisins
2 teaspoons butter
Pinch of salt.

Method:
- Roast the choice of nuts and raisins in butter for six minutes, then set aside.
- Boil the sago and cardamom in two cups of water, stirring intermittently for about ten minutes.
- Reduce heat, and add milk, sugar and coconut milk. Stir frequently for about ten minutes until the seeds are translucent, taking care not to let it get lumpy.
- Remove pan from heat and pour into dish.
- Top the dish with nuts and raisins mixture.

Acknowledgements

This book could not have been written and published without the help of certain people and organizations. It really *did* take a village.

First, I wish to express my appreciation for the writing program at Writers & Books in Rochester, New York, and the Serious Scribes writers' group in Chandler, Arizona. These groups were the "bookends" that helped me begin and complete the manuscript.

I gained valuable insight during the 2006 Desert Nights, Rising Stars writing conference at the Virginia G. Piper Center for Creative Writing at Arizona State University.

The research room staff at the Department of National Archives in Colombo, Sri Lanka was helpful, courteous, and accommodating during my visits when I pored over newspapers of the 1970s, mainly *The Sunday Observer* and *Ceylon Daily News.*

My gratitude also goes to H.A. Abhayagunawardhana, a civil servant, and to Ugantha Perera, an engineer. Both individuals demonstrate a great love for the written word. They provided me with encouragement and valuable editorial direction. In addition, I value the feedback I received from Senath Walter Perera, Senior Professor of English at University of Peradeniya in Sri Lanka. And I thank banker and friend Lalantha Goonetilleke for much encouragement over the years.

I am immensely grateful to the following people: Author Judith Starkston, for mentoring me during the publishing process; Editor Marsha Gilliam for her clever work, which pulled everything together; Billie Cox, who provided an unbiased evaluation; and Mel Weiser and Joni Browne-Walders for their constructive criticism.

I thank Lalith and Pushpa Wicks, Sondra Barr, Tina Shah, and Cathryn Creno for their help in honing the early stages of the manuscript.

I thank my extended family for their inspiration and support, and I thank my school friends from Bishop's College, Sri Lanka. They have patiently awaited the publication of this book. And last, but not least, I thank my husband, Siri, for being the ultimate sounding board on this long journey.

BIBLIOGRAPHY

The Chieftains of Ceylon: J.C. Van Sanden
Colombo, Plâté, 1936.

Sri Lanka: A Handbook of Historical Statistics: Patrick Peebles
G. K. Hall, 1982.

The Astrology Book: The Encyclopedia of Heavenly Influences:
James R. Lewis
Detroit, USA, Visible Ink Press, 2003.

Life and Planets: Hendrick de Silva Hettigoda
H. C Ebert Perera at Piyasiri Printing Systems, Sri Lanka, 1999.

ABOUT THE AUTHOR

Srianthi Perera grew up in Sri Lanka living next door to a young woman who played *A Maiden's Prayer* at twilight.

After studying English literature, she embarked on a lifelong career in newspaper and magazine journalism that took her to the Sultanate of Oman, Canada and the United States. Her work has appeared in the Sunday Observer (Sri Lanka), The Times of Oman, What's On (Dubai, UAE), Where Vancouver Magazine (Canada), The Arizona Republic and, more recently, in a cluster of community newspapers headed by Times Media Group (Phoenix).

She lives in Arizona with her husband.

As a child, she was not to know that her neighbor's mellifluous piano-playing would spark her debut novel. She's awaiting the next hint of memory.

Website: srianthiperera.com
Twitter: @srianthiperera
Facebook: srianthipereraauthor
Email: evocativejourneys@gmail.com

Made in the USA
Coppell, TX
27 September 2020